DEATH BY DUMPSTER

A LAUREN PRESCOTT MYSTERY

DEATH BY DUMPSTER

KAREN HANSON STUYCK

FIVE STAR
A part of Gale, Cengage Learning

GALE
CENGAGE Learning

Farmington Hills, Mich • San Francisco • New York • Waterville, Maine
Meriden, Conn • Mason, Ohio • Chicago

GALE
CENGAGE Learning®

LIBRARY OF CONGRESS CATALOGING-IN-PUBLICATION DATA

Stuyck, Karen Hanson.
  Death by dumpster / Karen Hanson Stuyck. — First edition.
    pages ; cm. — (A Lauren Prescott mystery)
    ISBN 978-1-4328-3106-6 (hardcover) — ISBN 1-4328-3106-2 (hardcover) — ISBN 978-1-4328-3102-8 (ebook) — 1-4328-3102-x (ebook)
    1. Women private investigators—Fiction. 2. Murder—Investigation—Fiction. 3. Dumpster diving—Fiction. I. Title.
PS3619.T89D43 2016
813'.6—dc23   2015025214

First Edition. First Printing: March 2016
Find us on Facebook– https://www.facebook.com/FiveStarCengage
Visit our website– http://www.gale.cengage.com/fivestar/
Contact Five Star™ Publishing at FiveStar@cengage.com

Printed in the United States of America
1 2 3 4 5 6 7 20 19 18 17 16

For Steve and Danny, once again

ACKNOWLEDGMENTS

Once again I want to thank the members of the Tuesday Writers' Consortium for their insightful suggestions, unwavering support, and friendship. Thanks to Irene Bond, Julia Mercedes Castilla, Lynne Gonzales, Guida Jackson Hume, Vanessa Leggett, Ida Luttrell, and Jackie Pelham.

CHAPTER ONE

Taking a deep breath, I knocked on the front door of the woman who was about to be the subject of my next magazine article. I wasn't sure what to expect from someone who called herself the Queen of Dumpster Diving.

The queen opened her door. In person, Caroline Marshall seemed taller and more striking than she'd appeared on television. Her prematurely silver hair was an interesting contrast with her unlined face and intense blue eyes, and her height—almost six feet, I'd guess—made her appearance even more memorable.

I extended my hand. "Hi, I'm Lauren Prescott from *Houston City Magazine.*" It still gave me a thrill to introduce myself as a professional journalist. For too many years I'd thought of myself as a full-time mother and wife who enjoyed writing in her spare time.

"Hi, Lauren, I'm Caroline." Smiling, she shook my hand, then invited me inside to meet the two women, students in her Living Frugally workshop, who would be accompanying us on our dumpster-diving expedition.

Before we headed out, Caroline gave us an introductory lecture. "I like to think of trash picking and dumpster diving as an exciting treasure hunt. Perhaps you'll find an antique table, an almost-new sofa, or a working computer. These are just a few of the discarded objects I've retrieved from the trash. In fact, the laptop I'm still using I found in a dumpster outside a college dorm at the end of the school year, along with a few textbooks that looked like they'd never been opened."

A plump, motherly woman named Ellen and I laughed. The other student, sour-faced Mary Alice, didn't.

"Of course," Caroline continued, "there were also many times when I didn't see anything remotely interesting. The fun part is never knowing what you'll find. I read about a young man who discovered a very nice engagement ring in a dumpster, and promptly went and proposed to his girlfriend!"

There were audible gasps. I jotted down the story.

"Any idea where this diamond dumpster is located?" Mary Alice asked.

Caroline shook her head. "Unsurprisingly, the guy kept that information to himself."

"What I wonder," Ellen said, "is how the girl he proposed to felt about that engagement ring. If it were me, every time I looked at it I'd be thinking about the terrible feelings that compelled someone to throw away something so valuable. And I'd also wonder if my fiancé would have asked me to marry him if he hadn't found a free ring."

Dour Mary Alice narrowed her eyes. "Do you ever hear about people coming to reclaim the property they threw away? Say the person who tossed the engagement ring later decided it would have been a lot smarter to sell it on eBay. If he learned who it was who took the ring from the dumpster, couldn't that guy be accused of theft?"

"No, taking discarded property is not stealing," Caroline said. Then she marshaled us all into her ancient SUV, giving me the honor of sitting next to her in the front.

We drove first to an affluent subdivision of large sprawling homes. "It's heavy trash day today." Caroline slowed the vehicle to a crawl. "You will be stunned to see what people throw away."

"I see something," Ellen called from the back seat. "Looks

like furniture."

It *was* furniture: a desk chair missing one wheel, a dining room chair with the cane seating broken, an old desk lamp, and a twin-sized mattress.

We all got out of the car to inspect the potential treasures. Caroline advised against the mattress—"too many possible health problems, including bed bugs"—and said that while both chairs could be repaired, she didn't think they were worth the effort. The lamp, however, went into the back of the SUV.

During the next half hour we found a few more treasures awaiting trash pickup. Ellen got excited about a discarded artificial Christmas tree and a box of old ornaments, while Caroline thought a dented file cabinet was a good find.

I myself didn't consider the "treasure hunt" all that thrilling. Maybe I'd spent too much time lately trying to get rid of my possessions before my move from my house to a much-smaller apartment. For the sake of my article, I hoped we'd find something more inspiring than broken furniture and a lopsided Christmas tree.

After that Caroline suggested we next try some apartment complexes. "The end of the month—today—is the best time to hit apartment dumpsters. Residents who are hurrying to move out often decide it's too much trouble to pack perfectly good furniture or transport perfectly good food. Instead they throw it all away."

"Food?" I asked. "Is it safe eating stuff you find in the trash?"

"Well, of course you have to be careful," Caroline said, "but in general Americans are much too fearful of food spoilage. Some of my best finds often come from dumpsters behind delis and high-end grocery stores. They toss out anything that's past its expiration date, and you can find wonderful day-old rolls and bread, delicious deli meat, and canned foods that are only being discarded because they've lost their labels."

She glanced back at her frugal followers. "It's best to hit the food dumpsters at night, after the day's food is discarded, but since I want you all to see what good meals can be made from these finds, I thought I'd let you taste some of my favorite free-food recipes at our potluck dinner tomorrow. You'll be surprised how tasty they are."

This was greeted with squeals of delight from the backseat. I was not convinced. "Uh, have you ever gotten sick from any of this free food?"

Caroline sent me a sideways glance. "You mean aside from the food poisoning, the salmonella episode, and my brush with botulism?" She laughed at my widened eyes. "No, I have not gotten sick from any found food. Occasionally I've had to sacrifice a bit of flavor, but I'd never sacrifice my health."

She turned her SUV into the driveway of a huge apartment complex and parked near a dumpster that seemed to be brimming with stuff. "Now this will be your first taste of real dumpster diving. I want everyone to put on her gloves. You need to be careful about broken glass or other sharp objects, and now's the time to get out your long stick with a bent nail on the end that I told you to bring. We're going to use them for poking through the trash."

I got some good photos of Caroline pulling out a silver golf trophy with her long stick, Ellen looking delighted that the plastic sack she'd retrieved contained unopened cans of soup and vegetables, and Mary Alice scowling at the cheap Mardi Gras beads she'd found.

A stern-looking woman approached us. "What the hell do you think you're doing? I'm the manager and I'll have you know this is private property."

Caroline, unfazed, turned to her. "I believe that parking lots are not private property, though of course the apartment complex is." She smiled. "Don't worry, we'll clean up after ourselves. We'll leave it exactly the way we found it."

The woman did not look appeased. "I'm calling the police."

Caroline nodded. "I'll be happy to talk to them. I just hope they won't be annoyed with you for bothering them about an entirely legal activity."

"We'll see about that," the woman muttered as she walked away.

"Maybe we should leave," Ellen said nervously.

"Nonsense," Caroline replied. "We still need to check the dumpster on the other side of the complex."

The group was noticeably less enthusiastic—or more scared—as we followed our leader to the next dumpster.

"Hey!" an angry male voice from behind us made Ellen jump. "Get out of here! You people delude yourself that you're being thrifty. What you are is disgusting scavengers—just like those blood-thirsty buzzards that feast on the last remains of the carcass."

A braver journalist than I would have taken a photo of the stocky, red-faced man advancing on us. Even from a distance, he reeked of liquor. I pocketed my camera.

Even Caroline looked disconcerted. "We're just leaving, sir," she said in the too-calm voice one uses with a snarling dog. "Back to the parking lot, ladies."

With the wild-eyed man still glaring at us, we made a hasty retreat.

As we headed back to Caroline's house, Mary Alice complained that she'd found nothing she could sell on eBay.

Caroline's mouth tightened. "Maybe next time you go out you'll find something you like."

"Well, most of what we found today is just junk."

"You'll be able to compare what your fellow students discovered in their trash expeditions tomorrow at the potluck dinner at my house," Caroline said, her voice only the tiniest bit testy.

She turned to me. "You're invited too, Lauren. Everyone brings some low-cost food. That might be something you picked up from a restaurant's dumpster or something made with ingredients from your pantry. The only rule is you can't go out and buy new food. You'll be surprised at how creative people can be. It's always a fun night."

Yeah, I thought, if we don't all come down with food poisoning. "I'll be there," I said, trying to look pleased about it.

Fortunately I could look forward to a non-frugal dinner tonight with one of my favorite people. As I drove away from Caroline Marshall's house, I decided to forget about tomorrow.

The evening was even better than I'd anticipated. For once everything was absolutely right in the world of Lauren Prescott. I glanced around my new, cozy apartment, took another bite of my slice of delectable pizza, glanced at my scintillating dinner companion, and sighed contentedly.

Paul O'Neal, my editor and—for want of a better word—romantic interest, chuckled. "Now that is the look of a woman who appreciates a fine pizza."

I smiled back. "And the fine company. Not to mention how relieved I am to have finally sold the house, had my divorce finalized, and moved in here. A lot of loose ends are tied up. I feel as if I can now officially begin the next phase of my life."

Paul raised his glass of Chianti. "To your new phase. May it be exciting, fulfilling, and everything you desire."

I clinked glasses with him. "I'll drink to that."

Surveying my tiny apartment, I knew many people would view this new phase as a definite step down. My whole apartment, after all, could easily fit into the great room of my old home. For twenty-five years I'd been married to a successful dentist, resided in a mini-mansion, and focused my energies on my picture-perfect family. I'd been a full-time mother, an active volunteer, and the CEO of all domestic matters.

Everything had abruptly changed when my husband absconded with all our money, most of our furniture, and the dental records that he realized could send him to prison. In very short order, I learned that everything I'd assumed about my long-time marriage and comfortable life was based on lies and I was in fact a clueless chump with no money, no husband, and no marketable job skills. What followed was, in the immortal words of Queen Elizabeth II, my *annus horribilis*.

But now, at long last, the misery was over. Fifteen months after my husband departed, I'd become an independent single woman. My one-time husband was no longer in the picture, my two beloved daughters were grown and out forging new lives for themselves, and, for the first time in my life, I was living alone, making all my own decisions, and responsible only for myself. And, perhaps best of all, I now had a writing job I loved and a supportive, handsome, witty man in my life who made me believe again in the possibility of romance.

That supportive man raised an eyebrow. "Do you mind if I inquire how your article is coming?"

"Not at all. I only mind when you harangue me about approaching deadlines."

"I do *not* harangue."

Right. I changed the subject. "I went trash picking today with Caroline Marshall and some of her students, and tomorrow I'm going to a student potluck dinner at her house. She's a fascinating woman—quotable, charismatic, a bit bizarre, everything you'd want in a subject."

"You're picking through garbage?"

"Caroline calls herself the Queen of Dumpster Diving. She claims she's furnished her house with items people throw away.

15

That's one of the skills she teaches in her workshop on how to live on practically nothing. She tells her students to think of themselves as the New Pioneers."

Paul rolled his eyes. "I wonder if people who have been out of work for the last year view becoming pioneers as a palatable option."

He had a point, one I intended to explore in my article. Could Caroline's frugal lifestyle really work for financially strapped, unemployed workers desperate to make their next mortgage payment? "I'm planning to sit in on one of her workshops later this week."

Maybe I could pick up a few useful tips myself. The money I made from my magazine articles barely covered my rent and basic living expenses, and my divorce settlement money constituted the tiniest of nest eggs.

"Sounds great. I'm just suggesting it might be a good idea to turn in the article as soon as possible."

"Why?" I asked. He normally told me to take my time and make sure I got everything right.

Paul looked a bit nervous, which also was unlike him. "It's premature to say anything for certain, but I've heard a rumor that our publisher might be considering selling the magazine. I hope it's not true, but it seems like a good idea to finish your article quickly to make sure you'll be paid for it."

And here I'd just been thinking that everything was going so well. What would I do for income if the only magazine that published my articles went out of business?

Paul leaned across the table and patted my hand. "There's absolutely no reason to get upset, Lauren. Nothing is definite. I've been hearing gossip like this for years, and, look, the magazine is still here."

For a cynical, hard-headed journalist, he was a remarkably tender man. "And, more importantly, I brought you a house-

16

warming gift."

"I thought the pizza was my house-warming gift."

He shook his head. "This is more in the line of dessert."

My cell phone rang before I could respond. For a moment I considered answering it. My elder daughter, Katie, had been calling quite a bit lately. Her husband was away on a long business trip to China and she was bored and lonely. Still, if it *was* Katie, she'd leave a message and I could return her call later. We independent women could choose to ignore ringing phones occasionally.

"So what's my present?" I asked Paul.

"Anyone ever tell you that patience is not your strong suit?"

"Patience is a highly over-rated virtue."

Paul sighed. "Don't get your hopes up. It's just something that I thought might make all the unpacking and the writing deadline a bit less unpleasant."

He walked over to a paper sack on the counter and returned with a jumbo bag of bite-sized Baby Ruths.

My eyes filled with tears.

Paul looked embarrassed. "I told you it wasn't much, not a real gift."

I shook my head. "No, it's wonderful. Perfect." If any tangible proof existed that I'd found a man who was the polar opposite of the critical, pretentious, never-satisfied man I'd been married to—a jerk who checked our wastebaskets looking for Baby Ruth wrappers—this was it. "Baby Ruths are my favorite food."

"I know," he said.

I got out of my chair and kissed him. His arms tightened around me, deepening the kiss. "If I'd known you'd be this grateful, I'd have bought you a whole carton."

I laughed. It took me a moment to realize that someone was knocking on the door of my apartment. I considered ignoring that, too, but the increasing insistence of the knocks convinced me that maybe I should check it out.

I looked out the peephole. My two daughters stood outside, each carrying a suitcase.

I opened the door. "What—what a surprise."

They stepped inside and I hugged each of them. "It's always wonderful to see you, but I wasn't expecting—"

"We just called you to tell you we were here, but you didn't answer your phone," Katie said. Her lips quivered. "I lost my job, Mom. My whole department was laid off yesterday."

"Oh, honey," I said, giving her another hug, "I'm so sorry." I managed not to say what else I was thinking: Every time she talked to me she complained about her boring job, for which she was grossly overqualified and underpaid, supervised by a man she called The King of the Cretins.

I looked over her shoulder at Emily, my younger daughter. "I thought you were in Austin, Em, in class."

"I quit school," she said matter-of-factly. "Don't worry, it's early enough in the semester that I got the tuition money back. I just decided that college was a waste of my time and your money."

"But you are such a good student," I said. Unlike her social butterfly older sister, Em had always been a straight-A student, the one whose grades we never worried about. Why, out of the blue, had she, my sensible, cautious, bookish daughter, suddenly made such an impetuous—and lousy—decision?

She shrugged. "Maybe I'll go back someday, when I have a better idea of what I want to do with my life. But until then I thought I could get a job and explore my options."

Em glanced from me to Katie, and the look that passed between them told me everything. This was the expression I'd seen when they'd broken an expensive vase playing catch in the house and came to tell me about it. I braced myself.

"Mom," Katie said, her large blue eyes imploring, "we both want to move back home with you for a while."

CHAPTER TWO

The next morning my daughters and I sat at my kitchen table, eating breakfast and watching Caroline Marshall do her thing on TV.

I had to admit that there was something larger than life about the woman. She made it sound imperative that every one of her viewers embrace her tightwad principles. Her blue eyes gazed earnestly into the camera as she said, "It will change your life for the better. I promise."

From the expressions on the faces of her mainly female studio audience, a lot of them were ready to drink the Kool-Aid.

I was less convinced. Stripped to its essence, Caroline's advice was not much different from cost-cutting information that had been around for years, though Caroline added her own twists to the message. I suspected her appeal had more to do with her striking looks, folksy manner of speaking, and aura of intense, focused energy.

"Did the pioneers who settled our frontiers whine that homesteading was too hard and they wanted to go home?" Caroline asked her audience. "No! Those brave settlers knew the only thing they could count on was themselves—their own strength, their own resourcefulness. In these bleak financial times we live in, with millions of our fellow Americans unemployed or going hungry, those are exactly the traits we need to thrive in this challenging economy. We need to become a new generation of tough-minded pioneers."

She leaned forward, a friend letting you in on a secret. "But don't take my word for it. Experience it for yourself. The first step is realizing that you *can* dig yourself out of debt, enjoy a satisfying, worry-free existence, even if you are unemployed or strapped for cash. Then I will show you how to put yourself in charge again and finally gain control of your own life."

"She's good!" my elder daughter said as the show segued into a commercial.

Her younger sister, Em, swallowed a mouthful of cereal. "Of course if you really embraced her new pioneers message, you wouldn't have a TV to watch on."

Katie, looking blurry-eyed from a night sleeping on an air mattress, scowled at her. "You are always so cynical."

"What I am is rational and therefore able to deduce that this is just another sales pitch. Her message plays to the audience's fears, their patriotism, and their nostalgia for a simpler life." Emily—unlike her sister, a morning person—produced a nerdy smirk.

Katie's pale face turned crimson. "Well, at least *I* managed to graduate from college."

"To everyone's amazement," Em shot back. "After an extra year and lots of special tutoring."

Before the battle could progress, I held up a palm. "Stop! I haven't had enough coffee to put up with your bickering." Only through great restraint did I manage not to add what else I was thinking: This phase of my life—Mommy Referee—was supposed to be over.

I sent them my I-mean-business look. "I need to work on my article now and I have to go to a dinner at Caroline's house tonight. But as soon as I get back, we're going to discuss your future plans. I suggest you give the matter some serious thought before I get home."

I was hoping that my maternal guidance, combined with the

21

experience of sharing a miniscule apartment with a cranky sibling, might convince them to revise their plan for an extended stay with Mom. In my favorite scenario, Katie decided to go back to her roomy apartment in Dallas before her husband returned from his business trip and Em resolved to head back to Austin and beg the powers-that-be to allow her to return to her classes and her dorm. While I loved my girls dearly, I sensed we might all do better right now with a little less family togetherness.

I headed for the room meant to be my office, which now was also crammed with an air mattress and suitcases. "Come take your clothes from my desk chair," I called over my shoulder. "I don't want to be interrupted while I write." I doubted very much that the no-interruptions would happen, but we independent women had to set our boundaries.

Eight hours later I'd made some progress on my article and, food contribution in hand, was heading for the potluck dinner. I was bringing a bottle of cheap wine and a cold pasta salad that Katie, an enthusiastic cook, had thrown together from ingredients she found in my kitchen.

I just hoped that this potluck dinner would be more interesting than my account of our trash-picking excursion.

Caroline had asked that I arrive before the other guests so we'd have time to talk. She greeted me at the door, then led me into the living room of her small, brick ranch house, which was furnished with elegant simplicity.

When I said how much I liked what she'd done to the house, she offered to give me a tour. As she walked me around, she told me how she'd bought the rundown house for a steal and then had undertaken all the needed cosmetic work herself. She'd refinished the hardwood floors, replaced the damaged linoleum flooring in the kitchen with sale-priced vinyl tiles, painted and wallpapered, and did a few "minor repairs" on the sheetrock and plumbing.

Her furniture was an eclectic mix of styles, much of it picked up at garage sales or from curbside discards. The living room held a nondescript couch covered with brightly colored throw pillows, upholstered side chairs that she'd draped with interesting Indian scarves, a handsome battered-oak coffee table. It should have been a characterless mishmash, but somehow it wasn't. Among her many talents, Caroline also seemed to have a knack for decorating.

She surprised me by saying that she'd just read my magazine articles. "I think you're a wonderful writer. And that's a talent I really envy because, while I'm an avid reader, I can't write a coherent paragraph. I especially loved your story about the murdered fitness guru."

"Thank you," I said, feeling inordinately pleased.

"I like your writing so much I'm hoping I can coax you into writing a book with me."

I stared at her, unsure of how to reply. Would she want to pay me with rescued canned goods? "Uh, what kind of book are you thinking about?"

"Maybe something along the lines of *Secrets of a Penny-Pincher*—my life story as well as tips on how to get started on your own frugal journey."

"Uh, what kind of secrets are we talking about?" I asked, but knocking on her front door interrupted us.

"It sounds as if my dinner guests are here," Caroline said. "We'll have to finish our discussion later."

The first guests to arrive were sour-faced Mary Alice and smiling Ellen, both of whom had been with me on the dumpster-diving expedition.

"This is so much fun," Ellen exclaimed. "I've brought a salad, using only vegetables from my home garden, and I baked this bread from scratch."

"They look delicious," Caroline said, and even I had to admit they did. I'd been feeling a bit apprehensive about how this potluck dinner might taste. I'd brought the wine because I thought alcohol might be a welcome addition to a meal of out-of-date food and wilted leftovers.

"Why don't you give them *your* contribution, Mary Alice?" Ellen said with a decided edge to her voice.

Mary Alice, who'd been inspecting the living room like a property assessor, handed Caroline a bottle of dry-roasted peanuts. "I found them on our dumpster dive."

Caroline smiled politely. "Oh, good, we can have them as hors d'oeuvres."

Ellen, who on our previous outing had struck me as the most affable of women, said, "You'll notice that Mary Alice has already started eating them." She nodded at the jar, which looked only two-thirds full.

Mary Alice scowled. "I had to make sure they tasted all right, didn't I?"

"Of course," Caroline said hastily. "I know I should remember this, but you two are neighbors, right?"

"Sisters," Ellen said grimly. "Twins."

"Fraternal," Mary Alice added, unnecessarily.

Astonished, I glanced from one to the other, finally noticing the similar gray eyes and long noses. In Ellen those features resided in a vaguely grandmotherly face of a short, plump woman, while, in Mary Alice, they appeared in a tall, hard-edged female with—at least in the times I'd been around her—an expression of chronic dissatisfaction.

Fortunately, other guests arrived then. Josie, a serene woman with long, gray hair that made her look like an aging hippie, arrived with her husband, Ed, a jowly geologist who informed us that he'd been laid off after "twenty-five years of loyal service to an ungrateful oil company." Right behind them was Nathan, a skinny young man with nervously darting eyes. He looked at me as if he were trying to determine if I was carrying a concealed handgun.

"Don't mind him," Josie whispered into my ear. "Nathan was in my dumpster-dive group. He's odd but harmless, a Ph.D. student in physics."

The last to arrive were Ethan and Margaret, a middle-aged couple who told us they'd given up their jobs to homeschool their three children and live off the land. They kept chickens and "gardened as a family." As their dinner contribution they'd brought homemade vegetable soup.

In the kitchen Ophelia, Caroline's assistant, cheerfully accepted each new food offering. I'd met Ophelia yesterday when I'd come to Caroline's house. A mousey woman whom I guessed to be in her fifties, she'd been an almost impossible person to interview. She answered my questions politely enough, but managed to make her responses so uninteresting that one had to wonder if being nondescript was part of her job description.

Clearly, though, she could cook. She pulled a cookie sheet of delicious-smelling stuffed mushrooms from the oven and arranged them on a platter.

Sitting in the living room, Nathan nervously eyed the plate of hors d'oeuvres Ophelia placed on the coffee table. "Mushrooms, you know, can be poisonous."

"Not these mushrooms," Ophelia said. "Poisonous mushrooms, such as those in the lethal Amanita family, have a distinct spore print, gill type, and base type."

Nathan did not look reassured. "How do I know that these aren't Amanita mushrooms?"

"You don't." Ophelia popped one of the mushrooms into her mouth and chewed with no immediate lethal consequences. "Maybe your safest bet is not to eat them." Perhaps, I decided, she was not quite so bland after all.

He glared at her. "I don't intend to." He patted the bulging pocket of his jacket. "I've brought my own food."

I helped myself to a mushroom, reasoning that Ophelia was too efficient to inadvertently poison us with fungi.

I could hear Margaret and Ellen chatting about getting children to appreciate organic vegetables. It sounded like a more pleasant topic than anything Nathan would offer. The two women smiled as I approached. "Do you have children, Lauren?" Ellen asked.

"Yes, two daughters, but they're past the age where I have to trick them into eating their vegetables. In fact, my older daughter is a very creative cook who's always trying out recipes with vegetables I never tasted before."

"Lucky you," Ellen said.

"Jealous, Ellen?" a grating voice from behind us asked. Ellen's bad twin had joined us.

"She doesn't cook for me that often," I said. "She lives in Dallas."

"Ellen's son and daughter-in-law moved in with her after they lost their jobs," Mary Alice said. "Neither of them ever helps with the cooking."

I sent Ellen a sympathetic look. "My daughter just got laid off this week, too."

"Is *your* daughter at least looking for another job?" Mary Alice asked.

Good God, if my sister was as malicious as this I certainly would not attend a class with her. "I assume she will soon."

Ellen scowled at her sister. "Don't talk as if *your* children are such prizes, Mary Alice. At least none of my kids ever threatened to put out a hit on me."

I could see my own incredulity reflected in Margaret's face. "A hit?" she asked.

Mary Alice looked embarrassed. "It was a joke. The girls have some anger-management issues—they take after their father. But they wouldn't actually kill anyone."

"You keep telling yourself that," Ellen said as she helped herself to a stuffed mushroom.

CHAPTER THREE

Perhaps it was only in hindsight that Caroline's potluck dinner seemed ominous. At the time, though, I merely thought it the strangest dinner party I'd ever attended.

The food was less bad than I'd expected. Some items—Ellen's home-baked bread and Ophelia's stew—were delicious, but others tasted odd. The salad from Ellen's garden, for instance, contained some bitter herbs or vegetables I'd not eaten before, and Margaret's soup seemed more like water-logged vegetables, though her home-canned peaches were tasty.

Since no one seemed to have coordinated what food everyone was bringing, it was a rather peculiar mix: soup and stew, salad, bread, canned fruit, an assortment of sandwich meats—none of which I would touch—that Josie and Ed had found "just last night" outside a deli, and a slightly stale bag of vegetable chips that Nathan had found in a grocery store dumpster. Still to come was a berry cobbler Ophelia had made for dessert.

The dinner conversation was stranger than the food. True to his word, Nathan did not eat any of the shared food, except for the veggie chips he'd brought. He munched on a sandwich from home, all the while providing the rest of us with a running commentary on the hazards of various foods.

He'd already told us, of course, about poisonous mushrooms. Now we got to hear about the highly toxic baneberry, which was sometimes confused with blueberries. An English family had been poisoned in 1972 when they'd made a pie out of the berries they'd gathered. "All but the mother died from it," Nathan informed us cheerfully. We also learned about toxic hemlock leaves, which, when made into a salad, could kill a diner within a few hours. The seeds and berries of the Jimsonweed were also responsible for many accidental poisonings.

I, and several others at the table, abruptly stopped eating Ellen's bitter-tasting salad.

"How come you know so much about poisonous food?" Mary Alice asked. She and her twin had wisely chosen seats far away from each other, with Mary Alice sitting between Caroline and Ethan at one end of the table, and Ellen next to Ophelia at the other.

"I researched the subject," Nathan said. "I'm a rational man of science who takes sensible precautions."

I myself thought him more of a paranoid nutcase, but thought it prudent to keep that assessment to myself.

"I think it's time to talk about something else," Caroline said. "Poisoning from plants is actually very rare."

"True," Nathan said, "but then there's also botulism and salmonella from processed food."

Ophelia cleared her throat. "I'm wondering what non-food items all of you found in your dumpster-diving expeditions."

Fortunately she was addressing an acquiescent group. Or maybe everyone was merely eager to contemplate any subject that didn't make them anxious about every bite of their dinner.

Ethan and Margaret's group had found six dining-room chairs, only half of them with broken cane seats; a blender that didn't work at all speeds, and a twenty-year-old set of encyclopedias. Ellen described the items found by our group, from the forlorn artificial Christmas tree and ornaments to the golf trophy and canned goods.

Once again Mary Alice said how disappointed she was that

she hadn't found something she could sell on eBay.

I didn't want to hear her complaints again. I excused myself and headed for the restroom. I presumed Nathan, who'd left the table a few minutes earlier, was on a similar quest.

Luckily, from my earlier tour of the house, I knew the location of the second bathroom, tucked in a far corner in the back. As I headed toward it, I caught a sound from behind the half-closed door of the room Caroline had called her office.

Why would anybody be in there now? I crept to the door, intending to discover what was going on.

Unfortunately, I didn't have a chance to quietly peer inside. The intruder chose that moment to stalk out—and spot me.

It was Nathan. He glared at me. "What are you doing here?"

What was *I* doing? "I'm looking for a bathroom. What were *you* doing in Caroline's office?"

I thought for a moment he wasn't going to answer, but then he said, reluctantly, "I was looking for some property of mine. I didn't find it."

Before I could blurt out my follow-up questions—What kind of property? Why would it be in Caroline's office?—he pushed past me.

When I returned from the bathroom, Ophelia was putting individual bowls of dessert on the table.

"Where's Nathan?" I asked as I resumed my seat. I was pleased to see that, after some of the unappetizing food I'd eaten tonight, at least her cobbler looked and smelled delicious.

"Oh, he's gone," Ophelia said. "Stopped in the kitchen to say he had to leave." Her dry tone seemed to indicate that she was not mourning his departure.

Mary Alice was digging into her dessert. For such a skinny woman she had a rather oversized appetite. "This is delicious, Ophelia. You put nuts and seeds in it, didn't you?"

Ophelia shrugged. "I tend to be a throw-in-whatever-is-at-hand kind of cook. I like to experiment with recipes."

Her culinary experiments, I thought as I sampled her tasty dessert, were considerably more successful than mine usually were.

"Well, I for one am stuffed," Josie announced.

Sitting across from her, Mary Alice eyed Josie's uneaten dessert. "You're not going to eat that?" When Josie shook her head, Mary Alice asked, "Mind if I do?"

"Be my guest." Josie handed it over.

Caroline smiled. "Would you like mine, too, Mary Alice? I know it will be delicious, but I ate so much of everything else I can't eat another bite."

For the first time in my memory, Mary Alice looked happy. "Thanks," she said, taking Caroline's bowl, too.

"Now I think we should go around the table," Caroline said, "and everyone tell the cost-cutting tip they found most helpful."

Ed grinned and said he intended to return to the deli dumpster on a regular basis. "Man, they're throwing away good food. Who needs to go out to a restaurant?"

Margaret said her family would continue to eat organic food from their garden, but she thought she'd check out more garage sales and thrift shops for used children's clothing. If Margaret's vegetable soup was a typical sample of her healthy organic food, her family had my sympathy. Probably she was the kind of smug mother who never let her children eat sugar.

Mary Alice, I noticed, was looking peculiar. "Are you okay?" I asked.

Frantically she shook her head. She seemed to be fighting for breath.

At the other end of the table Ellen stood up, her face white with alarm. "Mary Alice, what's wrong?"

Still gasping for air, Mary Alice suddenly lurched forward,

vomiting convulsively.

"Call 9-1-1!" Caroline screamed. *"Now."*

CHAPTER FOUR

"Do you think that lady is going to die, Mom?" Emily asked when I finally got back to the apartment.

"I don't know, honey. I hope not. She got medical help right away—that's always important." The paramedics had arrived within fifteen minutes, but Mary Alice was barely conscious when they wheeled her out to the ambulance, followed by her visibly shaken twin sister.

I took another therapeutic sip of white wine. I had to admit that it had been nice to come home to the concern and companionship of my daughters. While I still suspected that, in the long run, letting my children move back in with me would be detrimental for all of us, a kind of regression, it was nevertheless a comfort to have someone to talk to after witnessing such a horrific scene.

"That sounds like the worse case of food poisoning I ever heard of," Katie said. "Doesn't it usually take much longer than that before people get sick?"

I nodded. "I've always heard the symptoms don't occur until several hours after eating."

"And if it's food poisoning, wouldn't the other people at the dinner have gotten sick too?" Em asked, eyeing me anxiously. "You feel okay, don't you?"

"Just fine," I lied. Actually my stomach was feeling a trifle upset, but after spending the last hours first listening to a recital of various toxic plants and then seeing a living example of the most extreme gastrointestinal distress I'd ever witnessed, I suspected there was a large psychological component to my queasiness. Then again it *had* been a strange-tasting meal. . . .

"Did you eat all the same food that Mary Alice ate?" Em asked.

I tried to remember. "I wasn't paying that much attention, but she seemed to eat quite a lot of everything. I tasted all the food except the meat from the deli dumpster."

Before Em could jump to the obvious conclusion—the several-days-old deli meat was responsible for Mary Alice's illness—I added, "But a lot of other people at the dinner also ate that meat, and they didn't get sick." Yet.

"Maybe Mary Alice was allergic to some food she ate, which would explain why other people didn't get sick," Em said. "Or maybe she got sick from something she'd eaten hours earlier."

Could Mary Alice's allegedly homicidal daughters have decided that rather than springing for a hit man, they would do the job themselves? Maybe they'd slipped some weed killer or rat poison into their mother's coffee. After all, hadn't that other dysfunctional family, the Borgias, kept a private supply of arsenic on hand for any urgent assassinations?

I shook my head, trying to turn off my over-active imagination. "There's really no point in speculating about this now. Mary Alice's illness might not even be connected to what she ate. For all we know, this was a reaction to some medication she was taking or a disease we don't know about. Hopefully, she'll be fine by tomorrow."

Unfortunately, that best-case scenario was not the one that played out.

I myself was feeling okay the next morning, sipping my coffee and scanning the newspaper. I was more relieved than I cared to admit that I hadn't experienced any severe gastric distress.

My daughters didn't need to know how worried I'd been that I, too, might be heading to the emergency room.

The phone interrupted my contemplation of possible five-letter words for "Bohemian Rhapsody group" in the newspaper crossword.

"Lauren, hi, this is Caroline," a by-now-familiar voice said. "I'm afraid I have some bad news to report."

My previous sense of well-being deflated like a punctured balloon. "Mary Alice?"

"Yes, Ellen just phoned me. Mary Alice died last night at the hospital."

"Oh, my God." For a longish moment neither of us said anything. Then I asked, "Do they know what killed her?"

"They think some kind of poison, but they won't know for sure until after the autopsy."

"Uh, have you heard if anyone else from the dinner last night has gotten sick?" I told myself that I was asking not out of self interest but in my role as conscientious journalist.

"Not that I've heard of," Caroline said in a chilly voice, as if I was accusing her of personally harming her guests. "This wasn't food poisoning from spoiled food, if that's what you're getting at."

I wondered if some dinner guests *had* become ill, but just hadn't bothered to inform Caroline.

I was starting to recall in too vivid detail the scene of Mary Alice writhing, vomiting, and gasping for air. "That poor woman. What an agonizing death. Did Ellen mention if they were at least able to make her more comfortable when she got to the hospital? And did she say what time Mary Alice died?"

"No, it was a very short conversation," Caroline said.

I suddenly wanted to get off the phone with this unfeeling woman. "Well, thanks for calling."

"Wait!" Caroline said. "We still need to talk about you writing my book."

I took a deep breath and managed not to tell her what exactly she could do with her book. "I don't think this is really the time—"

"Under normal circumstances we could delay this discussion," she said, not letting me finish. "I realize I must seem crass and insensitive, but this tragedy has shown me that I don't have much time left. It's imperative that I get out my story now—before someone kills me, too."

"Kills *you*?" I asked, incredulous.

"Yes, but I can't discuss it over the phone. Come to my house tomorrow at nine and we'll talk." Without waiting for my reply, she hung up.

CHAPTER FIVE

At my knock, Caroline opened her front door and nervously peered up and down her street. Was she expecting an assassin to jump out of the azaleas? A car to zoom in for a drive-by shooting?

"Thanks for coming," she said, double locking the door after us.

"Of course." Caroline certainly looked as if she believed someone wanted to kill her. The poise and confidence she'd worn so casually the other times I'd seen her seemed to have disappeared overnight.

I still wasn't sure how I felt about ghostwriting her memoirs. Besides being uncertain if what she had in mind could be turned into a viable book, I was afraid she'd pay me next to nothing or want to barter my writing services for out-of-date canned goods. I was, however, definitely interested in hearing why she thought she was in danger.

I followed Caroline into the living room as she described the phone conversations she'd recently had with all the potluck dinner guests.

"So as of today no one else has gotten sick?"

She shook her head. "Not physically ill, though both Josie and Margaret became very upset when I told them Mary Alice had died. Then Nathan called and he wanted to hear all the grisly details: what Mary Alice had eaten, when she became ill, what were the first symptoms. It was quite unpleasant. I finally told him that I had an appointment and needed to get off the phone."

I recalled that Nathan had already left Caroline's house by the time Mary Alice got sick. Presumably he would have been unaware of the incident when he'd phoned. "Did Nathan say why he was calling?"

She shrugged. "It's hard to tell why Nathan does anything. He wants to come over and speak privately with me, but I said I was too busy today."

I thought about the way Nathan had stomped out of Caroline's empty study when everyone else was still at the dinner table. What had he been doing in there? And why did he now want to come over to talk with Caroline?

But clearly Caroline had other matters on her mind. "I didn't get you here to talk about the dinner, Lauren. I want us to get started on my book."

It seemed like a good idea to get a few of my questions answered before I told Caroline I was probably going to turn down her job offer. "You said someone was trying to kill you. What makes you think that?"

"I've received death threats in the mail. At first I didn't take them seriously. Now I do. That's why we need to write my book."

I personally didn't see how writing a book could stop death threats. Though if she wanted me to put the information into my article, I'd be happy to oblige. "Do you know who's making these threats?"

"I have . . . enemies. I'm not sure which of them is threatening me. But I want to write the book to tell my side of the story."

Her side of what story? I felt as if I was trying to hold a meaningful conversation with someone who only spoke Swahili. "Telling your story will stop the death threats?"

She sent me a sly look that said, Don't think I don't know

what you're doing. "I guess you'll just have to write my book, Lauren, to get all of your questions answered."

"I'm writing a magazine article about you."

"Your article is about my frugal-living classes, not me personally. Hopefully the magazine piece will make readers want to learn more by reading my book. We'll also have to give careful thought about how best to present the information about my suspects."

Her *suspects*? Exactly what kind of book was she expecting me to write? And what if the "death threats" she'd received in the mail were merely pranks? Malicious certainly, but not a real threat to Caroline's life. Though after Mary Alice's death, I could understand why Caroline would take those warnings very seriously.

She handed me an official-looking paper. "I have a nondisclosure agreement for you to sign before we get started."

I stared at her. What was such a secret that she'd had a lawyer draft a nondisclosure contract? What was she afraid I'd reveal? "I'm not ready to sign anything yet. Why don't we just focus on the magazine article for now."

The look she sent me was decidedly chilly. "You have enough information for the story. I want to start my book."

Clearly this was a woman very used to getting what she wanted. I remembered the way she'd barked orders at Ophelia last night, almost acting as if the woman was her servant.

I was not someone who enjoyed being barked at. I stood. "I have to go finish my article."

"Suit yourself." She walked me to the door. "But I want your decision about writing my book within twenty-four hours."

The blissful sound of silence greeted me when I returned to my apartment. Katie was spending the day with a friend from college and Em said she was going to begin exploring her career options.

I had just poured myself a cup of coffee when my cell rang: Paul. "Any chance you could have lunch with me today?" His voice sounded uncharacteristically tense.

"Sure. I have a lot to tell you." He didn't even know about the deadly potluck dinner or the ghostwriting job.

"I'll be there in half an hour. You can tell me then."

"Okay." The man was definitely acting strange.

But when Paul arrived, he kissed me hello and looked like his usual good-humored self. Maybe I'd just been imagining the stress in his voice. My own experience last night could easily have me seeing trauma everywhere.

We went to a quiet neighborhood Italian restaurant we both liked. "So what did you want to tell me?" he asked after we'd ordered.

I told him about last night's eventful dinner.

His eyes widened. "My God, the woman died?"

I nodded. "I don't think they're sure yet what she died from, but of course there's going to be an autopsy."

He peered at me, his eyes warm with concern. "Are you feeling okay? Did anyone else at the dinner get sick?"

"I feel fine, and I don't think anyone else was affected. Caroline told me she thought she was the intended victim of the poisoning. And she wants me to write a book for her that she says will deter the killer."

Paul, a journalist to his core, started peppering me with questions.

"She won't tell me who these enemies of hers are until I agree to write the book and sign a nondisclosure agreement."

"Nondisclosure agreement?" Paul rolled his eyes. "She's afraid you'll reveal the Queen of Dumpster Diving trade secrets?"

"I think she doesn't want me to reveal something more personal—like why her enemies are sending her death threats. But since I didn't sign the agreement, I guess I'll never know what those secrets are."

Paul skillfully plied spoon and fork to twirl his fettuccini. "Did she give you some idea of the kind of book she wants to write?"

"A memoir, I think, with some tips on how to live frugally thrown in. From what she's told me, the big drama in her life was her rejection of the materialistic values she grew up with and embracing frugality. It doesn't exactly seem like the basis for a riveting plot."

I tried to think of what else might constitute, in Caroline's mind, her story. "I guess her death threats could be dramatic. It wouldn't surprise me if she simply wants to use the book to thumb her nose at everyone who ever criticized her. The woman has a decidedly short fuse."

Paul raised his eyebrows. "I'd expect you to be more curious about what's going on, Lauren. Death threats, enemies, a mortally ill dinner guest—sounds pretty dramatic to me."

I was well aware that, in Paul's mind, lack of curiosity was a mortal sin. "Of course I'm curious. But I don't know if that's enough motivation to spend months trying to make Caroline's musings sound enthralling and then, after all my effort, receive pathetic pay."

"I thought ghostwriters made decent money."

I swallowed a mouthful of manicotti. "Pay was not mentioned, but remember, Caroline prides herself on being a cheapskate."

There was something in Paul's expression that seemed a little off, a shade too somber. All through lunch I'd sensed that something was bothering him. Impulsively, I took his hand. "What's wrong, Paul?"

"Am I that obvious?" He sighed. "I talked to the publisher this morning. He's decided he wants the magazine to fold. The next issue will be our last."

I stared at him. "So soon?"

He nodded, his expression grim. "Mark's like a spoiled kid who's grown tired of his once-favorite toy. I tried to convince him that if he holds on for a few years, the magazine could make a profit again. But he just wants to get rid of it and find something else to play with."

I shook my head, not knowing what to say. Then a new thought hit me. "There's not much point in me finishing the dumpster-diving story now, is there?" Not when the issue in which my article was slated to run was no longer going to be printed.

He looked, if possible, even grimmer. "I'm so sorry, Lauren. You'll get a kill fee for the article, of course. Maybe you can sell the piece to another magazine."

I glanced down at my half-eaten lunch, no longer a bit hungry. "So what will you do now?"

"I have no idea. I really wasn't expecting this. I knew revenues were down, but I never guessed . . ." He sighed. "I keep thinking of everyone who counts on the magazine to pay their bills, people who've worked there for years. And now, without warning, it's all taken away."

I nodded. "It sucks." Another thought struck me. He'd been surprisingly noncommittal when I dismissed Caroline's ghostwriting offer. "You think I should write Caroline's book, don't you?"

"I think you might look into it, find out what she's willing to pay and what exactly she'd expect from you."

I nodded. There was no harm in inquiring, but I wasn't getting my hopes up. Caroline was too cheap and her book idea too tenuous for this project to be anything other than a particularly frustrating volunteer job. And, in addition to

everything else, there was something about the woman—
something I couldn't put a finger on—that I didn't trust.

"So I guess we'll both be job hunting," I said. "Do you have
any idea where you'll look?"

"Not if I want to stay in magazine editing. A friend of mine
in Seattle is talking about starting a magazine. He'd like me to
be the managing editor."

"The magazine's in Seattle?" A city over two thousand miles
away from where I lived!

Apparently my dismay was written on my face because Paul's
expression softened. "At this point, the magazine is only talk.
It's not exactly the most opportune time to start a new publica-
tion. Jack is trying to raise the money, but it's probably all pie in
the sky."

We didn't talk much after that. Although we both tried to put
up a good front and at least pretend that everything would work
out, neither of us was very successful at it.

When I returned to my apartment Em was there, sitting at the
kitchen table paging through some books.

"I decided to begin researching my career options at the
library," she said.

"You might need to get a paying job while you're researching," I said. "It looks as if my magazine work is going to end.
Paul just told me that the publisher has decided that the next
issue will be the last."

"Oh, Mom, I'm sorry. I know how much you loved writing
for them."

I swallowed several times. "Well, I'm just going to have to
find someplace else that will print my work. Caroline Marshall
did offer me a job ghostwriting a book."

"Wow, a book!" Emily sounded genuinely impressed. "And
that certainly will keep you busy for a while."

"I need to get more information from Caroline before I decide whether I want to do it."

My cell phone rang. It was Caroline.

"Lauren, the police just left my place. They want to talk to everyone who was at the dinner."

"So, I expect they'll be contacting me soon."

"Undoubtedly. Speaking to them made me even more eager to get started on my book. I'm hoping you're ready to sign the agreement."

The woman was relentless! She'd only first mentioned the project to me a few hours ago, and already she was nagging me.

I took a deep breath and decided to be just as brash. "You didn't mention how much you'd pay me." At least this way I would have a concrete reason for refusing her offer.

She didn't even hesitate. "I researched how much ghostwriters are typically paid for a book. Since I want you to finish the project quickly, I'm willing to pay you ten thousand up front and another fifteen thousand when the manuscript is complete. If the book becomes a best seller, I'll give you a bonus. You okay with that?"

I swallowed. "Uh, that sounds fine." Also about ten times as much as I thought she'd offer. Even if the book turned out to be a dud, I would still be paid. Caroline might not be the person I'd choose to work for, but certainly I could endure a few months with her. After all, how difficult could it be to write her life story?

"Good," she said. "We'll get started tomorrow morning at eight. Expect to put in some long hours. After all, this is the book that's going to keep me alive."

I was still unclear on how the book was going to do that. "About keeping you alive . . . ?"

"We'll talk about it tomorrow. I have things to do now." Then she hung up on me—again. This woman certainly did not like long good-byes.

I turned to Emily. "I guess I'm going to ghostwrite a book."

"That's terrific. You've always said you wanted to have a book published someday, and here someone is paying you to write it."

Put that way, the job did sound more appealing. Even though it might not be the most interesting topic in the world, I would be writing a real book—something I'd dreamed of doing ever since I was a girl. I smiled at my daughter. Maybe things weren't so bad after all.

"I've got news too. Good news and bad news."

"What's the bad news?"

"After you left this morning Matt phoned Katie. He told her his project is taking longer than expected and he'll have to stay in China for at least another month. When Katie said maybe she could come to China to join him, Matt said she'd be too much of a distraction to him and they could save more money if she just found another job."

"Oh, dear." While in many ways a sweet man, Matt sometimes had an unfortunate tendency to put his foot in his mouth. "What did Katie say?"

"She said he shouldn't count on her being there when he finally managed to get back to Dallas. Then she hung up on him."

I winced. Poor Katie. "Do you know where she is now?"

"She went to see her old college roommate friend. Anne has a catering business and told Katie she could work for her. Katie said since there's no point in going back to Dallas, maybe she'd just stay here and be a waitress at rich people's parties."

"What's your good news?" I asked.

Em displayed the endearing little smile that had never failed to warm my heart. "I've been doing some research and I've decided what I want to be when I grow up."

"Oh?" With her brains, the girl could be anything she chose. I'd worry later about how to pay for medical or graduate school.

Em held up one of the books she'd been reading. "You know how I love solving mysteries. I've decided to become a private investigator."

I smiled weakly. "Are there college classes for that?"

She rolled her eyes. "Oh, Mother, you are incorrigible."

CHAPTER SIX

I was leaving my apartment for my first day as a ghostwriter when a police officer arrived to take my statement. I phoned Caroline to say I'd be late, then sat down with Officer Megan McCarthy to disclose what I knew about Mary Alice's death. Not much.

No, I hadn't seen anyone slip any suspicious items into Mary Alice's food and I didn't think she'd eaten anything unusual. I hadn't glimpsed any strangers slipping in or out of the house. Everyone I saw had been at the dinner table.

At last, a question that I could answer affirmatively! Yes, I *had* seen a conflict between dinner guests. Unfortunately Officer McCarthy didn't seem all that interested when I described the heated argument between Mary Alice and her twin sister Ellen at the beginning of the evening. Nor did she react when I recounted that Mary Alice said her children had "anger management issues" and had threatened to hire a hit man to take Mom out.

Either the police officer had already heard the stories or she was only interested in possible motives if they were accompanied by cold, hard facts. If I'd actually *seen* Ellen put something suspicious into Mary Alice's dessert, the police woman would have taken note.

Ellen, I had to admit, had been sitting at the opposite end of the table from Mary Alice and, as far as I could see, had no opportunity to mess with Mary Alice's meal. She'd also seemed genuinely shocked when her sister became ill. As for Mary Alice's children, I had seen no evidence of them or any skulking hit man either—unless the kids had hired one of the dinner guests as their assassin.

I sensed I was boring Officer McCarthy—or perhaps she was just thinking about what she was going to have for lunch. But her expression changed to something resembling interest when she asked what I knew about Nathan Evans.

"In his dinner table lecture about toxic plants did Mr. Evans specifically mention the Barbados nut? He might have called it by its scientific name, *Jatropha curcas,* or called it a physic nut, purge nut, curcas bean, or kukui haole."

I thought about it. "I'm not sure, but I don't think so." I hadn't been paying that much attention to Nathan's recital. After all, who wants to hear about poisons while eating a rather strange-tasting dinner?

The police officer tried again. "What explanation did Mr. Evans give for bringing his own food to the dinner and refusing to eat any of the communal offerings?"

"He did eat some of his contribution to the dinner, a bag of vegetable chips, though he didn't touch any food that anyone else brought. I assumed he was afraid of botulism and salmonella—topics that figured prominently in his speech—but he also just seemed kind of paranoid."

"Did he appear to know Mary Alice or display any animosity towards her?"

"Not that I noticed."

"Did you ever see him put anything into the communal food or on Mary Alice's plate?"

"I don't remember seeing him touch any communal food except his veggie chips, which were quite stale. He also wasn't sitting close to Mary Alice—she sat between Caroline and Ethan, several seats away from him—so it would have been difficult to put anything on her plate without anyone noticing."

Why, I wondered, was Nathan such a person of interest to the police? Sure, he'd refused to eat any food he had not brought himself and, yes, he had left the dinner early, but that still didn't explain why he'd want to kill Mary Alice.

It sounded as if the police had already decided that Nathan was guilty. I didn't like seeing anyone scapegoated, which was probably why I decided not to mention seeing Nathan in Caroline's study while everyone else was at dinner. Whatever Nathan had been doing in there, I doubted it had any connection to poisoning Mary Alice.

I figured it was my turn to ask a few questions. "What do these poisonous Barbados nuts look like?"

"From what I've heard, it's the seeds of the nut that are most often used as a poison. They're black, thin-shelled, and kind of oily. They could be ground up before being added to the food."

In other words, no one would probably notice a strange-looking ingredient in their salad, dessert, or soup. "Do they have any distinctive flavor?" I asked, remembering the bitter-tasting salad that I'd barely touched.

"The nuts are supposed to have a very pleasant taste."

"If anyone else ate a small amount would they get sick? Because one thing I did notice was Mary Alice ate rather large portions of everything."

"The Barbados nut is toxic in even small amounts," she said briskly, clearly getting impatient to leave. "People become sick fifteen or twenty minutes after eating them."

I shivered. In other words, Mary Alice had consumed these poisonous nuts at Caroline's house.

"Just one more thing," I said, "have you spoken to Nathan already?" Was it something he'd told them that had catapulted him into the leading suspect spot?

Her eyes narrowed. "We haven't been able to locate him. Do

you know where we might find him?"

"No, all I know is he said he was a Ph.D. student in physics."

"We know that, too." With a look that suggested I had been a big disappointment to her, the police officer departed, presumably to find a witness who would deliver.

I arrived at Caroline's house at 9:10. By 9:13 she had me sign the nondisclosure agreement.

Then, and only then, did Caroline deign to tell me more about the secrets she intended to reveal in her book. "As I've mentioned, someone has been trying to kill me. I want to use the book to make sure that they don't succeed."

I had to ask it: "How can writing a book stop someone from killing you?"

She sent me a patronizing, isn't-that-obvious look. "My book will identify my potential killers—present all the evidence to convict them. Since they obviously do *not* want that information to come out, they'll give up their attempts to murder me."

I could see several holes in that reasoning. "But wouldn't that make the killer more eager to kill you quickly, before the book is published?" Wasn't she in fact providing her assassin with a deadline for homicide as well as an incentive to get rid of the book's author—me? I had a sudden mental image of someone making another addition to a To-Do List: Get rid of ghostwriter ASAP, before she finishes book that sends me to prison.

Caroline shook her head. "Not if I make it clear that the incriminating chapters of the book will be published only in the event of my death."

Which meant that any semi-smart killer would delay the hit until after the book, minus the incriminating chapters, was published. Not many publishers would be eager to reprint a new book with an additional—and potentially libelous—chapter on who might or might not have killed the author.

Of course there was also the pesky issue of how exactly Caroline intended to notify her killer that she was writing a book that would send him/her to prison. "Are you saying that you know for sure who's trying to kill you?"

She shook her head. "But I have several strong candidates, and I intend to make sure *all* of them think that, if I die, the book will implicate them."

"*All?*" I asked. "How many potential killers are we talking about?"

She cocked her head, considering. "I can think of three possibilities—maybe four. And there may be some others I haven't identified yet."

Maybe I should start thinking about other job possibilities. Either this woman had more enemies than a crime boss or she had serious mental health issues. Neither possibility boded well for a happy working relationship.

"You mentioned there'd already been several attempts on your life," I said. "What exactly happened?"

"As I told you, I had anonymous threatening letters. They all said something along the lines of 'I'll make you pay, you bitch' and 'You'll get yours.' But the actual violence didn't start until a couple of months ago. I was out dumpster diving with a class and there was a homemade bomb waiting for me inside the dumpster—the one behind a grocery store that I always take my students to. Fortunately, that day I didn't poke around the bin because one of the students had come down with a stomach bug and we had to cut the class short. If we hadn't left early, I probably would have had my arm blown off. We were driving away when the bomb exploded."

Bombs? Maybe someone actually *was* trying to kill her.

"Then, of course, there was the attempted poisoning at the dinner at my house. Those toxic nuts that killed Mary Alice were intended for me. Normally I love sweets, but, luckily, I just wasn't in the mood for them that night."

Not so lucky for Mary Alice, I thought.

CHAPTER SEVEN

I wasn't entirely sure what compelled me to attend the memorial service for Mary Alice. I'd like to say I simply wanted to pay my respects to the woman who'd died so horribly after our shared dinner, but I had to admit I was also there out of curiosity. As a result, I felt uncomfortably like a passerby rubbernecking at the scene of a grisly accident.

Walking into the designated room at the funeral home, I was surprised to see several of my fellow dinner guests from Mary Alice's last supper already seated among the mourners. I knew, of course, that Ellen, Mary Alice's twin sister, would be there, but I hadn't expected to see Caroline and her assistant, Ophelia, or Margaret and Ethan, the homeschooling, back-to-the-land couple.

Then I gawked as I spotted the tall, skinny young man taking a seat. Nathan? The last I'd heard, the police were trying to locate him for questioning. Why was he here?

I slid into a back row just as a serious-looking bald man in a black suit walked to the podium and cleared his throat. "We are here today to celebrate the too-short life of Mary Alice Hatcher," he began.

I surveyed the audience as he covered the basic biographical details I'd already read in the newspaper obituary. At the time of her death, Mary Alice had been 55 (I would have thought she was older), the divorced mother of two daughters, and a recently retired high-school science teacher.

Could Nathan, the physics grad student, have once been Mary Alice's student? I wondered, my mind racing to create imaginary connections between these disparate people. Perhaps Nathan had poisoned Mary Alice at the dinner because she'd been a caustic teacher who'd given him bad grades and mocked his ambitions to become a scientist. Or maybe women with long noses and gray eyes reminded him of his sadistic granny and he'd vowed to kill them all, using his knowledge of toxic plants to plan the perfect, untraceable murder.

I told myself I had to rein in my over-active imagination. I'd seen absolutely no evidence at the dinner that Mary Alice and Nathan knew each other. A much more likely scenario was that Nathan had returned to town and heard from the police that Mary Alice had died from something she ate at the dinner, and he—like the rest of us dinner guests—had come to the memorial to pay our respects and appease our curiosity.

While the speaker droned on about the more mundane aspects of Mary Alice's life, I studied my fellow mourners. Nathan, to the left, sat quietly, looking a bit bored. He'd seemed a nervous, twitching kind of guy at Caroline's house. If he indeed had killed Mary Alice, I doubted he'd be acting this calm.

I could only see the backs of Ethan and Margaret, sitting in the row directly ahead of me. They seemed the kind of solid people who, in addition to eating organic and homeschooling their kids, would feel it their moral duty to attend funerals of everyone they'd ever met.

Caroline, sitting near the front, looked as if she'd pasted an earnest expression on her face and was now mentally running through her to-do list. Her assistant, Ophelia, however, seemed genuinely upset. Had she known Mary Alice personally? Perhaps she felt responsible that a guest had eaten toxic food at a dinner Ophelia was overseeing. Or maybe she was just of those supersensitive people who always cry at funerals.

As far as I could see, Ophelia and Mary Alice's sister had the only wet eyes in the audience. Ellen, in the front row, was sobbing so hard that the twenty-something girl with Goth hair seated next to her—her daughter, I presumed—was patting her on the shoulder, while also looking acutely embarrassed by her relative's emotionalism.

The man at the podium cleared his throat. "And now Mary Alice's sister Ellen and her daughter Eleanor want to share their memories of her."

Good. Maybe now I could learn something more personal than the organizations Mary Alice had belonged to.

Ellen walked to the podium. She was still red-eyed, but when she spoke her voice was steady. "Mary Alice was my twin sister—my older sister by three minutes, as she always pointed out." She waited for the polite laughter to subside before continuing. "She was also my dearest friend, someone who was always there for me through every major milestone in my life— the happy ones, like my wedding and the births of my children, and the miserable ones, like the death of my husband. Mary Alice was always by my side, holding my hand or offering encouragement and advice."

Encouragement? Hand holding? Was she talking about the same Mary Alice I'd met? The two sisters I'd seen at Caroline's dinner had looked as if they might break out into a fist fight at any minute.

Tears were now running down Ellen's cheeks. "I—I don't know how I'm going to go on living without her." She was still sobbing as she staggered back to her seat.

The young woman who replaced her at the podium was clearly Mary Alice's daughter. Tall, gaunt, with a prominent nose like her mother's, she also had Mary Alice's scowl. "It sucks to have your mother die," she announced.

It was hard to disagree with that, but she seemed to be waiting for someone in the audience to contradict her. When no one did, she said, "My mother and I didn't always get along. In fact, we often didn't. She had a lot of strong opinions that just struck me and my sister as wrong—like naming me for Eleanor Roosevelt and my sister for Emma Goldman." She glanced at a tall, sullen-looking teenaged girl in the audience—presumably Emma—who rolled her eyes.

I could see that these girls might indeed have what Mary Alice had called "anger management issues." In their emotional lexicon, would threatening to hire a hit man to off Mom qualify as *not always getting along*?

"But I miss Ma," Eleanor said, sounding rather surprised. "She could be a real bitch sometimes, but she taught me a lot. Once when I was in middle school an older girl on the school bus was bullying me—calling me names, kicking the back of my seat. I went home crying to my mother. She listened to me, then said, 'So what are you going to do about it?' The next day I, uh, made it very clear to the girl on the bus that I wasn't going to take her abuse anymore. And you know what? After that she left me alone."

From the audience Emma Goldman Hatcher snickered loudly, obviously enjoying the memory of whatever heinous thing her sister had done to the bully. Eleanor met her sister's eyes and smirked. It was the first show of good humor from either of them.

"That was the best lesson my mother taught me," Eleanor continued. "You have to stand up for yourself because no one else will. And I've never forgotten that."

Nathan, I noticed, had gotten up. He was now sauntering toward the door.

Eleanor watched him leave, her face impassive. "Well, that's all I wanted to say," she said. "Thanks for coming."

That was it? Rather than answering my questions, this service had only raised more. Why had Nathan once again left early? Why had Ellen depicted her relationship with her abrasive sister as something straight from the pages of *Little Women*? Why had Ophelia been crying? And could one or both of Mary Alice's surly daughters have decided the best way to stand up for themselves was by poisoning their overbearing mother?

I came home to the aromas of simmering spaghetti sauce and baking garlic bread wafting through the apartment. Heaven. My older daughter had not inherited her love of cooking and superior culinary skills from me, but I was nevertheless glad she'd somehow acquired them.

"That smells delicious, Katie," I said, giving her a kiss on the cheek. "I certainly hope I'm invited to this dinner."

"Don't have many other people to cook for right now," she said. A mask of too-familiar melancholy seemed to fall over her face. "I'd always thought that by this time in my life, I'd be cooking big family dinners every night for my husband and kids."

I squeezed her shoulder. "Someday you will, honey."

"I hope." She made a determined effort to look more cheerful. "But I actually had a good time today. I was over at Anne's. She has the sweetest little baby, Mom. Aaron's six months old and he's so cute. He giggles and smiles, and I love smelling the top of his head. That's such a wonderful baby smell. I told her I'd love to babysit for him anytime, and she's taking me up on my offer."

I smiled. "I used to sniff the top of your heads, too."

Emily, coming into the kitchen, shook her head. The maternal gene, she'd always said, had passed her by.

"Have you set the table yet?" Katie asked her sister.

"Yes, ma'am, exactly as ordered."

Katie ignored the sarcasm. "Then start cutting up vegetables for the salad."

I handed Em a chopping board and knife and got out the same for myself. "I'll help with the cutting."

As the three of us worked on dinner preparations, I asked my younger daughter how she'd spent her day.

"I applied for more jobs online and went to talk to Mrs. Owens to see if she had anything at the library I can do. She said they don't have any full-time openings right now, but she could use me part-time to shelve books and help out at the desk. I thought I could do that while I develop my investigator skills."

"Investigator skills?"

Emily's face grew more animated. "You'll be amazed, Mom, what you can learn from books: surveillance techniques, how to tail and track a mark, how to uncover hidden assets and other information that people want to keep hidden—all kind of things you'd never dream you could do."

Most of which, undoubtedly, I would not *want* to dream that she'd do. "Uh, exactly how are you developing these skills?"

"Well, right now I'm just reading about them, but eventually, of course, I'll want to try them out. I'm going to contact every private investigator in town to see if I can work for them, even if I have to be an unpaid intern."

Correctly interpreting the look on my face, she added, "They'd never have me do anything dangerous, Mom. I'm sure they only let experienced people do those jobs. I'd probably just have to do routine stuff on the computer." Her voice sounded wistful that she would not be allowed to do those dangerous, fun jobs.

Katie checked to see if the pot of water she was going to cook the pasta in was boiling yet. "Your education dollars at work, Mom. I'm using my college degree to work as Aaron's babysitter and do some waitressing, and Emily is going to be a part-time library aide and an unpaid intern."

At least, I told myself, I was grateful they'd found some paid work, even if it was part-time. After all, the girls wouldn't be in town long anyway. Staying with me was only meant as a brief transition period—in Katie's case, a visit while her husband was away in China and, in Emily's, a short break from school while she figured out what she was going to major in. I just hoped that was also the way my girls envisioned their stay at my apartment.

Katie, at least, seemed in better humor today. Maybe getting out of Dallas for a few weeks was just what she needed. She smiled over her shoulder. "I sent Matt an e-mail, Mom, saying I was having a great time with Aaron. It was wonderful to feel really appreciated by a guy."

"She, of course, did *not* mention that Aaron is six months old," Emily said.

"Yeah, and Matt freaked," Katie said, with visible satisfaction. In college, Matt, a quiet, more studious type than his wife, had always been intensely jealous of gregarious Katie's many male admirers.

I sighed. "You don't think it might be more productive, Katie, if you just talked to Matt and told him how lonely you've been with him gone so much?"

She sent me an exasperated, *Oh, Mother* look. "No. He knows that—or at least he *should* know it. Matt needs to learn that he has to stop taking me for granted."

With great restraint, I managed not to comment.

Em, busily chopping a cucumber, said, "Oh, Mom, I meant to tell you how I thought I'd practice my new investigative skills. I'll try to find out who poisoned that woman at the potluck dinner."

I stared at her. "The police are working on it, Em. I don't

think they'd appreciate your getting involved in their ongoing investigation." And I really, really, did not want her to antagonize someone deranged enough to put lethal nuts into food at a dinner party.

She brushed off my concerns as if they were hovering mosquitoes. "Oh, I won't tread on the police's toes. I thought if I'm not working at the library, I might come along when you do the interviews for your book. I might pick up some valuable background information. You could even use what I learn in your book. You're certainly going to write a chapter on the potluck poisoning, aren't you?"

At the moment I was not certain what I was going to do about anything. "I'm not sure yet what I'll write, but I'd appreciate your help with the research." It seemed a much better idea for Em to accompany me on interviews with Caroline's students than to go off on her own to find a psychopath interested in toxic plants.

Maybe Em could do some research for the book, perhaps collecting background information on cost-cutting tips housekeepers used in different eras. My research assignments would NOT involve trying to identify potential poisoners or criminal investigations of any kind.

Katie was dumping the cooked spaghetti into a colander. "Everything's ready, ladies. Let's eat."

CHAPTER EIGHT

When I reported to work the morning after the memorial Ophelia answered the door. "Caroline's on a phone call that I suspect might take awhile. Why don't you come and have a cup of coffee with me while you wait."

That sounded good to me. As Ophelia poured me a cup, we talked about the service for Mary Alice. "I thought it was incredibly sad," she said. "No one should die so horribly. And to think it happened after eating *my* food . . ."

"It wasn't your food that made Mary Alice sick. It was poisonous nuts."

Ophelia did not look reassured. "But the nuts were in the dessert I made. The police investigator took samples of all the food, including the leftovers on Mary Alice's bowl. The lab tests showed traces of Barbados nut in her cobbler."

My eyes widened. "I ate that cobbler, too."

"So did I. Apparently the nuts were only in the helping that Mary Alice ate. They tested the leftover dessert in the refrigerator and it was fine." She sighed. "And before you ask, I'll tell you what I told the police. I have no idea how those nuts got there. I certainly didn't add them. I dished up the dessert and brought the bowls to the table. None of them was intended for a specific person."

I tried to process all that she'd said. "Are you saying that anyone at the table could have gotten the serving containing the poisonous nuts?" Me, for instance.

"It appears that way," Ophelia said. "But that still doesn't explain how the nuts got into any of the cobbler. I didn't see anyone skulking around the kitchen during dinner, and I was there most of the time before that."

"When did you actually make the cobbler?"

"That morning. I baked it at Caroline's because her oven is better than the one in my apartment."

"Was anybody there while you were making it?"

She cocked her head, thinking. "There's usually a lot of people coming in and out of Caroline's house. I remember her walking through, but there certainly weren't any strangers sniffing around."

"I wonder if someone could have added the poisonous nuts after the dessert was on the table." If I recalled correctly, Ophelia had brought in a big tray of cobbler, and the bowls had just been passed around the table.

Could it possibly be that some maniac had wanted to kill and didn't really care who the victim was? After all, serial killers murdered people they'd never met. Sometimes their victims were a certain physical type, but sometimes the only trait the victims shared was being at the wrong place at the wrong time. But what did the people at the dinner have in common? Frugality? Attendance at Caroline's class?

Ophelia looked dubious. "But don't you think it would be risky for someone at the dinner to dump poisonous nuts into one serving in front of a table full of witnesses?"

"Yes, very risky." But didn't psychopathic killers get off on taking dangerous risks? And frankly, this seemed a method that only someone with a screw loose would use. Besides the high chance of getting caught, there was also the fact that so much could easily go wrong. What if no one ate the one poisoned serving?

There seemed so many easier and more reliable ways to commit a murder. Shooting, for instance. There was a good reason that few professional hit men favored poisonous nuts as their weapon of choice.

I wished I remembered more of what had happened around the time Ophelia set the desserts on the table, but that was when I'd headed for the bathroom. I'd been much more interested in Nathan's behavior—his rummaging through Caroline's office and leaving the party early. In fact the only notable thing I recalled of the latter part of the dinner was the gusto with which Mary Alice consumed her dessert.

"Poor Mary Alice." I shivered. "You know Caroline told me she thought she was the killer's intended victim."

Ophelia's smile was not pleasant. "Oh Caroline *always* thinks she's the chosen one."

"And yet," said a familiar voice from behind us, "the killer chose the food *you* made for the dinner in which to deposit the poisonous nuts. I wonder why that was?"

I could see the spots of red on Ophelia's pale cheeks as we both turned to face Caroline.

"I can only guess," Ophelia replied in an icy voice. "Perhaps he dumped the nuts in the first food that was available when no one was looking his way and the opportune moment occurred when we were passing out the cobbler."

Caroline raised a skeptical eyebrow. "He? Why not she?" She didn't wait for an answer. "I was just thinking that the cobbler was an ideal hiding place for those toxic nuts. After all, there were other chopped nuts in it already. No one would think anything of a few extra ones tucked in."

I could feel my mouth drop open as I glanced from Caroline's sneer to Ophelia's blazing eyes. Was Caroline accusing Ophelia of poisoning Mary Alice?

Apparently Ophelia had the same reaction. "If I had been trying to murder someone I'd have to be pretty damn stupid to add the poison to my own food, wouldn't I? As you have pointed out, Caroline, despite my many flaws, I am not stupid. Nor, for that matter, am I homicidal. And as you well know, there is a very big difference between wishing someone dead and actually killing her."

To my astonishment, Caroline laughed. Ophelia looked less amused, but at least she seemed a tad less angry.

As if nothing at all had just happened, Caroline turned to me. "I guess we should get to work now. Let's go to the living room. Ophelia will be working in the office."

Having received our marching orders, Ophelia and I stood. "Oh, one more thing," Caroline told her assistant. "Nathan Evans keeps calling to get an appointment with me. I don't want to talk to him. That kid is a major pest."

Ophelia nodded, but the muscles in her jaw tightened. Did she resent being Caroline's gatekeeper? Or did she feel that Caroline was mistreating Nathan, a guy who, after all, had attended Caroline's class?

As I followed her to the living room, my mind reeled with more questions. Why did Caroline not want to talk to Nathan? And what did Ophelia mean when she said Caroline knew all about wishing someone was dead?

After the acrimonious beginning to the morning, the next hour with Caroline was relatively uneventful. She shared her "vision" for her book. It would emphasize that living frugally meant being in charge of one's own destiny. "Money," she said with authority, "does not make you happy; it and the luxuries it buys are only a quick fix for desperate people."

To illustrate the point she rambled on about her privileged childhood. "Constant shopping was my parents' favorite pastime and consumerism, my family's religion, but, like all addictions, the fix—that wonderful new possession—only provided a brief jolt of pleasure. Then we needed another extravagant purchase to make us feel worthwhile."

Did she really think that anyone would regard this as a startling insight? Well, maybe some die-hard shopaholics might, but it didn't seem likely that they'd be picking up a book on penny-pinching. "Perhaps we should focus first on specific tips that your readers can use in their daily lives. I thought we might expand on some of those excellent class handouts you gave me. Did you write them?"

Unlike Caroline's rambling and self-absorbed speaking, her handouts had been refreshingly down-to-earth and straightforward. I sensed she was at her best when she was being practical rather than philosophical.

"I dictated the articles to Ophelia," she said stiffly. "They were my ideas that she typed up."

Kind of like I would be "typing up" her book? "Maybe we could use some case histories of how people incorporate these frugal principles into their daily lives."

"I was thinking the very same thing," Caroline said. "There was a hairdresser in one of my classes, Patricia Somebody— Ophelia will know her last name—who bartered for everything. She cut a mechanic's hair for a whole year in exchange for getting major work done on her car. Then there was that couple— you met them at our dinner—who homeschool their kids and grow all their own food. They exchange their produce for other items they need. And, oh yes, there was another woman a couple of months ago who threw big garage sales from her dumpster-diving finds."

Caroline looked inordinately pleased with herself. "You can get these people's contact information from Ophelia. She keeps all the records and has a better memory for the different students than I do. She'll probably have some more ideas on people to interview."

"You mentioned before that this book would keep you alive

and protect you from your enemies," I said. "Maybe you could elaborate on that a little more?" Without more specifics, I was having a hard time imagining anyone working themselves into a murderous snit over Caroline's provocative ideas on materialism.

She waved her hand dismissively. "We'll have to get to that another day. I have an appointment now."

She stood, glancing at her watch. "Ophelia," I heard her call from the hall, "Lauren needs some information."

When Ophelia appeared, I apologized for interrupting.

"Don't worry about it," she said. "After working with Caroline for so long, I'm used to it. What do you need?"

She went to the computer and shortly came back with the required contact numbers. "I also added the names of a few more people you might interview."

I thanked her. "If you don't mind my asking, why didn't you write this book? You certainly know the subject inside and out, and Caroline as much as admitted that you were the one who wrote those great class handouts."

Ophelia's smile was only a trifle bitter. "I'll bet she didn't say I *wrote* the handouts, did she?"

"She might have said she dictated the information to you."

Ophelia snorted. "Caroline has dyslexia, so she has a hard time writing anything. But she tells herself that I am merely transcribing her ideas. The important thing, you see, is *her* vision and her ambition."

I wondered once more how this woman could continue to work for someone who treated her so badly.

As if she was afraid she'd offended me, Ophelia said, "I'm not saying I'm a real writer, like you are. I can string words together, but my style is nonexistent. Since Caroline has illusions of reaching the best-seller list, she wanted a pro to write her book."

"Books on frugality aren't likely to become best sellers, no matter who writes them." I shrugged ruefully. "Probably the topic isn't sensational enough."

Ophelia narrowed her eyes. "Oh, if Caroline told the truth about her life, instead of—"

Before she could finish that thought, Caroline's voice interrupted from the hallway. "I had to come back to the house for my cell phone," she explained. "Now that you've got the phone numbers, Lauren, I know you'll want to get started on those interviews right away. I want to read your complete outline of the book by the end of the week."

Then, in case I was too dim to grasp her subtle message, Caroline wiggled her fingers good-bye.

As I walked out the front door, I heard her say, "And you and I, Ophelia, need to get a few things straight."

After all the veiled—and not-so-veiled—hostility I'd witnessed at Caroline's, I was looking forward to a relaxed dinner at home. Katie had volunteered to cook and suggested I invite Paul to join us. He had enthusiastically accepted, saying he was eager to get to know my daughters.

"Oh, good," Katie said when I told her. "There are a lot of things Em and I want to find out about him as well. Tell him to come at seven. Unless, of course, that's too late for him. He is quite a bit older than you, isn't he?"

Well, maybe dinner wouldn't be as relaxed as I'd hoped. "Yeah, two whole years older. But for this special occasion, I'm sure he'll be willing to stay up past nine."

Katie rolled her eyes. Em said, "Don't worry, Mom. It will be fun for us all to get acquainted."

It was more like a tribunal with food, I thought, as I glanced around my dining-room table. What lunacy had allowed me to believe that having Paul and my daughters share a meal was a good idea?

Paul was his usual charmingly inquisitive self. Smiling, he asked the girls how they were enjoying their visit and how they were spending their time.

Katie, normally friendly and gregarious, answered curtly that she'd been doing some babysitting for a friend.

Paul, of course, could not leave it at that. He was at heart a journalist. Some people—Katie, for instance—experienced his interest as more akin to interrogation.

I could see my daughter's lips tighten as she answered that the baby was six months old, yes, she enjoyed sitting for him, and, no, she didn't do it every day.

Paul, fortunately, switched his focus to Em.

Generally my reserved daughter, Em seemed delighted to talk about herself. At length. She told Paul about her search for a new direction for her life, her part-time library work, her attempts to find a job or internship at a private investigative agency.

"Oh, what kind of detective work are you interested in?" Paul asked.

"I'm not sure yet. All the different kinds of researching and surveillance that investigators do sound really interesting. When I hear about the woman who was poisoned at that potluck dinner I keep thinking how a PI would use those skills to solve the case."

"Being an investigative reporter is a bit like that. I did that for a few years, when I worked on a newspaper. I loved having the time to develop a story and really delve into a subject."

"That does sound cool," Em said.

Also less dangerous than being a PI, I thought. And it required a college education. "Sounds fascinating," I said brightly.

"Yeah, too bad all those newspaper jobs have dried up," Paul said. "So you're planning to be in town long enough to take a full-time job, Emily? I didn't realize you were going to be here that long."

I wanted to dump my glass of wine on his head.

Em suddenly looked less friendly. "My plans aren't that concrete yet. I'm still checking things out."

Katie narrowed her eyes. "And who knows how long that will take?" she said, smiling sweetly at Paul. "No telling how long we'll be here."

Quickly I interjected, "Katie and her husband live in Dallas." *And eventually she is going to move back there.*

"Though lately my husband has been spending more time in China than in Dallas," Katie said grimly.

Fortunately, this time Paul had enough sense not to ask a follow-up question.

This gave Katie a chance to step into the role of Grand Inquisitor. "How about you, Mr. O'Neal? What are *your* plans now that your magazine is folding?"

Well, turnabout was fair play, wasn't it? I also was eager to hear Paul's answer.

He smiled at her. "That's a question I wish I knew the answer to. For now I'm tying up loose ends at the magazine and exploring my job options."

"Are those options based in Houston?" she asked.

"Mom mentioned something about you starting a new magazine in Seattle," Em added.

Paul turned to me, his expression inquisitive, assessing.

Stop, all of you! I wanted to snap. Not only were the girls embarrassing me with their lack of manners, but they were revealing way too much to our observant guest. I could just imagine how he must be interpreting their questions, probably envisioning vulnerable, needy Lauren tearfully telling her daughters how upset she was that Paul the Magnificent was about to soon move out of her life.

Just to set the record straight, I had not told the girls any such thing. I might have matter-of-factly and unemotionally mentioned that Paul *might* be moving to dismal, rainy Washington state to work on a risky start-up magazine, but they had inferred everything else.

"The magazine is a very remote possibility, just a friend's pie-in-the-sky idea." He turned to Katie. "By the way, this is a delicious dinner. You mother told me what an accomplished cook you are."

"Thanks," Katie said. "I do like to cook when I have people to cook for. My father gave me cooking classes taught by a famous French chef as a Christmas gift one year. He has a great appreciation for fine cuisine."

And fine everything else, I wanted to add—except that the high-flying creep happened to also be their beloved father. It seemed unkind to point out that Daddy's superb taste and compulsive spending were a big factor in his turning to insurance fraud and falsification of criminals' dental records to supplement the income from his dental practice.

"Well, it seems it was money well spent," Paul told Katie, refusing to rise to the bait. "And you were obviously an excellent student."

With as much heartiness as I could muster, I announced, "I for one am ready to sample Katie's famous chocolate mousse." We needed to get this dinner over with before I had a mental breakdown or dropped dead from mortification.

The rest of the dinner was conspicuously more bland, with all participants reverting to their best behavior. Paul inquired about my progress on Caroline's book and we all talked about movies we liked. It was too bad, I thought bitterly, eating chocolate that I barely tasted, that they hadn't opted for that tactic an hour and a half earlier.

But finally the interminable dinner was over and I was walking Paul to the door. We stepped outside, closing the door behind us.

"I enjoyed meeting your daughters," he said, leaning down to kiss me. "It was an interesting evening."

Interesting? It was not the adjective that I myself would have picked.

Back in the apartment, cleanup noises were coming from the kitchen and it sounded as if the girls were arguing. I sighed, remembering the blessed solitude and quiet time to write that I had been looking forward to when I'd moved into my cozy apartment with my very own home office.

Except I had experienced very little solitude and certainly no quiet because the girls had arrived hours after I moved in. If this awkward dinner had done nothing else, it showed me that I needed, desperately needed, some space: physical space where I could sit and write in my office cubbyhole without having to move someone's clothes to find a seat. Emotional space where I wasn't required to be the mediator-in-residence, soothing everyone's else's feelings, and had time to contemplate what I wanted and needed at this point in my life.

"Mom?" Katie called as I walked by. "Aren't you going to say something?" There was a faint pleading note in her voice that reminded me of when she was a little girl asking, "Are you mad at me, Mommy?"

"I've got a bad headache, Katie. I need to take something and lie down for a little while."

"I'm sorry if I was rude to your friend," she said, the words coming out in a rush. "It's just that he's so different from Daddy."

Which was one of the things I most liked about Paul, I thought but did not say. "What do you mean?"

Katie put down her dishcloth, obviously thinking about it. "Well, he asks an awful lot of questions, doesn't he?"

"It's a journalist's job to ask questions," Em said. "I think Mr. O'Neal is very smart. I like him."

"You do?" I asked, feeling as if I'd been holding my breath and just got a lungful of air.

"I don't *dislike* him," Katie said. "I guess I just expected him to be more like Daddy." And she missed her father. She and Em had gone to see Rob a couple of times in prison, but Katie in particular had found the visits with her once supremely confident and ebullient parent upsetting.

I gave her shoulder a squeeze. "By the way, Paul told me he enjoyed meeting both of you and said again how delicious the meal was."

"You know, Mom," Em said, following me into the hallway. "After Mr. O'Neal talked about how interesting investigative reporting is, I wanted to be sure to remind you that I'd like to come along when you do those interviews tomorrow. They don't need me at the library for the next two days."

"Okay, you can come and observe, but you've got to let me do the interviewing."

"Great! I will be a totally silent onlooker." She sent me a huge grin. "Seeing you work is going to be exciting. And maybe I'll even get some leads on the Potluck Poisoning."

She made it sound like the title of an old mystery novel. Which was not a good thing, if she was also envisioning herself as the intrepid amateur sleuth who solved the case. "Remember," I said in my Stern Mother voice. "You promised to be a *silent* onlooker."

"Yes, ma'am. We private investigators always like to sit quietly in a corner and observe our suspects."

Suspects? "Emily," I began.

But she interrupted me, her eyes twinkling. "Chill, Mom, I was just kidding."

CHAPTER NINE

Patricia—"call me Pat"—Holly opened the door of her thirties-era stone cottage and, smiling at Em and me, invited us to come inside. Which was not, we instantly realized, an easily accomplished feat.

"Watch your step," Pat said. "It's kind of crowded in here."

Kind of crowded? There was barely a five-foot-wide corridor through the maze of stacked boxes and piles of things—clothes, books, magazines—on every available chair or table. This was a woman with serious hoarding issues.

"I need to get my stuff better organized," she said apologetically, "but I just never seem to have the time."

In my personal opinion, she needed to throw away about 75 percent of her "stuff" before she even thought about organizing. "I know how hard it is," I said instead. "A few months ago I moved from a four-bedroom house into a two-bedroom apartment. You never know how much you've accumulated until you're faced with packing it all up."

"Tell me about it, hon." She nodded energetically, her long, straight, brown hair falling onto a cheerful face devoid of any makeup. "So what did you end up doing with all that furniture—put it in storage?"

"No, I only kept what I needed to furnish my apartment. I got rid of the rest of it—donated most of it to charity."

She shuddered. "That must have been really hard—parting with beloved things you've had with you for years."

"It was." Clearly Pat didn't plan on parting with any of her beloved possessions anytime soon. I myself was wondering where we could find a few unoccupied chairs to sit on for the interview.

Fortunately Pat had already considered that. "I thought we could talk at my kitchen table. There's more room there."

Her kitchen, in fact, was surprisingly uncluttered. A weathered oak table sat in one corner, surrounded by four chairs (not matching, but all functional). Completing the look were bright blue-and-white curtains that looked as if they'd been sewn by a not-quite proficient seamstress, wood cabinets, faded blue tile countertops that looked original to the house, and an older model stove and refrigerator. All in all, it was a sun-filled and surprisingly cheerful room—a little oasis of normality after we'd trekked through two rooms that seemed more like storage sheds.

Pat offered us herbal tea, which we both accepted. As we sipped, I told her about Caroline's plan to include frugal-living tips from former students in her book.

Pat looked annoyed. "Caroline said I was her former student?"

"You're not?"

"I've spoken at a few of Caroline's classes about my bartering, but I was never her student. Years ago though, I took several classes from Eloisa Hart, Caroline's old boss. I was *Eloisa's* student, as was Caroline. She later became Eloisa's employee."

A warm smile lit her wrinkled face. "Eloisa was a wonderful person—generous, smart, and a born teacher. At a time when the idea of penny-pinching brought back nightmares of the Great Depression for a lot of people, Eloisa made frugality fun. It was as if she was teaching us the secret to mastering this complex game. The grand prize was a life of independence and self-sufficiency. She called her class Living on Next to Nothing."

"That sounds like a good game to learn," Em said with

conviction. "Did you manage to acquire everything in your house through bartering?"

So much for our agreement for my daughter to sit quietly and let me conduct the interview.

Pat leaned forward, warming to her subject. "Some of it I got through bartering, but I also find a lot of bargains shopping garage sales. And lately I've really gotten into couponing. With everything on the Internet now, it's a whole new ballgame."

She nodded at a laptop sitting on her kitchen counter. Unlike almost every other possession I'd spotted in her house, the computer looked new. "You don't have to just clip coupons from the newspaper; you can get tons of them on the Internet. And there are good online bartering sites, so you have a lot more people available to barter with."

Before Em could ask another question, I interjected, "Are you willing to offer tips for Caroline's book?"

"I'm more than willing to help anyone who wants to get started saving money though, to tell you the truth, I'm not too thrilled that Caroline is the one who profits from my advice."

Caroline did not seem very popular with anyone. "You don't like Caroline?" I asked.

Pat shook her head. "I don't, but this isn't about my liking or disliking. It's about Caroline being a shameless opportunist who's taken credit for other people's work. First she took over Eloisa's business when she died. Remember, Caroline had only been Eloisa's assistant, but suddenly she's talking about herself as the oracle of frugality. Sure, she spiced up the presentation and did a good job marketing, but it was still Eloisa's material. And *Eloisa* lived the lifestyle she preached, the way Ophelia does now. Ophelia is the one who cooks from scratch and is a coupon whiz. Hell, she even taught Caroline how to dumpster dive."

"So why isn't Ophelia writing her own book?" I asked. "Why

isn't she teaching the classes herself?"

"That's a good question. I asked Ophelia that once, and she gave me some b.s. about not liking to be in the public eye. She's a talented painter, by the way. She says that this is a perfect job for her—it helps people, it's part-time, and gives her enough time and money to paint. Ophelia got into frugality, you know, because she believed those sayings about starving artists. If she had to be an impoverished painter, she said, she was going to live damn well on her pennies." Pat shrugged. "I can see not wanting to go on TV, but what I don't get is how she can keep working with Caroline."

I wondered that myself, particularly after the way I'd seen Caroline treat Ophelia.

"But you didn't come here to hear me complain about Caroline. So what do you want to know about bartering?"

She told us about how she'd started out exchanging hair cuts and perms for services she needed: mechanical work on her car and minor home repairs. "Then when the economy got so bad, I realized that there were a lot more people eager to do the same thing. Since then, I've bartered everything from dog walking to weaving lessons and got an almost-new laptop, a barely-used treadmill, and a ton of other good stuff in exchange. I have a friend who traded wedding photography for house painting, and another who was a website designer traded her skills with a carpenter. She made him a website and he made her a deck for her house."

Internet barter clubs and websites now even let someone trade their goods or services for credits that could be used later, she said. "For instance, you do so many hours of babysitting or dog walking and then bank your time and use it later to get something that you need. And if you want to do face-to-face bartering, you can always go to a swap meet." Her eyes sparkled. "Now *that's* my idea of fun."

An hour and a half later, our interview over, she led us back through the maze to her front door. "I've enjoyed talking to both of you. You tell Ophelia I say hi."

Margaret Galen was about as different from Pat as two people could be. A tall, brisk woman with cropped, blond hair, Margaret waved Em and me into her neat-as-a-pin house, while the sounds of children's voices wafted from another room. "I can give you forty minutes while the kids do their homework."

She ushered us into a living room with hardwood floors, two sofas, upholstered in an ugly brown material undoubtedly picked for its ability to hide stains, and built-in bookcase that held neatly organized books and plastic bins filled with toys, arts supplies, and notebooks.

I glanced around the room. "Your house is certainly immaculate. I'm envious." Although I'd prefer more color and a few warm decorative touches in my own home, I could only admire the uncluttered order of the place.

"With three children, you have to be organized," Margaret said. "Otherwise there's utter chaos."

The way she said the words, it was clear that Margaret thought of mess and disorder in the way others viewed plague and pestilence.

Em and I sat on one of the mud-colored sofas, while Margaret chose a straight-backed wooden chair across from us. "How do you do it all—the homeschooling, gardening and cooking, along with parenting and running a household?" I asked. Even thinking about it all made me feel exhausted.

"I only sleep four hours a night."

Em grinned. I, on the other hand, realized Margaret wasn't kidding. I doubted the woman was even capable of making a joke. Perhaps she was just too tired.

With predictable succinctness, Margaret then outlined her

frugal philosophy. Boiled down to its essence, it was, "Make do with what is available. If it's not available, do without." Easily stated, not so easily accomplished in our consumer-driven society, I thought, particularly when one had children—those little folks who all wanted the right clothes, the latest video game, and their own cell phone.

Except, her kids didn't want those things, Margaret claimed. "They know how important it is to live simply, using one's own resources. From the time they were little, my children worked in the garden. Even toddlers can pull weeds, and they love feeling as if they're contributing members of the family. When they're a little older, they help prepare the food, too."

As if on cue, a tall girl with freckles appeared carrying some plates. "This is my oldest daughter, Lucy. She wants you to taste the zucchini bread she made from the squash in our garden."

The girl smiled shyly as she handed each of us a plate with a hefty slice of warm bread.

Em and I each took a bite. "This is delicious," I said.

"It's awesome," Em added. "Best zucchini bread I've ever tasted."

"Do you do a lot of baking?" I asked Lucy.

She nodded. "I love to bake and to cook, too. I like to invent recipes that hide vegetables so my brother will eat them. He's seven and he says he hates vegetables."

"But he likes Lucy's food," her mother said proudly. "You wouldn't believe all the pureed vegetables she puts in her spaghetti sauce, and the whole family loves it." She glanced at us. "I need to go check on the other two. If you like, you can interview Lucy."

"Do you like being homeschooled?" Em asked the minute Margaret left.

Lucy nodded. "Sometimes I wish I had classmates my own

age, though we do get together with other kids who are home-schooled. We go to museums or on field trips."

I sent Em a look: *My* interview, remember? "Your mom mentioned that if you kids want something special—say some expensive clothing or toy—you work for it."

Lucy enthusiastically bobbed her head. "I really, really want an iPod. Mom says I can do extra chores to earn money, but so far I've only saved fifteen dollars, and I can't even buy a used one for that."

"How much do you get paid for doing chores?" Em asked.

"It depends," Lucy said. "It has to be something that's not on my chore list, of course. But Mom usually pays me fifty cents an hour for doing extra cleaning and twenty-five cents an hour for babysitting."

Which explained why she only had fifteen dollars. "Why don't you sell your zucchini bread?" Em said. "I'd buy it."

Lucy looked as if she'd just been offered a pile of Christmas presents. "You would? I can get you one of the loaves I baked today, if Mom will let me." She hurried out, returning shortly with a plastic-wrapped loaf. "Mom said I could sell it to you for one dollar. Is that too much?"

Em dug into her purse. "Oh, I think it's worth five dollars," she said, handing the girl the money. "And I'll think of you when I eat it for breakfast."

Lucy beamed at her. "Oh, thank you." Glancing over her shoulder, she whispered, "If you'd like more bread, or some cookies or cakes, I wrote down my phone number for you."

Her mother returned then and Lucy excused herself.

"You didn't have to buy the bread from her," Margaret said. "We don't need charity."

"It wasn't charity," Em said. "I loved the piece she gave us and asked if I could buy a loaf."

Margaret looked slightly less annoyed. "I only have a few

more minutes I can spend with you." The woman was as tight with her time as she was with her money.

"Did you learn anything new from Caroline's class—any techniques you're using?" I asked.

She thought about it. "I learned about dumpster diving. I'd heard about it—my sister-in-law took Caroline's class several years ago—but I'd never tried it. I intend to check the dumpsters behind college dorms at the end of a semester for school supplies."

"So the dumpster-diving information was the most useful thing for you?"

"It was certainly the most useful new thing I learned from Caroline. Ophelia taught me a lot, too. She gave us all a comprehensive list of resale shops where I found some great, barely-used kids' clothes. She also handed out some terrific thrifty recipes. The woman's a real inspiration."

On our way out, Em took a few photos—the kids' chore chart, the huge garden, Lucy stirring a pot of stew. "It was nice meeting you; keep in touch," she called after us.

"I think we have another Martha Stewart in the making there," I said as we climbed into the car. "And I bet if her mother had stayed out of the room longer, she would have sold us her home-baked cookies, muffins, and pies."

"If they're half as good as her bread, I'd buy some of each," Em said. "I feel sorry for those kids, stuck here all day, always under their mother's thumb."

"I think Margaret views it as giving them skills to live a frugal, self-sufficient life."

"Maybe it's *her* idea of a free and independent life, but those kids have no experience of all the other options out there. Maybe what *they'd* prefer is eating take-out pizza, being around children their own age, and wearing clothes that no one else has worn first."

"From what I saw, the kids looked happy enough," I said. Lucy seemed a pleasant and energetic girl, and, when we'd met them briefly, her little brother and sister had appeared cheerful and polite.

"Maybe they just don't know any better. You know what else I noticed? Considering this is Caroline's book, nobody we talked to seems to like her very much, do they?"

"I noticed that, too," I said. "But everyone seems to love Ophelia." Except, perhaps, her boss, Caroline Marshall.

CHAPTER TEN

I rang the doorbell to Caroline's house, and once again it was Ophelia who answered the door.

"Hey, Lauren, Caroline just called to say she's running late for her appointment with you. How about having a cup of coffee and a muffin with me while you wait?"

"That would be nice." Also a welcome reprieve from what I anticipated could be a testy conversation.

We settled down at the kitchen table with our coffee and fresh-from-the-oven blueberry muffins. "Ever since I started working on this book, I've had the best homemade baked goods," I said. "These are delicious, and a couple days ago I had wonderful zucchini bread made by Margaret Galen's eleven-year-old daughter Lucy. Is that a hallmark of frugality: high-calorie bread, muffins, cakes, and cookies?"

Ophelia laughed. "You mean we use our sugary baked goods to compensate for all the other bitter deprivations? I think a more likely explanation is that a lot of us cook from scratch, often with fresh items from our gardens, and the results are frequently tasty."

"Or maybe you and Lucy just happen to be exceptionally good bakers."

She smiled. "That's also a possibility. But I'm more interested in your interviews. How'd they turn out?"

We sipped our coffee while I told her about them. "Everyone sends you their regards. In fact, I got the impression that they all associate this enterprise more with you than with Caroline."

"Better not tell Caroline that. She's already angry with me. We had a big fight Tuesday after you left."

"Caroline feels competitive with you?"

Ophelia sighed. "She thinks she should be queen of the hive, while the rest of us are busy worker bees."

It seemed the perfect opportunity to ask what I'd been wondering for days. "So why don't you quit?"

Ophelia stared into her coffee, as if searching for an answer. "I ask myself the same question. You must think me some kind of . . . I don't know, wimp or masochist."

She waved aside my assurance that of course I didn't think that. "The only way I can explain my reluctance to leave is to tell you how it used to be when Caroline and I first started out. We met when we both worked as assistants for Eloisa Hart, helping her with her frugal-living classes. We were Eloisa's entire staff, and we soon became good friends. When Eloisa had a recurrence of her breast cancer, Caroline and I carried on while she was in the hospital. But, unfortunately, Eloisa never recovered."

Ophelia took a bite of muffin. "It was Caroline's idea that the two of us continue Eloisa's classes and expand the business. At first everything went well. Each of us had our own area of expertise. Caroline liked public speaking, marketing, and being in the spotlight—which I loathe—while I focused on the content of the classes, working behind the scenes. We were a team."

"So, what happened?"

Ophelia shrugged. "I guess the simple answer is media exposure. When the economy turned bad, living frugally became a timely topic. And Caroline is good on TV and in interviews—attractive, articulate, inspirational. Suddenly everyone wanted to interview her, take a class from us, and, for the first time ever, we started making real money."

I began to sense where this was going. "But Caroline didn't want to share the profits with you?"

"She no longer wanted to give me half. She was the more valuable commodity in our business, she told me, the public face of our brand. It was as if she started believing her own press."

Ophelia looked me in the eye. "Which, of course, doesn't answer why I'm still working with her. I've been tempted to walk out and let her try to run everything by herself, but the truth is I am well paid for what I do, and most of the job I like."

A pounding on the front door interrupted our discussion. Frowning, Ophelia went to answer it.

From the kitchen, I heard snatches of her conversation. "She's not here, Nathan, but I'll tell her you came to talk to her."

From the rising volume of Nathan's voice, I surmised he was not happy with her suggestion. "Tell her she can't avoid me forever. She won't get away with stealing my family history. We'll sue her if she publishes the diary."

Apparently Ophelia managed to calm him down with assurances that she'd talk to Caroline and relay his message. I heard the door close and Ophelia returning.

She'd just sat down again when we heard a car pull into the driveway. "Oh, that's Caroline. I need to talk to her about Nathan. Could you just give us a minute?"

"Sure." I stood up. "I'll just take a bathroom break."

I'd reached the hallway outside the bathroom when I heard Caroline's and Ophelia's voices. If I were a better person, I would have closeted myself in the bathroom then and not eavesdropped. But I wasn't and I did.

"Nathan was here again, a few minutes ago," Ophelia said.

"Doesn't that man ever give up?" Caroline said. "He's like a stalker."

"He says his family will sue if you don't return their diary.

They believe you stole the book from them."

"Stole it? That's absurd. Eloisa gave it to me."

"I believe she lent it to you to read, not to own."

"Whatever," Caroline snapped. "I can't imagine why they're getting so agitated. It's not as if they were even interested in the diary until they heard I had it." Her voice changed, sounding more contemplative. "There must be something in the book the family doesn't want to get out. I wonder what it is. Maybe they'd pay me *not* to print it."

"You are shameless," Ophelia said, her voice heavy with disgust. "Do you *ever* think of anyone besides yourself?"

When she replied, Caroline's voice was frigid. "This earnest righteousness of yours is becoming tiresome, Ophelia. In fact, I'm growing very tired of *you*. Perhaps it's time you find another job."

"Don't think you can get rid of me that easily," Ophelia said. "I know where to find all the skeletons in your closet, and I won't hesitate to reveal them."

"Get out *now!*" Caroline shouted. "Before I do something I'll regret."

The slam of a door suggested that Ophelia had left.

Okay, how do I handle this? I took a deep breath. Should I just stroll into the kitchen, saying, "Maybe this isn't the best time for us to discuss your book. Should we reschedule?" Or maybe I should pretend that I hadn't heard a word of the argument and act as if nothing had happened.

At the very least it seemed wise to downplay my blatant eavesdropping. Tiptoeing into the bathroom, I closed the door, flushed, and noisily washed my hands. Then, and only then, did I return to the kitchen.

"I wondered where you were," Caroline said.

"Bathroom. Before that, I was sampling Ophelia's muffins." I looked around. "By the way, where's Ophelia?"

"She had to leave." Caroline gestured toward the living room. "Let's talk in there."

She seemed very cool considering that she'd just thrown her business partner and one-time friend out of the house. Did the two of them always argue like that? Tomorrow would they be calmly working together again?

I sat on a chair across from Caroline and told her what I'd come to say: Right now the book seemed a little too much like a textbook, with generic advice that sounded like class handouts. "It might help if we had stories about real people using a specific cost-cutting technique, sharing their experience and tips on how to get started. The women I interviewed this week—Pat and Margaret—were great, but we need a lot more of those personal stories, people the readers can identify with."

Caroline cocked her head, considering. "How's this for a title: *How to Live Twice as Well on Half the Money?*"

"Not bad. You'll have to be able to substantiate that claim, of course. It would be terrific if we could have you doing some financial makeovers for a family, showing the actual savings after implementing the techniques."

To my surprise, I was actually starting to feel more excited about the project. "We could also show the day-to-day expenses of a family that's been living frugally for a while. One of the women I interviewed this week, Margaret Galen, has a huge garden where her family grows almost all their food. The zucchini bread her daughter made was delicious. We could even print some of their recipes."

She looked thoughtful. "I do like the idea of showing real budgets and the actual savings people can achieve. Why don't you get with Ophelia to set up some interviews?"

You mean the same Ophelia you just kicked out of your house? I wanted to ask, but didn't. Instead, I nodded. I'd much prefer working with Ophelia anyway.

"I thought of another true story we might add to the book," Caroline said. "Wouldn't it be great if we had little snippets from a real family's experience going through the Great Depression? They managed to get by and live happily, despite incredible odds against them."

"Where do we get this true account?"

Caroline smiled. "Oh, I have an actual woman's diary. Best of all, she documented everything she did to save money. She wanted her daughters to be able to use her advice when they set up their own households. I thought we could use a short diary excerpt at the top of each chapter, kind of serializing her story."

I felt a shiver of unease. Surely Caroline was talking about a *different* diary. "Uh, whose diaries are these?"

"The grandmother of a good friend—in fact, the friend who got me hooked on frugal living. It was her grandmother who taught her about penny-pinching. Eloisa's own children were bored by the subject, so she gave me the diary before she died. I know she'd be thrilled that I used it in my book, letting another generation benefit from her grandma's advice."

Remembering Nathan's heated words from earlier that afternoon, I myself was less certain of that.

CHAPTER ELEVEN

The next day when I arrived at Caroline's house Ophelia once again answered the door. Apparently she and Caroline had made up since yesterday's argument.

I handed her a cellophane-wrapped basket that had been sitting on the front steps. "Someone dropped this off."

She peered at the typewritten note and read aloud, "For Caroline, in appreciation for all you've done for me. From A Former Student."

Studying the objects visible through the wrapping, she said, "This looks like a lot of the items we demonstrated in our workshop on handmade Christmas gifts." She placed the basket on a table that already held a small stack of letters.

I followed Ophelia into the kitchen. "Something smells wonderful."

Her smile was almost girlish. "I'm baking cinnamon bread; it's Caroline's favorite." She must have seen my look of surprise because she added, "It's a peace offering. I hate it when Caroline and I fight."

To my way of thinking, it should have been Caroline giving the peace offering, but I kept my opinion to myself. "I'm sure she'll appreciate it," I said, sounding, to my ears, both lame and dishonest.

She smiled ruefully. "You must think I'm really pathetic to be trying to make amends. But you're seeing Caroline at her worst, Lauren. She isn't always so short-tempered. She's just been

89

under a lot of stress lately. We've been friends and business partners for a long time and she needs me, even if she doesn't realize it."

I nodded. I wondered how Caroline would describe their relationship. Did *she* think she needed Ophelia?

The buzzer rang and Ophelia went to take her bread from the oven. Returning to the table where I was sitting, she said, "But you had some questions to ask me."

I nodded, pulling out my notebook. "By the way, have you read the diary that Caroline wants to use in her book? I just skimmed it last night."

"I only read the beginning pages, and that was years ago. What did you think?"

I shrugged. "To be honest, I thought what I read was rather dry."

"Well, Eloisa's grandmother wrote it for her female descendants as a way to pass on housekeeping tips and recipes and to relay a bit of their family history. I don't think she ever expected anyone else to read it."

"I understand that. But what I don't understand is why Caroline wants to include excerpts of it in her book."

Ophelia chuckled. "Mainly to piss off Eloisa's daughter—who, incidentally, is also Nathan's mother. We didn't realize the Nathan connection until recently."

"I can't imagine why Eloisa's daughter would care if Caroline prints excerpts. Believe me, nobody else will be fighting to publish the diary, and nothing I've read so far seems like it would embarrass the family. Do you think they feel protective of the secret recipes passed down from generation to generation?"

Ophelia grinned. "Nothing as high-minded—or rational—as that. I think Janice, Eloisa's daughter, just hates Caroline's guts. She wants the diary back because Caroline has it. Janice always felt her mother gave Caroline more attention and affection."

Lovely. So Caroline wanted to publish a dated and not-very-interesting diary merely out of spite.

"If I were you, I'd forget about that and focus on the rest of Caroline's book. I have some ideas on how we can quantify the amount of money saved by adopting different cost-saving methods. I'd already put together the numbers because I thought we could use the information in class."

The two of us were going over Ophelia's research when Caroline arrived. She, apparently, had been out jogging while Ophelia baked for her and the two of us worked on Caroline's book. But we, of course, were—in Ophelia's words—"the busy worker bees."

Caroline greeted both of us. "Who sent the basket?"

"Some grateful student," Ophelia said. "Looks like the presents are all from our homemade gifts workshop. Open it so Lauren can see everything."

Caroline ripped off the cellophane. "I wonder why the student didn't sign her name." She pulled out a glass jar filled with a floury mixture with chocolate chips.

"Instant Cookies," Caroline and Ophelia both said at the same time. Caroline explained to me, "These are the ingredients for the cookies. All you have to do is add an egg, some butter, mix, spoon the batter onto a cookie sheet, and bake."

Next she retrieved a small glass jar from the basket. Smiling, Ophelia said in a too-cheerful voice, "And who wouldn't *love* some homemade preserves on their breakfast toast?"

Caroline laughed. She picked up a small knitted teddy bear with embroidered eyes and mouth. "And what child wouldn't adore a teddy bear made especially for her or"—she held up a thin wooden object—"his own carved whistle?"

The two of them grinned at each other. For the first time, I glimpsed the kinder, gentler Caroline and saw the affectionate

91

bond between the two of them.

"I know, let's sample these preserves on the cinnamon bread," Ophelia said, practically clapping her hands together like a little girl planning a picnic.

Caroline nodded. "What do you say, Lauren? Want to taste some mouth-watering and thrifty homemade treats?"

"Why not?" It was surprisingly nice to see the two women getting along for a change.

Ophelia cut generous slices of warm bread for us while Caroline poured mugs of coffee. Ophelia slathered some of the homemade strawberry preserves over her bread, but Caroline and I chose to eat ours plain. We ate in companionable silence for a few minutes. Then Ophelia picked up the toy whistle and blew out a few reedy noises.

"This bread is delicious," Caroline told her. "How are the preserves?"

Ophelia took another bite. "Good, but there's some taste—a spice, I think—that I can't quite identify."

I noticed that her face looked sweaty. Suddenly, groaning, she clutched her stomach.

"Ophelia! Ophelia, are you all right?" Caroline asked. But Ophelia had already slumped to the floor, unconscious.

Chapter Twelve

Ophelia was dead.

I kept repeating the words to myself, as if repetition would somehow make it real, make this nightmare believable. For the second time in a month, a woman had died at Caroline's house—no, two women had been *murdered* there. Because surely Ophelia's terrible convulsions were not the result of natural causes.

The paramedics had arrived quickly. But, despite their best efforts, they had not been able to revive Ophelia.

Only minutes earlier, she had been reminiscing happily about that first holiday workshop. "Remember, Caroline, how someone in the audience said she'd rather shell out twenty dollars for a store-bought teddy bear than spend months knitting one, and you—who'd never knitted a stitch in your life—said, 'But think of how much love you put into a homemade toy, how much of yourself goes into your knitting.' "

The two of them had chuckled at the memories as we sipped coffee and munched on warm cinnamon bread. Ophelia had slathered her bread with the homemade strawberry preserves that a grateful former student had sent.

She'd been the only one to eat the preserves—and now she was dead!

"Can't you understand?" Caroline was yelling at the policeman who'd come to take our statements. "Someone is trying to poison me! The preserves were sent to *me*!"

"Is there some reason you didn't eat the jelly, ma'am?" the officer, Sergeant Martinez, asked her.

Caroline looked at him, her eyes narrowing. "Yes. I don't *like* preserves."

She hadn't touched the dessert containing the poisonous nuts either, I recalled. Perhaps she just didn't care for sweets. Or maybe the threats she'd received, followed by Mary Alice's death, had made her understandably wary about sampling any homemade food. Yet Ophelia had had no qualms about eating the preserves. Was Caroline just a more suspicious person? Or had she *known* that the preserves were toxic—and known, too, that Ophelia would eat the food?

I shook my head, trying to dislodge those unwelcome thoughts. Why would Caroline want to kill Ophelia? If she didn't want to continue working with the woman, there were certainly less drastic ways to get rid of her. On the other hand, it might be difficult and expensive to sever a partnership with a woman whom she'd been in business with for years—and Caroline hated to part with her money. Only yesterday I'd heard Ophelia warn, "Don't think you can get rid of me that easily, Caroline. I know where the skeletons in your closet are hidden."

Could Caroline have decided that Ophelia's death would simplify the situation? No severance pay necessary, no division of assets to worry about, no hidden skeletons jumping out of the closet. Only a funeral to attend.

The police officer turned to me. "You didn't eat the preserves either?" When I shook my head, he asked, "Is there anything else that only Ms. Smythe ate or drank?"

"We all had cinnamon bread and coffee," Caroline said. "Ophelia and I both drink it with skim milk. Lauren also added quite a bit of sugar."

I could feel my cheeks grown warm, remembering my ex-husband's jibes about my sugar consumption.

Sergeant Martinez was eying the gift basket. "Your students often send you gifts?"

"No, they usually thank me in person or sometimes send a note, so this package seemed strange, especially since I didn't know who it came from."

He looked up. "That jar of jelly the only thing you took from the package?"

Caroline thought about it. "Ophelia took out the jar of Instant Cookies, though she didn't open it, and a hand-knit teddy bear." She looked at me. "What else, Lauren?"

"A wood whistle," I said. "Remember? Ophelia picked it up and blew it."

"Oh, right." Caroline looked exhausted, as if she'd aged ten years in the past couple of hours.

The officer stood. "Don't either of you go out of town. We'll be getting back to you."

Caroline, I noticed, was rubbing her stomach. "Are you okay?" I asked. Could she also have been poisoned?

"I can't stay in this house."

Involuntarily I glanced toward the kitchen, where Ophelia had slumped to the floor and never gotten up again. In the room next to that, another woman had died at the dining-room table. No, I wouldn't want to stay here either.

"You could spend the night at my place," I said. Though God knew where she would sleep. An air mattress in the hallway?

"No, thanks," Caroline said. "I'm just going to pack a few things and get the hell out of here."

"Where will you go?" I called after her.

"Don't know," she called back. "Anywhere except here."

She seemed surprised when I followed her to her bedroom. Had she expected me to just walk out the back door? "I'll call you when I get settled," she said.

"Okay. Want some help packing?"

An unreadable expression crossed her face. "No, thanks. I just think I need some time alone to process everything."

I couldn't remember ever seeing Caroline so jittery. Even after the horror of Mary Alice's death, she'd been upset but still in control.

"Talk to you later, Lauren," she said.

I would have liked to talk about the events of the afternoon—my way, I guess, to "process" trauma. Instead I said good-bye and headed to my car.

It was only when I was driving away that the realization struck me. Caroline was afraid of *me*!

When she phoned me the next day, Caroline did not mention where she was, nor did she mention Ophelia. All she said was, "Do you still have Eloisa's diary?"

"Yes."

"Good. I want you to give it to Nathan Evans. It was written by his great-great-grandmother, and his family might like to have it." She gave me his phone number. "I'd appreciate you taking care of that today."

"I thought you wanted to keep it to use in your book."

"I've reconsidered my position. Nathan's family is eager to get it back."

They'd been eager before, but Caroline said she had no intention of returning it. What made her change her mind?

"And please photocopy the diary before you return it."

She hung up before I could offer any further comments. But ever the industrious worker bee, I headed to a copy shop to duplicate the diary and then phoned Nathan.

"What made Caroline decide to give it back?" he asked, sounding incredulous.

"I have no idea." Though I could speculate.

"Okay, let me get it tonight. Where do you live?"

For some reason I didn't want to tell him. I guess seeing two women die right in front of you can make a person feel paranoid. "I'm going to be out tonight." Paul and I had plans to go to dinner. "How about I drop it off?"

We made arrangements to meet at a coffee shop I suggested. It had the advantages of being far from my apartment and fairly close to the restaurant where Paul and I would be eating. It was also a popular gathering spot. There would be lots of witnesses if Nathan turned violent.

"There he is," I said to Paul as we entered. "The tall, skinny guy at the corner table."

Nathan had spotted me, too. "I remember you. You're the magazine journalist who was at the dinner at Caroline's."

I nodded and handed him the diary.

He barely glanced at it. "You're not planning to use it in your magazine article about Caroline, are you?"

"I'm co-writing a book with Caroline now. We won't include any excerpts from the diary."

When Paul and I turned to leave, Nathan said, "Just one more question. What did you think of the diary?"

It was a strange question, though Nathan, of course, was a pretty strange man. His eyes seemed too bright, his body taut with tension. There was something off, something threatening about him.

"To be honest, what I read was a bit dry, though I can understand why your family wants it back."

"You do?"

"Of course. Your great-great-grandmother wrote it to pass down her recipes and housekeeping advice to the women in her family. It seems only fair they receive what was written for them."

Did he relax a bit or was I just imagining that? "Yes, that's what my mother thinks. She used to have no interest in her family history, but she's gotten into genealogy. Now she wants every family memento she can lay her hands on."

It sounded reasonable, but I did not for a minute believe that it was the complete explanation. "And it also probably irritated your mother that it was Caroline, a woman she can't stand, who had possession of the diary."

"Irritated?" Nathan barked out a bitter laugh. "The way Mother sees it, everything that bitch has, she got by stealing from our family." He raised an eyebrow. "Just a friendly word of warning. If I were writing a book with Caroline, I'd make damn sure I got my money up front."

Paul touched my arm. "I think we better get going."

Nathan nodded. "Thanks for delivering it, Lauren. I thought Ophelia was the one who ran Caroline's errands."

Did he not know about Ophelia's death? Though how would he know—unless he'd been involved in her murder? "Ophelia," I said, "died yesterday."

His face grew pale. "Dead? What happened?" If he'd been aware of her death, Nathan was a very fine actor.

"It looks as if she was poisoned."

A series of unreadable expressions crossed Nathan's face. Then, inexplicably, he burst out laughing. "I get it now," he finally managed to say. "Caroline's sudden generosity. She must think that my family is *murdering* people to get the diary." The thought sent him off on another round of laughter.

He was still laughing as Paul and I left.

Chapter Thirteen

I did not see Caroline again until we met at Ophelia's memorial service.

We had talked on the phone because Caroline, control freak that she was, wanted to ensure that I'd given Nathan the diary. Remembering Nathan's advice, I reminded Caroline that I hadn't yet received my first promised paycheck.

"Is there some reason you need the money this instant?" she replied tartly.

"Yes, my rent, utility bills, and groceries, among other things." Did the woman think I was writing her book merely for the pleasure of her company?

"Oh, rent," she said, disparagingly. "Perhaps we should do a little bartering. You and your daughters can move into my house. I'm sure it's much bigger than your apartment. As I said, I've decided to move out, but you could live there in exchange for writing my book."

Did she seriously think I would jump at the chance to move into a place where two women had recently been killed? "I've already signed a year's lease," I said, "and I'm fine with my apartment. I'd prefer payment in cash, check, or money order, as we agreed in our contract."

"I had hoped that you might be a bit more flexible and, well, sensitive about getting your money, considering the recent tragic events."

With some effort, I managed not to slam the phone down in

her ear. *She* was calling *me* insensitive and selfish? How could I have been naïve enough not to realize that Ms. Stretch-Your-Pennies would be unwilling to part with them, even if she'd promised to do so. I needed to find another job with someone who wouldn't try to cheat me out of my pay—or have homicidal poisoners visiting her house.

But now, as Caroline caught sight of me at the memorial service, she flashed me a dazzling smile, as if our testy conversation yesterday had never taken place. Of course she'd acted the same way with Ophelia: one minute Caroline was ordering her old friend out of her life and the next day everything was back to normal.

My tolerance for abuse, however, was considerably lower than Ophelia's. I nodded coolly at Caroline and took a seat several rows behind her.

I was happy to see that a lot of people had shown up to remember Ophelia. Most of them I didn't recognize, but as I scanned the room, I noticed that almost every student who'd been at Caroline's deadly dinner was there: Nathan, Mary Alice's twin sister, Ellen, gray-haired Josie and her husband, Ed, Margaret Galen and her husband. Ahead of me I spotted Pat Holly, the bartering expert I'd interviewed.

Catching sight of me, Pat smiled and waved. I waved back. The auburn-haired woman sitting next to me said, "Oh, are you a friend of Pat's?"

"I interviewed her a few weeks ago. I liked her."

The woman offered me her hand. "I'm Cecily Holt and I *am* a friend of Pat's." Her expression darkened. "And I *was* a friend of Ophelia's, a good friend."

I introduced myself and said I'd also been very fond of Ophelia.

"Did you interview her, too?"

I nodded. "I'm writing a book with Caroline about frugal living."

"Poor you," she said. "I once had the misfortune of working for Caroline. If Ophelia hadn't been there as mediator and general calmer-downer, I would have probably quit after a week. But I stayed a year, putting in sixty-hour weeks, being Caroline's personal assistant/indentured servant. Finally I mustered up my courage to ask for a raise, and Caroline fired me on the spot. She said I had a bad attitude and wasn't a team player— faults she hadn't mentioned until I asked for more money."

A string quartet started playing a Bach fugue. It was soothing and intricately organized, rather like Ophelia.

The performance did not stop Cecily's conversation, though she did lower her voice. "I still don't understand how Ophelia could have put up with that woman for all those years. She's the only person who worked for Caroline and still managed to stay on friendly terms with her, but finally even Ophelia had enough."

"What do you mean?" I whispered.

"I had lunch with her last week. She was very upset, said she'd just learned that Caroline was trying to push her out and establish a solo business. Ophelia discovered e-mails Caroline had sent about her plans to have her own reality TV show, online classes, and how-to books and kits. Her dumpster-diving kit, for instance, would include a booklet of tips, work gloves, a collapsible stick for sorting through the bins, and a log where the person could document discoveries at various dumpsters.

"Caroline never mentioned any of this to Ophelia. Apparently she just intended to take the stuff she and Ophelia had developed and repackage them all under her Queen of Dumpster Diving brand. Ophelia said the queen was about to find out that she wasn't the clueless doormat Caroline thought she was."

And yet the last time I'd seen the two of them together

Ophelia was obviously trying to play nice. "But the day Ophelia died, she'd baked bread for Caroline."

Cecily raised her eyebrows. "Maybe she was taking a page from Caroline's old passive-aggressive playbook." When I looked confused, she leaned closer. "One night years ago the three of us were sampling our homemade beer, and Caroline got a bit tipsy. She started telling us stories about her former marriage. Her then-husband had had the audacity to request she provide home-cooked meals. So she made him a tuna casserole and added a bottle of ipecac—the stuff you use to make someone throw up. He got so sick that he never asked her to cook for him again."

Such a sweetheart, our Caroline. I needed to extricate myself fast from her toxic presence. "But only Ophelia got sick that last day," I told Cecily. "And it wasn't from her bread. Both Caroline and I ate that and were fine."

She scowled. "Ophelia was too kind-hearted. I would have laced Caroline's bread with cyanide."

The string quartet had stopped playing and a man I didn't recognize stepped up to the podium. Facing forward to focus on the speaker, I had the prickly sensation that someone was watching me.

Cecily apparently noticed the same thing. "Uh-oh," she whispered. "Caroline looks pissed. She doesn't like seeing us talking." She flashed a conspiratorial grin. "Too bad."

I listened while speaker after speaker stood up to eulogize Ophelia. I learned that in addition to being a talented artist and an expert at all things frugal, Ophelia had gone out of her way to assist anyone in need. She'd once briefly owned a health-food restaurant where, one former waitress reported, "She gave away food to anyone who couldn't afford to pay. She just wanted to help people any way she could."

Cecily leaned toward me. "Check out Caroline."

I looked. Caroline did look grim, but grief, I knew, had many faces.

Cecily, however, didn't see Caroline's grief. "She's so envious she can barely contain herself. She's furious that anyone might suggest Ophelia was the real frugality expert, the only one who wanted to do good in the world."

I was less sure that all of that could be read into Caroline's expression. The one thing that *was* clear to me was that Cecily disliked—really, really disliked—Caroline.

Finally Caroline stood up to give her remarks. She described how she and Ophelia had met as coworkers and then later started their own classes and workshops. She said how smart, helpful, and loyal Ophelia had been over the years. But her delivery seemed too facile, as if she were talking about some long-time employee she barely knew. I suspected Caroline's real regret about Ophelia's death was that she'd have to find someone else to do the heavy lifting.

"Now wasn't that touching?" Cecily whispered before standing to deliver her own tribute.

Cecily's eulogy could not have been more different. Voice shaking, she told how Ophelia had provided "a pure shining light" that had led Cecily out of "a very dark place. When no one else was willing to help"—she looked pointedly at Caroline—"Ophelia was always there for me. I intend to do everything I can to see that the murderer of this wonderful human being is brought to justice."

To my astonishment, the attendees burst into applause, some shouting out their agreement.

Then another surprise as Ellen, Mary Alice's twin, marched to the podium. "I hadn't really intended to speak today. I didn't know Ophelia well. In fact the last time I saw her was also the last time I saw my sister. Mary Alice died—she was poisoned—after a potluck dinner at Caroline's house. While there were ten

103

of us at the dinner, only Mary Alice got sick. She was gone by the next morning."

She waited for the shocked gasps to dissipate. "Now, a few weeks later, I learn that another good woman was murdered, apparently also poisoned at Caroline's house. Once again, only one of the people eating the food died—a very disturbing coincidence, don't you think?"

Ellen managed to shush the audience. "I am not—I repeat NOT—saying that I have any idea who this evil killer is. I can see no connection at all between the two victims, other than where they died. Mary Alice and Ophelia didn't know each other. The only thing they had in common is they both left us way too early. We must—all of us—make sure that the monster who killed these two women is apprehended and punished, before he or she destroys more innocent lives."

This time the applause was deafening. The anger in the audience and the frustrated desire to *do something* were palpable. The tall man who'd begun the service came back to the podium and rather nervously announced he hoped everyone would stay for refreshments in the church hall.

Roughly half of the audience obediently stood and made their way to the exit. Caroline, I noticed, was one of the first to slip out. For a moment I envisioned the clusters of people still milling around in the sanctuary as a growing mob set on vigilante justice. I told myself that was ridiculous.

Cecily, in the middle of one particularly loud group, motioned for me to join them, but I shook my head, waving good-bye. I was ready to head home.

I'd just started walking to my car when I heard a familiar voice call my name.

Lovely. Caroline. Just the person I wanted to talk to now. Still, I couldn't very well run away from her, particularly as my car was on the opposite side of the lot.

Suddenly Caroline was at my side. "I need you," she began, her voice rasping.

How many times had I heard her begin her sentences like that? "I can't," I said, looking her in the eye. "*I need* to get home." I turned in the direction of my car.

"Wait!" Her hand clutched at my sleeve. "Please."

The desperation in her voice made me stop and notice how frightened she looked. "I need to show you something," she said. "So you can understand."

Reluctantly I followed her. What could she possibly want to show me? A bank statement showing why she was so reluctant to pay me?

We stopped at her car. There was a piece of paper pushed under her windshield wiper. I could see her name scrawled in block letters.

Caroline gingerly extracted the paper. "I've read it already, but I put it back the way I found it. I'm not sure why. I—I just couldn't take it into my car." Her hand trembled as she handed the page to me.

I stared. With a black marker someone had printed: YOU'RE NEXT. DO YOU THINK THIS MANY PEOPLE WILL COME TO <u>YOUR</u> FUNERAL?

CHAPTER FOURTEEN

"Now do you see?" Caroline wailed, gazing wild-eyed around the church parking lot. "It has to be someone from the memorial service who wants me dead—someone who was sitting right there in the church."

"Probably somebody is just trying to scare you," I said, trying to sound reassuring.

"You mean in case I'm not scared enough from the two attempts to poison me at my own house?" Caroline asked, her voice dripping with sarcasm.

Well, at least she was getting her old nastiness back. Scared, vulnerable Caroline was harder to deal with. "No, what I mean is that the writer of that note might be someone other than the killer."

Nervously Caroline glanced around, as if she expected somebody to jump out at her from behind a parked car. As far as I could see, we were the only people there. The rest of the mourners were still in the church.

Caroline pointed at the note in my hand. "Whoever wrote that had to have put it here only a little while ago. Maybe he's watching right now to see how I react."

Despite myself, I shivered. "When you came out of the church, did you see anyone near your car?"

She shook her head. "There were a couple cars driving out of the lot, but I couldn't see who was in them."

I tried to remember who from the memorial service had left

the church before me. Cecily, who certainly disliked Caroline enough to put a hate note on her windshield, was still in the sanctuary. Ellen, who might blame Caroline for her twin sister's death at the potluck dinner, had also been in the church. I wasn't sure where Nathan had been as the service ended.

Of course there was also a possibility that someone had put the note on her windshield before the service started, waiting until Caroline had parked her car and headed into the church. Then, after delivering the hateful message, the poison-pen writer could have joined the other mourners.

Unfortunately, I couldn't recall when specific people had arrived at the service, though I did remember that both Caroline and Cecily were already seated when I got there.

It was equally possible that whoever left the note hadn't even attended the service. He/she would only have to have surmised that Caroline would likely be at Ophelia's memorial service and been aware of what kind of car she drove. So unless a witness came forward who'd seen someone put the message on Caroline's windshield, we weren't likely to learn the writer's identity anytime soon.

"Do you have time for a cup of coffee?" Caroline asked. "There's a little café just down the street. I—I'd really like to talk."

If she had not sounded so hesitant, so unlike the take-charge, demanding Caroline I was familiar with, I probably would have declined the invitation. This Caroline evoked in me a stab of something surprisingly like pity. "Okay, though I can't stay very long."

I followed Caroline's car to a coffee shop a few blocks from the church, and we both parked in the lot behind the restaurant.

Inside we settled into a booth at the back and ordered coffee and, in my case, a blueberry muffin. As soon as the waitress left Caroline pulled something from her purse. "The first installment," she said, handing me a check.

I glanced at it, making sure it was for the amount we'd agreed upon. "Thanks."

Strangely, I felt a bit disappointed. Certainly I could use the money, but Caroline's nonpayment of what she owed me had made the decision to stop working for her a no-brainer. Now that I was being paid, the choice became more difficult. How much flak was I willing to put up with in order to get a paycheck? I needed to think about that.

"Now about my book: you did photocopy those diaries before you returned them to Nathan, didn't you?" When I nodded, she said, "Bring a copy to the house tomorrow. I want to read it more carefully to figure out why the family is so eager to get the diary back. I'd bet my last dime that it has nothing to do with old recipes or preserving family history. There's something in there that they don't want published."

I took a sip of my coffee. "I have absolutely no idea what it could be."

"I know you don't," Caroline said. "That's why *I'm* going to read it."

I reminded myself that I really, really needed the money. "So you've moved back into your house?"

"Yes, it's financially irresponsible not to. When I thought about it, I realized I wasn't actually any safer at the hotel I was staying at, and it was costing me a bundle. Ophelia would have told me to stop being a coward and return to my house."

I took a bite of my surprisingly good muffin. "I thought the memorial service was touching and very well attended, didn't you?"

"Very nice," she said in a I-do-not-wish-to-pursue-this-topic voice. "Now about my book. Besides the frugality tips, I was thinking you should start a new section on the recent poisonings."

A new section on the poisonings? What exactly would this chapter include?

But Caroline had already started issuing her instructions. "I know you've written before about murders. I read your story about that gym owner who was killed while he was jogging. I envision a long chapter like that in my book. People are always interested in hearing about true-crime cases, and maybe your interviews will encourage the cops to get their asses in gear to find the poisoner."

Could this woman possibly be more self-centered? "Let me get this straight. You want me to investigate the poisonings and then write about them in the book?" Nothing like two grisly murders to help sell a frugal-living text.

"That's about it. Hopefully once you expose the killer, he or she will stop trying to kill me."

I started to tell her that, contrary to her inflated expectations, I was neither a private investigator nor a solver of crimes. Yes, when I wrote my article about Stan Harris, I did happen to discover who'd murdered him, but only *after* the killer tried to eliminate me, too. Cold-blooded criminals, I'd learned, are not thrilled to have nosy journalists poke around in their homicidal business.

Then I stopped myself. A warning voice in my head said, Cash her check before sharing your doubts. Maybe tomorrow I would try to talk Caroline into focusing on the other sections of her book. And if she refused, I'd at least have the money in my account before she decided to stop payment.

Caroline drained her coffee and motioned to the waitress. "Separate checks, please."

As we walked to our cars, I was so busy imagining the waitress showing her coworkers Caroline's ten-cent tip that at first I didn't register Caroline's shriek.

She was staring at the very flat tire of her car. It looked as if someone had slashed it. With trembling fingers, she pulled another note from under her windshield wipers. Like the previous message, this one was also hand-printed with a black marker.

I read the message over her shoulder: NOT MUCH TIME LEFT, CAROLINE.

CHAPTER FIFTEEN

I will say this for Caroline: when under pressure, she was decisive, action-oriented, and, unfortunately, bossier than usual. Within two minutes of reading the second anonymous message left on her car, she had called the police officer who'd come to her house after Ophelia died, told him of the day's events, and inquired, "Am I just supposed to sit here waiting for this murderer to kill me while the police turn a blind eye?"

Her approach wasn't tactful but it seemed to be effective. Although Sergeant Martinez apparently took exception to the "turning a blind eye" part, he nevertheless told her he would come to inspect things.

"When can we expect you?" Caroline asked. Then suddenly looking notably more nervous, she scanned the street and the parking lot. "No, the only person in sight is my ghost—uh, assistant who's helping me with my book, and she was with me all the time."

She listened for another second, said, "Okay," then motioned for me to follow her. "He wants us to go back into the restaurant and wait for him. He said not to touch anything." She scowled at the paper she was still holding. "Maybe they can get some fingerprints off these letters, but I doubt it. Whoever is pulling this isn't some idiot."

I followed Caroline back into the café. She seemed more angry than scared by the tire slashing, but I kept imagining someone violent following us from the church to the café.

Maybe right this second he was still watching us!

"I just want a glass of water," Caroline told the waitress who approached us. "Someone slashed my tire in your parking lot." She managed to make it sound as if the waitress was personally responsible.

"Gosh, that's awful," the waitress, a gray-haired, tired-looking woman, said. "That's never happened before. Did you call the police?"

Caroline nodded as I scanned the café to see if anyone looked familiar or secretly sinister. But no one did, and the two people sitting at the counter and the couple at a back table had all been there when we'd arrived.

"Hon, would you like something?" the waitress asked me. "You're looking a bit peaked."

The only thing I really would have liked was to crawl into my nice warm bed and pull the blankets over my head—after first making sure that my children were home and the door and windows were all securely locked. Maybe I'd have a glass or two of fortifying white wine, too, and a mood-enhancing Baby Ruth.

"How about a nice cup of tea?" the waitress asked.

It was not my remedy of choice, but it would have to do. I nodded. At least holding the warm cup in my hands might make me stop shaking.

Fortunately we did not have to wait long for Sergeant Martinez to arrive. I felt marginally calmer the minute he walked in the door.

After inspecting the slashed tire, the officer studied the two notes. Carefully he placed them in evidence bags. "There's a lot of animosity in these messages," he said to Caroline. "Who do you think sent them?"

"Obviously someone who hates my guts." Her voice seemed to be losing some of her earlier belligerence.

Sergeant Martinez turned his shrewd eyes on her. "And are

there a lot of people who feel that way about you?"

Caroline looked as if she were trying to summon some of her usual bravado, but this time she didn't manage to pull it off. "Unfortunately, there are quite a number."

The police officer seemed to take pity on her. "Why don't we go back into the restaurant to talk."

Although I wasn't thrilled that he wanted me to stay for questioning, too, I did feel a bit safer. If someone actually was watching us, I figured they were unlikely to pull another malicious stunt with a policeman nearby.

At our old table the sergeant pulled out a notebook. "Now who are these people who hate your guts?"

"Well, I've stepped on a lot of toes in my business over the years. I've fired several employees who couldn't meet my standards. I guess I can be rather short-tempered and sometimes a bit unreasonable."

A *bit*? I remembered the stories Cecily had been telling me at the memorial service about Caroline's tyrannical behavior at work, of how Caroline had fired her because she asked for a raise. Of course, maybe working for peanuts was part of Caroline's "employee standards."

"Can you give me some names?" the police officer said.

Caroline produced quite a few. Cecily—no surprise—was one of four people whom she'd fired "and things ended acrimoniously, I'm afraid." Patricia Holly, the barterer-extraordinaire whom Caroline had me interview for her book, was also on the fired list.

"But I thought Pat was a former student," I blurted out. "You said she was so good you wanted to include her in your book."

"She is excellent at bartering," Caroline said coolly, "but she was a very mediocre employee. I fired her because she was always late for work."

"And she also left acrimoniously?" the sergeant asked.

"She wasn't exactly friendly when I accused her of walking off with a sizeable amount of my office supplies, but I decided not to press charges. We're cordial now."

Nothing like refusing to press criminal charges to cement a friendly relationship. Remembering the towering piles of stuff in Pat's house, I could see her leaving with some office supplies. But an out-and-out thief? Never.

Caroline took a sip of her water. "Someone else who I know loathes me is Janice Evans. She's the daughter of my former boss and mentor. Janice was jealous because her mother liked me better than her, and because she thought I stole the business after Eloisa died—which I didn't. Of course she never blames herself for being a whiny, ungrateful brat who treated her mother like crap."

Caroline leaned forward, scowling. "If Janice had the brains to plan these murders, she'd be at the top of my suspect list, but she's dumb as a stick. Her son Nathan, though, might be doing the deed for her. He's a physics grad student who also signed up for one of my classes."

"Wasn't Nathan Evans at the dinner where the first poisoning took place?" the sergeant asked.

Caroline nodded. "He's quite the authority on poisonous plants, *and* he refused to eat any of the communal food at the dinner. He was also at the memorial service I just left—as were Cecily and Pat."

The police officer was jotting it all down. "Anyone else who might want to do you harm?"

Caroline considered. "Well, my ex-husband and I are not friendly, but we haven't had anything to do with each other in years. Last time I heard he was living somewhere in Central America."

Sergeant Martinez looked up. "Isn't that where Barbados

nuts come from?"

Caroline shrugged. "Could be, though I don't think he would have gone to all the trouble to fly back and dump the nuts in my dessert." She sent the police officer a pointed look. "Are you telling me that it was Barbados nuts that killed Ophelia, too? Is that what was in the preserves?"

He seemed to hesitate. "No, no Barbados nuts."

"So what exactly did kill her? You certainly should have the results of the autopsy by now."

"The M.E. said she was poisoned by oleander. It's apparently a very fast-acting poison."

Caroline stared at him. "There was ground-up oleander in the preserves she ate?"

He shook his head. "Not in that. There were traces of another poison, but it was the faster-acting oleander that killed her."

"I don't understand," I said. "If the oleander wasn't in the preserves, where was it? The only thing Ophelia ate was a slice of her homemade bread—which Caroline and I also ate—but only she covered it with the preserves."

"It was in the whistle, which was whittled from a twig of oleander," Sergeant Martinez said. "Was she the only one who tried out the whistle?"

"Yes," Caroline whispered. Her face had turned ashen, as if all the anger and defiance that had been giving her cheeks color had been leached out by the autopsy results. "I used to love those whistles. On the TV program where we demonstrated how to make them, I was the one who showed how they worked. Ophelia would carve them and I—I'd blow on them."

CHAPTER SIXTEEN

"You know, Mom, maybe you should stay away from that woman," Katie said. "People around Caroline seem to have an unfortunate habit of dying."

Em sent her an incredulous look. "But this is a wonderful opportunity for us to solve a crime. I'll be able to develop my detective skills and Mom can use what I learn in her book."

I took a restorative sip of my wine. I was too wiped out to even tell Em what a bad idea that was.

Sergeant Martinez had had us go over every detail of the memorial service. After that he said I could leave, but Caroline wanted me to wait with her until someone from a discount garage came to change her tire. By the time I got home, I felt as if I'd been hit by a Mack truck.

"Mom," Katie repeated, "you need to stay away from Caroline."

"Right now I don't even know where Caroline is. She said she was going into hiding."

"So you've given up writing her book?" Em asked.

"I'm hoping we can do it by e-mail and phone. I can e-mail her the chapters as I write them." The idea of not having to deal directly with Caroline held definite appeal. Tomorrow morning I intended to cash her check. Then I'd e-mail her to set up the arrangements for telecommuting.

"Good," Katie said. "It's hard to poison someone by phone or computer." She paused. "I wasn't going to tell you until later, Mom, but I might be returning to Dallas soon."

Her sister and I turned to look at her.

My older daughter suddenly looked more vulnerable. "Matt and I have been talking. He's coming home from China in two weeks. He told his boss that from now on, he can't spend so much time working out of the country. Matt told him the long absences are hurting our marriage and that being with me and starting our family are more important to him than advancing in the company."

Tears were glistening in her eyes. This was what she'd needed to hear from Matt: She and their marriage counted more with him than his high-paid, demanding job. "Oh, honey, that's wonderful," I said, giving her a big hug.

Em, a less sentimental sort, said, "Did Matt's boss mention when he'd be receiving his last paycheck?"

"No!" Katie was too happy to even acknowledge her sister's cynicism. "His boss said he understood. When Matt gets back, he's going to be based in their Dallas office."

"Good." Em smiled. "I guess this means I'll soon have more room here to spread out."

I sighed. She was already occupying the bedroom formerly known as my study. How much more space did she need? But my cell phone rang, interrupting the thought.

"It's me," Caroline said. "I can't tell you where I am."

I didn't particularly want to know anyway. "You okay?"

"I've been better. I'm calling about my book."

"I was going to e-mail you about that. I figured we could handle it all online and by phone. I can e-mail you my finished chapters and you can send me your corrections."

"No," Caroline said. "That won't work. Someone could find my location by tracing the IP address to my computer. It would lead the killer right to me."

"I guess I could send them by mail. You could get a P.O. box so nobody would know where you're living."

"That would take forever. I figured what's best is for you to come with me. Then we can really focus all our attention on the book and bang out a first draft."

"Come with you?" I repeated stupidly. "Where?"

"I can't discuss that over the phone. Just pack a suitcase, your notes, and your laptop. I'll be in touch."

Caroline disconnected before I had a chance to tell her my answer. No way was I going into hiding with her.

After my stressful day, dinner out with Paul was sheer bliss. For once it was just the two of us together, savoring our meals and each other's company in a quiet little Italian restaurant. We'd lingered over coffee and a shared tiramisu, just talking, catching up on each other.

Paul was writing a series of educational brochures for a nonprofit organization as a freelance gig. The work, he said, was interesting. Best of all, from my perspective at least, it was in Houston.

"I told my publisher friend in Seattle that relocating doesn't sound very appealing to me." He set his large warm hand over mine. "I have too many ties to Houston."

As romantic speeches go, no one would immortalize his words in *The Best of Odes To Love*. But to me his words were more moving than any verses by Keats or Shelley.

I squeezed his hand. "I am very glad to hear that." Okay, so I was no Elizabeth Barrett Browning either, but Paul didn't seem to mind.

"I was thinking," he said, "that we might go somewhere together at the end of the month, for a week, if you can get away, or else a long weekend."

"That sounds lovely," I said.

"Maybe Cancun?" he suggested. "Or Savannah? Or Santa Fe?"

"All of them sound great." In truth, I'd be happy to go anywhere with him. In the weeks since my daughters moved in, Paul and I had seen less and less of each other. I'd feared that what I'd hoped was a budding romance was about to die from neglect. A chunk of time alone together was exactly what we needed.

I was still feeling elated as we walked up the stairs to my apartment. Before I unlocked the door I turned to him. "Paul, I can't tell you how much—" I paused at the sounds coming from my living room. No, it couldn't be . . .

Quickly I unlocked the door. Oh, yes, dear God, it could. "What are you doing here?" I asked Caroline. She was sitting in the middle of my couch chatting with my daughters, acting like, well, an invited guest.

"Coming for you, of course." She cast an appraising eye over Paul, smiling a bit too flirtatiously for my liking. "I've already met your charming daughters; won't you introduce me to your handsome friend?"

I'd swear that the tips of Paul's ears were red when I introduced him to Caroline. "Maybe I should be going. I know the two of you have things you need to talk about."

The look he sent me was a pointed reminder of his advice about how to deal with this woman. Don't let Caroline push you around, he'd said. If she wouldn't agree to my demands for more reasonable working conditions, I should tell her to find another ghostwriter.

"Oh, don't go," Caroline told Paul. "You can stay here and talk to me while Lauren packs."

"Lauren packs for what?" I asked.

"I thought I e-mailed you to be ready to leave for our retreat so we can focus on writing my book." She sounded like a parent reminding a child of family plans.

Except I wasn't a child. "Then you must recall that I never agreed to that suggestion. You apparently forgot to tell me when you wanted to leave, where you intended to retreat to, and how long you intended to stay there."

Paul smiled slightly as he settled into a chair. Em and Katie, sitting across from Caroline, looked enthralled.

Caroline, on the other hand, appeared mightily annoyed. "I didn't want to convey that information over the Internet or phone in case someone intercepted it."

Instead she'd driven her car to my apartment, leading anyone following her to me and my daughters. "We're not on the Internet or cell phone now," I said.

"And we promise not to tell anyone," Paul chimed in. He nodded at Em and Katie. "Right, girls?"

"Right," they chorused, nodding vigorously.

Caroline clearly wanted to squelch this insurrection. But perhaps realizing that she was outnumbered, she deigned to answer—partially. "I have airline tickets for the two of us for a flight tonight." She glanced at her watch. "In three hours we're going to Colorado."

"Three hours?" I said. "Colorado?" Where in Colorado?

"I've been here waiting for you for over an hour," she said, her voice accusing.

"Which I, of course, was totally unaware of."

Caroline glanced disapprovingly at Kate and Em. "Your daughters said you were gone and couldn't be reached. I said in that case I'd wait here for you."

I felt a wave of maternal affection for the two brave girls who, under enormous threat of Caroline's torturous presence, had refused to give out my location. I opened my mouth to reply, but Paul spoke first.

"Lauren is not going anywhere with you," he announced. "So

maybe you'd better leave for the airport to make sure you don't miss your flight."

I had been about to say basically the same thing. But that didn't matter. There was a principle involved here. I glared at Paul. Who did he think he was—my mother?

Caroline did not even glance at me. "You make all of Lauren's decisions for her, Mr. O'Neal?"

Paul's look was frigid enough to freeze bathwater. "Lauren and I have already discussed this. We both think you're making unreasonable demands on her."

"It's hardly unreasonable to ask a writer to come with you to a quiet location to collaborate on your book."

I opened my mouth to debate the point, but Paul beat me to it. Again. "Not when what you're really requesting is for her to go to an unknown location with a woman whose two previous guests were fatally poisoned."

Caroline looked as if she were on the verge of throwing a punch. "Are you implying that *I* poisoned those women? I'll have you know that *I* was the intended victim."

"All the more reason to not be in your company, wouldn't you say?" Paul asked.

"I think—" I began.

Both of them ignored me. Glaring at Paul, Caroline said, "The place we're going to is perfectly safe. A comfortable, furnished house in an out-of-the-way town that no one's ever heard of. My grandmother used to live there."

"Nothing like being a sitting duck in a remote, isolated location." Paul's face was growing redder by the second. "The part you don't seem to grasp, Ms. Marshall, is that you're asking Lauren to put her life in danger. And for what? An ill-conceived book that probably will never even be published."

Caroline stood, practically shaking with rage. My God, was she really going to hit him?

"Okay, settle down!" I shouted, finally getting their attention. "Caroline, sit. Paul, be quiet. We are going to pretend now that we are rational adults."

For about thirty seconds I thought this was going to work. Caroline sat and Paul, looking sulky, shut up.

Caroline leaned toward me. "Lauren, I really need your help. When we don't have any interruptions we can whiz through the book, but I can't do it alone."

"But is it really safe there?" Em asked, looking worried. "Couldn't somebody follow you or figure out you'd hide at your grandmother's house?"

"Oh, trust me, Emily, your mom will be perfectly safe," Caroline said. "No one even knows about this place. Since Grandma was a bit paranoid, that house is more secure than Fort Knox. And I made sure that no on will follow us. The plane tickets are not in my name."

"Whose name are they in?" asked Em.

"Lauren's."

What? "Why did you use *my* name?"

"Nobody will be looking for *you*," Caroline said in an isn't-that-obvious voice. "But don't worry, I'm paying for everything."

Paul made a noise deep in his throat. "That settles it. Lauren is NOT going with you."

Oddly enough, that *did* settle it. Have I mentioned before that I have a major problem with people telling me what to do? Undoubtedly this is a direct result of my more than twenty-year marriage to a sanctimonious tyrant who always knew precisely what I should be doing, never mind that *he* spent his spare time committing white-collar crimes. One thing I'd learned from my divorce: I'd never again allow anybody to make my decisions for me.

I glanced from Paul to Caroline, weighing my options.

Caroline's eyes were pleading with me. "It should only be a

few weeks, a month at most." She swallowed, looking embarrassed. "And I really don't want to be there alone."

I glanced at my daughters. "Could you guys cope for a few weeks without me?"

Em rolled her eyes. Katie said, "Of course we could. But Mom, if it's dangerous—"

"I'll be careful," I told them. Then, turning to Caroline, I said, "Wait here while I pack."

CHAPTER SEVENTEEN

I had a lot of time during the flight to Denver to contemplate the soundness of accompanying Caroline into the middle of nowhere. With some time to cool off, I was less sure if I *had* made my own reasoned decision or if I'd just angrily reacted to Paul's command by doing the opposite.

Nevertheless, I didn't think that going with Caroline was as risky as Paul believed. I doubted the killer would follow us to Colorado. But that wasn't the main reason I'd agreed to Caroline's request. I'd seen the fear and vulnerability she'd tried so hard to hide and realized how much she needed me. That was when I'd decided to go with her. Showing Paul that I couldn't be pushed around was merely an added bonus.

Still I didn't want to be too overconfident about our safety. Throughout the trip I watched our fellow passengers, checking to see if anyone on the plane seemed especially interested in Caroline or me. No one seemed to be.

In Denver we learned the bus we were supposed to take didn't leave until seven in the morning. Caroline seemed to think I should feel grateful that we got to spend the night in a cheap motel rather than in a chair at the bus station.

After a terrible night's sleep, I climbed onto the bus the next morning, wondering what in the world I'd gotten myself into.

"Not far now," Caroline said when we finally staggered off the bus a couple hours later. "We just have to pick up Granny's car and drive to the house."

"Is it close by?" I asked hopefully.

"Yeah, only an hour or two. Or at least it is when the mountain roads aren't completely fogged in."

Granny's car turned out to be an ancient van that an old friend was housing in his garage. It required the assistance of jumper cables for the vehicle to start.

"Uh, Caroline, don't you think it might be a good idea to get a more reliable vehicle?" I asked, imagining us stuck on a deserted road in a van that refused to move.

She looked as if I'd just suggested she buy her own helicopter. "That sounds needlessly extravagant. This van has been running reliably for twenty years."

To my relief, the van, with a few fits and starts, got us up the mountain. We had to stop first for groceries, since the nearest store, Caroline explained, was twenty miles from the house.

As we made our way on the narrow winding road, Caroline grew increasingly chatty. "When I was a kid, I spent my summer vacation with Granny. I loved it out here."

"Did your whole family come?" I asked.

"No, just me. My brother thought spending time there was boring and Mother didn't really get along with her mother. Granny was too eccentric and free-spirited for her, and Granny said Mother was a snob and social climber."

"Your grandmother *told* you that?"

Caroline shrugged. "It was true. Granny just wanted me to know that there were different options besides the status-conscious, materialistic life my parents had, and I could choose the one I liked best."

Our trip finally concluded on a dirt road with only one building in sight. Granny's house looked more like a big log cabin. It was surrounded by a cluster of quaking aspens and a formidable mountain range. I couldn't imagine that many killers would be able to trace our convoluted path from Houston or, for that matter, be willing to make the interminable trip to get here.

It suddenly occurred to me—a bit on the late side—that this would be one hell of a difficult place to leave if my collaboration with Caroline didn't work out.

Caroline unlocked the cabin door and motioned me inside with a small smile. She clearly was waiting for some reaction from me.

I stepped into a large room and stood there, trying to take it all in.

"So what do you think?" Caroline asked.

"It's something else, isn't it?" I said. The room looked like a furniture showroom—if, that is, the buyer was drawn to flashy and dated furniture. The pieces themselves were a hodgepodge of different styles, as if someone had started to decorate the room in one look and then abandoned that idea to start on another scheme.

"Unique, isn't it?" Caroline surveyed the mess with affection. "My favorite is over there." She gestured toward a corner that contained a big, gilt-edged mirror, an arrangement of peacock feathers in a big vase on the floor, and two chaise longues upholstered in crimson satin. "I call it the Victorian bordello."

"I'd say that's a fairly accurate description."

There was also a section of angular fifties-era pieces—lots of blond wood—next to some uncomfortable-looking geometric furniture that I guessed was a stab at Art Deco. Granny clearly was a woman of eclectic tastes.

Fortunately, she'd believed in a functional kitchen, allowing us to put our groceries in a pantry and working refrigerator.

"When I was here, Granny and I loved to go to garage sales and flea markets. On heavy trash day, we'd drive down to the valley to see if anyone was throwing away something interesting." She gazed fondly at her grandmother's collection. "Granny called what we did 'rescuing and restoring abandoned furniture.' I think that's what inspired me to get into dumpster diving. Searching through dumpsters is a lot like Granny's scavenging trips."

I smiled. "She does sound like fun." We should definitely work Granny into the book. Caroline seemed much warmer when she talked about her beloved grandmother.

"Oh, she was." Caroline ran a finger across the kitchen table, scowling at the resulting dust. "But she was never much of a housekeeper. We're going to have our work cut out for us trying to make this place livable."

"Before I do anything else I need to call my children to tell them we got here safely."

"Sure." She pulled out what I presumed was a dust cloth as I went to retrieve my cell phone.

I pawed through the oversized purse I always use for traveling but couldn't locate my phone. I'd packed very quickly. Could I have inadvertently tossed the phone into my suitcase? I checked but didn't find it.

"Uh, Caroline, I can't seem to find my cell. Could I borrow yours for a quick call?"

Caroline looked up from her dusting. "Oh, I don't have mine with me. I planned to buy a disposable cell phone. It's harder for someone to trace calls from them."

So we were out in the middle of nowhere with no cell phones? "Is there a land line?"

She shook her head. "We had it disconnected when Granny died."

"Guess I'll just have to e-mail my daughters then."

"Sorry, there's no e-mail either," Caroline said, not sounding remotely sorry. "We don't have Wi-Fi, so no Internet connection. Though of course you can still use your laptop for writing my book." That, her tone implied, was the only important issue.

"But my girls will be worried if they don't hear from me," I said. "They expect me to call or e-mail."

Caroline shrugged. "They're big girls and I'm sure they're not worrying. Actually it's better that you don't contact them. That way no one can hack into their e-mail accounts to find out where we are."

"It wouldn't be *better* for me or my children," I said, starting to feel annoyed. Did she want us to be out here in the boonies with no contact with the outside world? "And there's no reason for anyone to be hacking into my daughters' accounts. Unless the killer followed *you* to my apartment, he or she has no idea who my daughters are."

Caroline's eyes flashed. "Did the killer have a *reason* to do anything he's done—murder two women, slash my tires?"

"Oh, the killer had a reason," I said. "We just don't know what it is."

I wrestled with a lot of unwelcome thoughts as I started sweeping the kitchen floor. S*mart move, Lauren, coming out here alone with an insane person. It's going to be a long walk back to town—IF you can remember the way and Ms. Control Freak doesn't tie you up to keep you here.*

After a minute of sweeping, I said, "Maybe we should see about getting your grandmother's phone reconnected."

"Why? It seems an unnecessary expense."

"You're not worried that we might be cornered by a killer and not be able to summon help?"

"I don't think the killer could have followed us out here," Caroline said, in the patient, reasonable tone an adult uses with someone impatient and a bit slow.

I wondered what had happened to frightened, vulnerable Caroline who, only hours ago, had claimed to desperately need my company because she was scared to come here alone. And what suddenly made her so confident that the poisoner wouldn't somehow manage to track her down?

I tried a new tack. "Of course you're planning to buy a disposable cell phone anyway, so we can make do with that. Are we going to drive to town today to get it?"

"Oh, it's too long a drive to go every day. That's why we stopped on the way here to pick up supplies. But we'll go in a week or so, and I'll look for a phone then."

A week or so? I HAD to figure out a way to get out of here—soon.

We spent the rest of the morning cleaning. Then we had a lunch of peanut butter and jelly sandwiches and apples for dessert.

"This place is really starting to shape up," Caroline said as we ate, looking around with approval.

Rather than launching into more cleaning after lunch, I insisted that we spend the afternoon working on the book.

I'd started interviewing her about Granny when I heard a noise. It was a very distinctive and familiar sound. "Do you hear *The 1812 Overture*?" I asked Caroline.

She looked puzzled. Then she looked guilty.

"That's the ring tone on my cell phone." The distinctive choice that my daughters had insisted would always let me know that it was my phone that was ringing.

I followed the ringing to Caroline's bedroom. The sound was coming from her suitcase! I rummaged through her clothes until I found my cell, though by then it had stopped ringing.

I turned on Caroline. "You *stole* my cell phone?"

"I didn't *steal* it," Caroline said, looking only a little sheepish. "I would have returned it to you."

"When were you planning on doing that?"

"When I was sure we were safe!" she said, sounding testier. "What's the point of coming all the way out here if this murderer can track us by our cell phones or our e-mails? A disposable phone—which, eventually, I *will* get—doesn't pose that danger."

This woman, I realized, was seriously paranoid. And I had been too stupid to see it. I was so furious—with her and with my gullible self—that I was, for one of the few times in my life, speechless. Trembling, I clutched my cell and hurried to the front door.

"Where are you going?" she called after me.

"Outside, to phone my daughters."

I stepped out the door and took a deep breath. Several deep breaths. Then I punched in Emily's number.

"Mom!" Em answered. "We've been phoning you." Well, at least there was cell-phone reception out here.

"I misplaced my phone." No need to worry her about *why* it had been misplaced. "It took forever to get here, but we're here. So what's up with you two?"

"You're always so OCD about phoning the minute we step off the plane, we were starting to worry that you forgot how to charge your cell."

"Sorry to worry you." I did NOT suffer from OCD!

"Guess what Katie and I have been doing?" She didn't wait for me to guess. "Since neither of us had to work today, we decided to investigate your case together so you'll be able to come home sooner."

"What do you mean you're investigating my case?"

"Well, Caroline's case. We've only done Internet research so far. It's amazing what you can find if you just know where to look. Did you realize that several people have filed lawsuits against Caroline? Katie and I are trying to think of some excuse to go talk to them."

"No!" I finally managed to interject. "Do NOT contact those people. Do NOT investigate, Emily!"

"You don't have to yell. I'm not a dumb little kid."

No, she was a dumb, reckless *big* kid. I tried to modulate my voice. "This is a very determined and devious killer, Em. You don't want to interview someone who might have poisoned two women." And undoubtedly would have no qualms about poisoning two more. "Promise me that you'll leave this to the police to deal with."

"I promise we'll be careful, Mom."

Did she think I was born yesterday? "Not careful investigating, Emily—NO investigating."

"We're losing the signal, Mom. Talk to you later. Love you."

I loved her, too. I also wanted to wring her skinny little neck for hanging up on me.

CHAPTER EIGHTEEN

I tried to convince myself that my daughters were taking their mother's advice and steering clear of potential psychopathic killers—but I was having trouble believing my arguments. Certainly the girls wouldn't *knowingly* contact a murderer, but if they insisted on "investigating the case," they might unknowingly provoke a dangerous and/or insane person into targeting them.

In short, I needed to get home sooner rather than later.

"So the girls are fine—right?" Caroline asked when I returned to the house.

I nodded. I still was annoyed about her hiding my cell phone and even more annoyed that she didn't seem the least apologetic for doing it.

"I told you they would be. Now that you've reassured them that you arrived safely, I know you'll refrain from using your cell. We'll keep our fingers crossed that the killer didn't manage to track the call."

I glared at her. Could she possibly be more self-centered and insensitive? "Actually after talking to them, I realized I need to get back to Houston."

She stared at me as if I'd suddenly sprouted a second head. "You can't do that! We have work to do. And you've made a commitment."

"I will still write your book, but I'll write most of it from Houston. I want to leave at the end of the week."

Actually I'd like to leave tomorrow, but I figured the girls would be okay for a few more days and we really needed to get some work done on Caroline's book. "That will give us five days to finish the interviewing and the outlining. I can do the actual writing by myself."

"You promised you'd stay here with me!" she shouted. "What's suddenly so urgent that you have to run home?"

What was she, eight years old? "The only thing I *promised* was to write your book, which I *will* do. Some family matters have come up that require my attention."

Her eyes narrowed. "What kind of family matters?"

"Private ones. Don't worry, Caroline, you'll be fine here alone. I would advise buying that cell phone, but, as you said, no one followed us and it's a very secure house."

"How do you know that no one followed us here?"

"That's what *you* told me only a few minutes ago, and I think you're probably right." She looked as if she wanted to argue, but I kept talking. "Of course now that my stay here is limited, we'll have to start making better use of my time. No more cleaning, only working on the book."

"Then we'd better get back to work, hadn't we."

I was under no illusion that she'd just agreed to my terms. More likely, she was only giving herself time to figure out how she was going to keep me from leaving.

Nevertheless we worked until dinner time, ate a slapdash meal of tuna casserole and canned green beans, took a short after-dinner walk, and then went to bed early.

The walk, over that hilly dirt road, convinced me that there was no way I could walk back to town, wheeling my suitcase. I definitely required a motorized vehicle.

The next several days followed basically the same pattern. Caroline was more distant—basically the way she'd acted back in Houston—but we did make progress on her book.

In fact, things were seemingly going so well that I had to give myself a lecture about my bad attitude: *Why do you have to be so suspicious, Lauren? It's likely that Caroline is NOT just pretending to accept your leaving and Em is NOT trying to hide something whenever you talk on the phone. Undoubtedly everything is exactly as it seems—just fine—and, in a few short days, you'll be back with your unharmed daughters, finishing Caroline's book at your desk, and asking Paul O'Neal out to dinner.*

Yes, that scenario sounded lovely. Unfortunately, I couldn't make myself believe it. Deep in my bones, I knew something was up. And it wasn't something good.

The day before my scheduled departure Caroline appeared at breakfast with a woebegone expression and dark circles under her eyes. Over bowls of instant oatmeal, she asked, "Did you hear any strange noises last night?"

"What kind of strange noises?"

"Noises from outside, near my bedroom window, around two in the morning."

I shook my head. "I was fast asleep. Maybe it was some kind of animal outside." I didn't want to speculate on what kind of animal. If it was outside, I didn't much care.

Caroline didn't seem reassured. "I looked out the window, but I didn't see any animals."

"Maybe it was just the wind," I suggested.

"Or maybe it was a prowler. I had this creepy feeling that someone was out there."

I suspected the fear on Caroline's face was designed to make me stay with her. She'd probably realized that I'd agreed to accompany her to Colorado only after she'd told me how frightened she was of being here alone. Except this time I was feeling less empathetic. "If you're really scared, you can come back to Houston with me tomorrow."

She glared at me. "I can't return to Texas until the police have the killer in custody." She paused. "During your extensive conversations with your daughters about their ventures into detective work, did they happen to mention how the police are progressing?"

How did she know what my daughters talked about in our phone conversations? Did she crack open a window and eavesdrop on what I was saying in her front yard?

"They didn't say anything about the police case." In fact, my last conversation with the girls had mainly been about how excited Katie was that Matt would soon be home from China. Even Em had sounded pleased for them.

"Maybe I should phone that HPD detective myself." Before I could say anything, she added, "I didn't mention it before, but I brought a disposable cell with me. I just didn't want to use it until it was essential."

In other words, if it was a concern of Caroline's, rather than of mine, cell use was permitted. Fuming, I watched her head for her bedroom. A minute later I heard her voice demanding to speak to the police officer on the case. Then, unfortunately, she shut her bedroom door.

A good fifteen minutes later she returned to the kitchen. I looked up from my laptop. "Have the police learned anything?"

She shook her head. "Not really, though the detective said I probably should stay out of town for a while. Apparently someone broke into my house a few days ago. My neighbor reported it but didn't have any way to contact me."

She ran her hand through her hair, looking agitated. "I just phoned my neighbor. She didn't think anything was stolen, though the place was a mess, desk drawers dumped out, flour and sugar all over the kitchen floor. She cleaned up the kitchen and her husband boarded up the broken window. They think it was probably some kids who just wanted to vandalize the place."

Caroline and I exchanged a look: Not likely.

"So you can see why I don't want to return to Houston just yet," she said.

Before she had a chance to launch another appeal for me to postpone my return trip, my cell phone rang. I glanced at it. "It's my daughter. I have to take the call."

I moved out of Caroline's earshot. "Hi, honey."

"Hey, Mom," Katie said. "I need to talk to you when Em's not around."

"What's up? Did something happen?"

"Maybe. I'm not sure exactly, but I think so."

I took a breath. "Tell me."

"You know how Em gets, Mom, when she's so obsessed about something; she's like a pit bull with a T-bone. Well, she's like that now, certain she's going to find the person who poisoned those two women."

I groaned. "She told me she was doing all her detecting online."

"Well, yeah, she did a lot of that. But now she says she needs to branch out."

"Branch out how, precisely?"

"She wants to do surveillance on some of the people she researched. I went with her two days ago. It was really boring, sitting around watching this nerdy chemist."

"Nathan?" He was the only chemist I could think of.

"Yeah. As far as I could tell, she learned nothing. When I complained about being bored, she drove me home."

So far this sounded less dangerous than I'd expected: computer work, watching while nothing happened.

"But then Em started thinking up excuses to talk to her suspects. 'Suspects,' that's what she calls them. She phoned a few of them, pretending to be somebody taking a survey or a reporter doing an interview."

This was definitely not good. "Has she met face to face with any of these, uh, suspects?"

"I don't know," Katie said. "She won't tell me because she says I'll run tattling to you. But I think she's meeting somebody right now."

I hoped to God that whoever Em decided to talk to was not guilty of anything besides looking suspicious. "I'll be home tomorrow night, sweetie. So don't worry. Em and I will have a good long talk." Assuming, of course, that Emily managed to not provoke a crazed killer before I got back.

"But that's not the worst of it, Mom." She paused long enough for me to envision what could be worse than having my daughter out interrogating potential murderers. "I think somebody is following us."

This time I didn't even attempt to sound calm. "What makes you think that?"

"When Em and I went out to dinner last night I kept feeling as if somebody was watching us. But when I turned around to look, nobody was there."

I started to say something reassuring, but she cut me off. "I kept trying to tell myself that all Em's talk about killers was making me imagine things, but when we got back to the car, there was a restaurant napkin under our windshield wiper. It said, 'Back off. Remember what happened to the curious cat.' "

CHAPTER NINETEEN

"What do you mean you have to leave right now?" Caroline asked, incredulous. "You're going tomorrow morning!"

"Tomorrow may not be soon enough." By then one or both of my daughters might be dead.

When I explained why I had to leave, Caroline, to her credit, did not announce, "Well, I'm glad to hear the killer is still back in Texas." What she did say was, "Even if you could find a seat on a plane today, the earliest you'd get there is the middle of the night. Why don't you have your daughters go stay with a friend or in a hotel tonight? I'd also advise them to stop this investigating."

I raised my eyebrows. "You think?" Of course it wasn't Caroline who I was upset with. That designation belonged exclusively to my younger daughter, Emily, who, in addition to everything else, was not answering her cell phone.

What if she was interviewing the killer right at this moment?

Doubting that it would make one iota of difference, I dialed Em's number again and left a second message: "Emily, stop your snooping and call me this minute. I could not live with myself if you get yourself killed." I figured that covered all the bases: Simple, direct orders that she couldn't "misinterpret." And ladling on the maternal guilt.

Of course if she didn't listen to my messages, it didn't matter what I said. I turned to Caroline. "Good idea about having the girls spend the night somewhere else."

I punched in the number of my best friend, Meg. She had a large house with extra bedrooms, the girls adored her, and—best of all—she could be counted on to keep them safe.

The phone rang many times before going to voicemail. "I'm not in the country right now," Meg's voice announced, "but as soon as I'm back, I'll return your phone call."

Oh, no, how had I forgotten? She was off on a three-week-long cruise of South America. I was pondering whom to call next when my cell rang.

"Hey, Mom," Emily said cheerfully. "You'll be glad to know I'm still alive."

I couldn't decide if I wanted to scream at the little smartass or burst into tears of relief. "Emily, I've been so worried. Please tell me you're at home now." *With your sister next to you, the door dead bolted, and windows securely locked.*

"I'm walking to my car. Don't get yourself agitated, Mom. That note was just trying to scare us."

"Well, it worked for me," I snapped. "You DO realize that the person who wrote that message is not a practical joker. He or she has already *killed two women* and was warning you that YOU could be the next victim."

"I'm being careful."

"You can't be that careful if the killer is aware that you're looking for him."

In typical Emily fashion, she chose not to address that particular point, instead changing the subject. "I have learned *so much* the last couple days, Mom! I've talked to almost everyone who was at that dinner at Caroline's."

"What did you learn that was so interesting?"

"Well, for one thing, I figured out possible motives. I'm not entirely sure who the killer is yet, but right now I think it's most likely to be Mary Alice's twin sister Ellen, Nathan Evans, or Caroline herself."

I was aware that the last mentioned person was standing a few feet from me, pretending not to be listening to my every word. "Why do you think that?" I asked, trying to keep my voice casual as I moved to my bedroom.

"Well, Mary Alice's daughters told me that their mother and her sister were having a big fight over whether or not to sell their parents' home that they'd jointly inherited. Apparently Ellen really needed the money now, but Mary Alice was adamant that she wanted to keep the house."

"Hmm," I said as I walked into my bedroom and closed the door. I vividly remembered how angry Mary Alice and Ellen had seemed at the dinner. "But while that gives her a motive to kill Mary Alice, it doesn't make sense why she'd go on to kill someone else. She and Ophelia barely knew each other."

"Oh, the only reason she would kill again was to make it look like Mary Alice had not been the killer's intended victim. The second murder was just a cover-up. Mary Alice's daughters said Ellen is ruthless and smart, though they didn't accuse her of murder."

"In other words, this is your theory."

"*One* of my theories. I talked to Nathan Evans, the grad student who refused to eat any of the communal food. His whole family hates Caroline—he says she stole all of his grandmother's ideas and made a profitable business out of them. He told me that Caroline finally returned their family diary, but his mother still wants to sue Caroline for stealing her mother's business. When Caroline heard that, she called Nathan before she left for Colorado. She told him if his family ever attempted to sue her, she'd expose some embarrassing family secrets that she'd learned by reading a copy of his great-great-grandmother's diary."

"What secrets?" I hadn't read any secrets in the book.

"Something about his great-great-grandmother and great-

great-grandfather not being married. I think his great-great-grandfather was still married to another woman when their children were born. Apparently Nathan's mother was mortified to learn that her ancestors included a bigamist and a bunch of possibly illegitimate children."

Could that have been why Nathan had been so intent on retrieving his family diary from Caroline? Except he hadn't known that she'd kept a copy for herself so she could look for dirt to use against his family.

"Of course Nathan intended to kill only Caroline, not Mary Alice or Ophelia," Em said. "But the wrong woman just kept being poisoned."

"I understand why he'd assume that Caroline would be the one to sample the gift basket, since it was sent to her house, but how could he know for sure that she'd eat the one serving of cobbler that contained the Barbados nuts?"

"I still need to work that out," Em admitted. "My last theory, by the way, is that Caroline herself did both poisonings, with Ophelia the intended victim. Mary Alice was just collateral damage. It infuriated Caroline that people were whispering that Ophelia was the brains of the business—the real expert—and she decided to eliminate the competition."

That made even less sense than Em's other ideas. Would Caroline be hiding out here at Granny's house if she was the poisoner? She couldn't have left the message on her car windshield because she'd been with me in the café when it was delivered. Although, of course, it was possible that the poison pen writer was unconnected to the killer.

"I really need to do some more research," Em said, "to figure out which one of those people is the actual murderer."

"Emily Prescott," I said, "have you not heard one word I've said? Do NOT do any more investigating until I get back in town tomorrow night. Go home right now and stay home, and don't open the door to anyone. Do you hear me?"

"I hear you," she said. "Well, I guess I'll see you tomorrow, Mom. Bye, love you."

Was I only imagining that she was blowing me off—or at least blowing off my warnings? *Dear, silly, over-protective Mom. She means well but always imagines the worst* . . .

I took a deep breath and then punched in another phone number. "Hi, Paul," I said when he answered. "I'm wondering if you could do me a very big favor."

CHAPTER TWENTY

"I'm afraid I have some bad news for you, Lauren," Caroline said to me the next morning.

I looked up from the suitcase I was zipping closed.

"The van won't start. I'm not going to be able to drive you to the airport after all."

"Oh, dear," I said.

She looked a trifle confused, but humorless people, I've noticed, frequently don't pick up on sarcasm. "Maybe you'd better reschedule your flight for later in the week. It might take a while to get the car repaired."

Did this woman think I'd been born yesterday? "That won't be necessary. Luckily, I already arranged to have a driver pick me up here."

She glared at me before remembering that anger was not part of the role she was playing. "Well, that *is* lucky."

Luck, I thought, had nothing to do with it. "I figured that you can never be too careful, relying on an old car like yours, so I arranged for a driver when I made my plane reservation."

A loud knock on the door saved Caroline from having to reply. I picked up my tote and my suitcase. "Thanks for your hospitality."

She tried out a smile that came off as more of a grimace. "Have a safe trip. I'll be in touch."

As I drove away, I thought about Em's theory that Caroline had murdered Ophelia. Could she possibly be right? Certainly

143

Caroline was a selfish person with a notable streak of ruthless-ness. And she'd clearly resented Ophelia and didn't want to share the spotlight with anyone.

Nevertheless, I still believed Caroline was convinced that someone was trying to kill her. She was not pretending to be frightened; she was genuinely concerned for her life. If Caroline knew that she was the only killer in the vicinity, why would she be hiding out on this mountaintop, afraid of her own shadow?

As the driver skillfully navigated the winding mountain roads, I considered Em's other two suspects. Unfortunately, I felt as ambivalent about their homicidal tendencies as I did about Caroline's. I'd seen Ellen's expression as her sister convulsed at the table—a wrenching mix of horror, astonishment, and concern. It was a look that was hard to forget—and even harder to have feigned. Sure, she and Mary Alice had bickered earlier in the evening, but there's a big leap from annoyance to pre-meditated murder, and I doubted that Ellen had taken it.

Which left Nathan. Admittedly, he'd had the best chance to covertly add the Barbados nuts to the dessert when he left the table to go to the bathroom. He'd also displayed a sophisticated knowledge of toxic plants, a refusal to eat any of the communal food at the dinner, and a resentment of Caroline. Maybe it was just because Caroline had told me so many times, but I was inclined to believe that Mary Alice and Ophelia had never been the killer's intended victims, that the poisoner had merely failed to eliminate his true target—Caroline.

But despite the facts that Nathan had opportunity as well as the necessary knowledge, I had a hard time seeing him as a cold-blooded assassin. Of course, I also had never imagined my former husband as capable of criminal activity—and the man now resided in a federal penitentiary. So maybe my nose for fer-reting out felons was not to be trusted.

I'd spent too much of last night talking on the phone to my

144

agitated children and my thankfully-calm friend Paul. (It was yet to be determined if he was still my boyfriend, but his willingness to house my whiny daughters certainly qualified him as a very good person.)

Katie had been relieved to be spending the night somewhere other than our apartment, but Em had been outraged that I felt they "needed a babysitter." Paul, bless him, just told me that the girls were fine, everything was working out, and he'd meet me this afternoon at the airport.

I checked my phone messages as the driver dropped me off at the Denver airport. There was only one: Caroline wanted me to call her. Yeah, I'd have to do that. Maybe tomorrow or perhaps the day after.

I expected to see only Paul when I arrived in Houston, but, to my surprise, both of my daughters were there with him, chatting animatedly with each other.

"Mom," Em exclaimed when she spotted me, "you won't believe what happened."

I kissed everyone hello. "What happened?"

"Nathan Evans killed himself," Em said. "And he left a note confessing to both the murders."

I stared at her. "Are you sure?" I finally managed to blurt out.

"It was on the radio news. We heard it on the drive to the airport. It said Nathan used Barbados nuts, just like before, but this time he poisoned himself."

I shuddered, remembering Mary Alice's death. Not an easy way to go, but I could understand Nathan, in a fit of conscience, feeling he should die the same way one of his victims had.

"Did the report you heard mention what he said in the suicide note?" I asked.

Paul nodded. "He admitted killing Mary Alice and Ophelia,

and said he couldn't live with the guilt of murdering innocent people. His body was found early this morning at the university lab where he worked."

I shook my head, remembering the lanky man I'd first encountered at Caroline's potluck dinner. "What a terrible waste." A waste of a fine mind, of a potentially long life filled with contributions to science. And for what? Some ridiculous notion of avenging his family honor and keeping Caroline from revealing to the world that, generations back, some of his ancestors hadn't been married. It was a secret that no one, aside from possibly Nathan's mother, cared a whit about.

Em suddenly looked on the verge of tears. "Do you think I drove him to kill himself, with all of my prying questions?" she whispered. "I didn't want him to die, only to stop murdering people."

"No," I said firmly, "it was *not* your fault, Emily. You and your questions did not make Nathan do anything."

She looked as if she was trying hard to believe me. "You know he was actually kind of a nice guy, though even he admitted he was irrational on the subject of Caroline."

Paul looked thoughtful. "He told you he was 'irrational' about Caroline?"

Em nodded. "Yeah, his word."

"Seems kind of detached for a cold-blooded murderer," Paul said. "You'd think he feel justified in his hatred of the woman who he repeatedly tried to kill."

He insisted on carrying my bags for me. The smile he sent me and the way his hand lingered as he picked up my luggage sent an unexpected jolt of pleasure through my body. Would we actually be able to resume our relationship at the very nice spot it had been immediately before Caroline barged into my apartment?

As we headed for his car, I felt myself grin at the prospect.

I had taken only a few happy steps when my cell phone rang. I'd turned it back on when the plane landed. Glancing at the caller ID, I briefly considered not answering it, then thought, Why delay the inevitable?

"Hello, Caroline."

"I have been calling and calling," she said. "Why the hell didn't you pick up?" Fortunately, she didn't seem to require an answer because she rushed on. "I have the most exciting news. Nathan Evans killed himself after confessing to all the murders. The police called me this morning. Isn't that wonderful?"

"It certainly should be an enormous relief for you."

"You know I always suspected it was him," Caroline said. "His grandmother, my mentor Eloisa, was a sweetheart, but the rest of the family were vipers. And they were SO jealous of my success."

I was beginning to suspect that this was not going to be a short conversation. "Well, Caroline, thanks for calling to share your news. I'll talk to you soon."

Unsurprisingly, Caroline did not take the hint. "I haven't told you the best part yet. With the killer out of the picture, I'm returning to Houston. So we can get back to working together on the book, Lauren! You can pick me up at the airport tomorrow evening."

With considerable effort I managed to stifle my groan until after we said good-bye.

Chapter Twenty-One

I would like to be able to report that all of my problems were over once I returned home, but, unfortunately, they weren't. Yes, I felt immensely relieved that a double murderer was no longer out poisoning people and putting threatening notes on windshields—particularly when one of those windshields belonged to my daughters. I was also glad to be home again with Em and Katie and apparently back on good terms with Paul. Still I couldn't seem to shake my belief that this tidy ending was too tidy—diabolical poisoner confesses and then helpfully offs himself.

It wasn't that I possessed any evidence indicating that Nathan was *not*, in fact, the killer. I barely knew the man. Still, on the couple of occasions on which I'd met him, he had not struck me as a man who'd poison people or, for that matter, commit suicide. Certainly he was smart enough and knowledgeable about poisonous plants, but he didn't seem sly or devious in the way this particular killer would have to be.

Other issues also puzzled me. Why, for instance, would Nathan suddenly develop a conscience? I found it hard to believe that Em's penetrating questions had pushed him into guilt over his deeds or convinced him that it was only a matter of time before the police arrested him.

"I keep going over and over everything I said to Nathan," Em told me after Paul dropped us off at my apartment. "I'm sure I didn't say anything that would make him think I believed he was a killer. I asked him the same questions I asked the others who were at Caroline's dinner, and he knew I was questioning everyone, not just him."

Katie joined us at the kitchen table. "Maybe his suicide didn't have anything to do with what you said to him," she told her sister. "Maybe the guilt was eating away at him and he'd planned on killing himself for a long time. You just happened to show up right before he got around to doing it."

"Maybe," Em said, though she didn't look convinced.

"Well, at least you can stop playing detective now," Katie said, "and quit endangering our lives while you muck around in other people's business."

Em glared at her bossy, know-it-all older sister, and I held up my palm, trying to hold off the inevitable.

"We were never endangered," Emily said, ignoring the hand. "Somebody put a note on our car. So what? It's not as if he shot at us or tried to kill us—which, in case you're interested, is what 'endangered' means."

"There was somebody following us!" Katie shrieked. "And the note on my car threatened to hurt us if you didn't stop sticking your big nose where it didn't belong."

"*I* never saw anyone following us," Em retorted. "You probably just saw someone who was walking down the street."

"Shows what a great detective you are, if you don't even notice that someone's tailing you."

"Girls!" I said loudly. "Enough!" How old did sisters have to be before they stopped bickering? If, of course, they ever stopped. I had no trouble at all envisioning eighty-year-old Emily shouting at eighty-two-year-old Katie about something altogether trivial.

Em shot her sister a dirty look as she said, "I'm going to take a shower. I'm glad you're back, Mom, though staying at Mr.

O'Neal's place wasn't as bad as I thought it would be. He's a cool guy."

"Yeah," Katie said. "He's not much like Daddy, but he's nicer than I thought. Funny, too."

Well, at least the two of them agreed on something, I thought, feeling inordinately pleased that they were warming to Paul.

My sense of euphoria lasted roughly ninety seconds. Katie waited until she heard Em close the bathroom door to grab my arm and hiss at me, "Mother, you have to do something about Em and her detective fixation. She acts as if this is all some mystery-solving game, like Clue, instead of a way to get herself killed."

I sighed. I didn't like the idea of Emily Prescott, P.I., any more than Katie did. "Maybe now that Nathan is dead, Em will decide to focus on something else."

Katie rolled her eyes. "I wish. You know how she gets, Mom. She's obsessed with crime investigating. She'll move on to another crime, but maybe next time the criminal won't be accommodating enough to kill himself instead of her."

Unfortunately, I did know how obsessed Emily could get. The problem was I didn't have a clue what I could do about it.

I was still considering ways to ensure that Em did NOT encounter any more crimes requiring her intervention when Emily walked out of the bathroom and her cell phone rang. She answered it.

"Nathan Evans's mother?" I heard her say. "Uh, I'm very sorry for your loss, Mrs. Evans."

She listened some more. "Well, I guess so. Maybe you could come here, to my mother's apartment. Tonight? Well, let me check."

She held her hand over the receiver. "Nathan's mother wants to talk to me. She found my phone number among his things. Is it okay if she comes here in half an hour?"

When I nodded, she got back on the phone and gave Mrs. Evans directions.

When she hung up, she said, "I'm glad you're going to be here, Mom. Mrs. Evans sounds pretty agitated." But when I started to ask why Mrs. Evans wanted to talk to her, Emily was already heading for the bathroom. "I'll tell you later," she called over her shoulder. "I need to get dressed and dry my hair before she gets here."

Nathan Evans's mother, Janice, bore a distinct resemblance to her skinny son, though her flamboyant clothes—long gauzy skirt, linen tunic cinched by a large silver belt and accessorized with lots of expensive-looking turquoise jewelry and strappy turquoise sandals—indicated a very different fashion sense.

I remembered Caroline's disdain for this woman. According to her, when Caroline had been working for Eloisa, Janice had been a hard-partying college girl who was a huge disappointment to her frugal, serious-minded mother.

We introduced ourselves, then Janice got to the point. "From what I gather, you were one of the last people to speak to Nathan," she told Em. "I—I am trying to make sense of what happened." Her voice broke and she had to struggle to regain her composure. "I want to know everything: What did you two talk about? Did he seem depressed or upset or frightened? Was he drunk or high—or acting peculiar?"

Em looked puzzled. "We really didn't talk long, but I didn't think he was, uh, acting peculiar. Was Nathan often drunk or high? Because he didn't seem to be on anything when I saw him."

"No!" Within the course of a few seconds, Mrs. Evans's expression changed from anger to confusion and then to raw-boned anguish. "As far as I know, my son never experimented with drugs or drank more than a few beers, but the person the

151

police described—that isn't the son I knew. My Nathan was a supremely rational man: calm, analytical, emotionally detached, as many scientists are. He was never violent, not impulsive, not depressed. He never hurt anyone. The only reason he took Caroline's class was to help me." She looked suddenly on the verge of tears. "If it wasn't for me, Nathan would never have had any contact with that terrible woman."

Emily gave her a few seconds to regain her composure, then asked gently, "Why did he think that taking the class would help you, Mrs. Evans?"

She sent Em a watery attempt at a smile. "Nathan believed that hatred damaged the person carrying the emotion—in this case, me. He knew I'd loathed Caroline for years, blamed her for taking my mother from me—pretending she was the perfect daughter Mother always wished she had—and then, after her death, taking over Mother's business and assuming all the profits for herself. At the time my mother became ill, I was a big-spending sorority girl, not remotely interested in frugality, the family business, or anything, really, except my own pleasure. I think if Mother had lived longer, we would have become closer. Eventually, I settled down, got married, and had a son. Mother would have loved being a grandmother. Nathan, in fact, is very like her."

She apparently noticed her use of the present tense, once again fighting tears. "Nathan only contacted Caroline because he wanted me to make peace with her—to give up my hatred and resentment. He naively thought if he could convince her to give back my great-grandmother's journal—the ultimate symbol for me of Caroline stealing whatever she could get from my family—that I might be able to forgive her and move on with my life."

"And Caroline did give the journal back to you."

Janice's look was more bitter than appreciative. "Yes,

reluctantly. It really didn't change how I felt about her. When I heard about the poisoning attempts, I had no doubt that Caroline was the intended victim. I envisioned all her enemies lining up, applauding at her funeral."

So much for her son's hope to dispel Janice's animosity toward Caroline, I thought. She, in fact, seemed a much better candidate for a killer than her son. I wondered suddenly if Nathan had believed that his mother had tried to murder Caroline. Could he have committed suicide and confessed to crimes he didn't do in order to shield Janice?

Janice was studying Em. "So, you see, don't you, why I need to understand what was really happening to my son in those last days. I desperately need to understand."

Em nodded sympathetically. "I wish I could help, Mrs. Evans, but I only met Nathan that one time. For what it's worth, he didn't seem depressed or agitated to me. He was friendly, but kind of pressed for time. He said he had some appointment he had to get to, but he answered all my questions and promised to call if he remembered anything else. I'm sorry I can't tell you more."

"He'd call you if he remembered anything else about what?" Nathan's mother asked.

"About the dinner at Caroline Marshall's house where the guest was poisoned. I was talking to everyone who'd been at that dinner."

Her eyes narrowed. "And why were you doing that?"

I could see two red blotches spread on Em's cheeks. "I was trying to find out who poisoned those two women."

"Why not leave that to the police?"

Em's face seemed to grow a shade redder. "Well, the police didn't seem to be getting anywhere, and my mom—who's ghostwriting a book for Caroline—had to go out of state with Caroline because Caroline was afraid someone was trying to kill her. Also, I think I might want to become a private investigator, so this seemed like it could be good training as well as a way of getting my Mom back in town."

Surprisingly, Nathan's mother seemed to accept this rather convoluted explanation. "So did you find out who the killer is?"

"I haven't learned anything definitive yet," Em said. "I'd only been working on it a few days, but I was beginning to put together a few of the puzzle pieces."

Katie, who'd been shamelessly listening, decided to enter the conversation. She told Mrs. Evans about the message left on their windshield and—shooting a defiant look at her younger sister—having someone follow them.

"Your questions must have riled up someone," Mrs. Evans said. "Nathan, by the way, would never leave notes on a windshield. He might have texted you reasons why you were investigating the wrong people, but threatening you with a hand-written message was not something he'd do." She looked Emily directly in the eye. "I want to hire you to find out who killed Nathan."

Absolutely not, I wanted to say, but managed, with some effort, to remain silent.

"You understand that I'm not a real, licensed private investigator," Em said.

Nathan's mother waved her hand dismissively. "As I said, whatever you were doing, you managed to rattle someone's cage. Your questions were upsetting somebody. Very possibly that person killed my Nathan."

Which was all the more reason for Emily to stay out of it, I thought. Because if Janice's version of events was true, this killer had had no compunction about murdering Nathan Evans and making it look like a suicide. I suspected that he/she wouldn't hesitate to add an additional victim—my daughter—to the kill sheet.

"I don't think that Emily is the woman for your job," I said quickly. "Have you talked to the police?" Let them rattle the killer's cage.

"I have. They seem convinced that it's suicide and I'm just a hysterical mother who can't accept reality. They're so relieved to have their case solved that they don't want to even consider the possibility that they might be wrong."

I hesitated. I didn't want to be cruel, but this had to be said. "What if Em learns that Nathan did indeed kill himself?"

Janice sent me a hard, level look. "Then, I'll just have to deal with it, won't I? But at least I'll know what really happened. And I don't think that's what Emily is going to learn."

Only if Em were short-sighted and reckless enough to take on this no-win assignment. "Em," I began.

"I'll do it," Emily told Janice. "I'll start tomorrow."

CHAPTER TWENTY-TWO

To my surprise Emily wanted to come with me to pick up Caroline at the airport.

"Really?" Given my choice, *I* would not be driving to the airport tonight.

"Well, I figured I might be able to get some useful information for my investigation of Nathan's death."

"From Caroline? She was in Colorado when Nathan died. I can vouch for that. I, unfortunately, was with her."

"I know that," Em said. "But she might be able to tell me about Nathan's motive for wanting to kill her or about the feud between her and Mrs. Evans."

Don't get your hopes up, I almost said before deciding for once to keep my opinion to myself. If Emily was with me at least I'd know she wasn't out interviewing homicidal psychopaths.

As we drove to the airport, she filled me in on what she'd learned so far about Nathan's death. A night janitor had found his body shortly after midnight, in the university lab where Nathan worked.

"Mrs. Evans showed me the suicide note—or a copy of it. The police found it on the table next to the food Nathan had eaten—a salad that had Barbados nuts in it."

"Was the note handwritten?" I asked, trying hard not to imagine Nathan grimly eating the salad that he knew would make him terribly ill within minutes.

"No, it was typed on a computer. A really short message that said, 'To whom it may concern, I poisoned those two women. I can't live with the guilt any longer. Nathan.' Even his name was typed." Emily paused, studying me. "His mother says Nathan didn't write it."

It did seem as if anyone could have typed such a generic confession, but that didn't mean that Nathan hadn't. "Did she say why she thought that?"

Em sighed. "She said the note didn't sound like him. If Nathan had written a confession, he would have gone into more detail—which two women he'd poisoned, why he killed them. She said he's a scientist, 'a precise, analytical man who would have felt compelled to explain how and why he did such a ghastly thing.' "

Em glanced out the car window, then added, "Oh, and she said Nathan would never use the words 'I can't live with the guilt any longer.' He'd think the expression was too hackneyed and melodramatic."

I wondered. If a man who was normally rational and unemotional suddenly found himself acting violently and irrationally, would he write a reasoned suicide note?

From the little I knew of Nathan, probably he himself could not explain why he'd turned to murder. Perhaps he'd botched two attempts to kill Caroline and accidentally killed two bystanders. Or he might have been a sociopath who just wanted to kill somebody. Maybe his actions had been the result of some kind of psychotic break.

"It would be very hard for any mother to believe her son would murder anyone," I told Em. "It would be perfectly understandable if Janice Evans needs to think that someone else killed the women and then wrote a bogus suicide note, setting Nathan up. That doesn't mean it's true."

"I thought of that," Em said. "Maybe Mrs. Evans is just in

denial. Instead of wanting me to find out what really happened, she could have hired me to pin Nathan's crimes on someone else."

I exited the freeway onto the feeder street leading to the airport. "So, do you think that Nathan is the poisoner?"

Emily made a face. "I honestly have no idea, but I intend to discover what really happened, whether or not it's what Mrs. Evans wants me to find."

The minute Caroline Marshall walked into the airport waiting area, I could tell that she'd left vulnerable and almost-likeable Caroline back in Colorado. The woman who greeted us with a phony smile and started issuing orders was the bossy, confident, obnoxious woman I'd first met.

"I am so glad that unfortunate episode is over," she explained as we walked to my car. "I just wish it hadn't consumed so much of my valuable time."

"Or killed two innocent women," I couldn't stop myself from adding.

She sent me a look. "That goes without saying."

"So you feel confident that Nathan Evans is the murderer?" Em asked her.

"Of course. Why else would he confess?"

"But what I don't understand," Em said, "is why Nathan would murder those women. From what I heard, he was kind of a nerd; he never was violent before."

Caroline issued a dramatic sigh. "Well, Janice, Nathan's mother, had an absolutely toxic hatred of me. Maybe she convinced Nathan that I was an evil monster who'd stolen her mother from her. Janice never could admit that she was the one who'd alienated Eloisa with her own obnoxious behavior. Of course, her mother preferred me—any sensible person would."

Behind Caroline's back, Em rolled her eyes at me.

"Besides being a spoiled brat," Caroline added, "Janice was emotionally unstable. Eloisa was evasive about it, but I gather that Janice was in a mental hospital for a while. Maybe Nathan inherited that psychosis—or whatever it was that sent his mother to the nut house."

I was speculating on what kind of emotional instability could have sent Janice to a mental hospital when I suddenly heard what else Caroline was saying.

"I had time to read your manuscript on the plane, Lauren, and frankly I thought it was quite boring."

"I'm sorry to hear that." I didn't say what I was really thinking: *Maybe that's because the subject of the book—you—is a bore.*

"It needs to be more dramatic and well, juicier. I told you before you should include a section on these poisonings."

Caroline, as I recalled, had also suggested that I discover the killer and write the account in the book.

"I think that's an excellent idea," Em said before I could respond. "Everyone loves to read a true-crime story—and it certainly is, uh, juicy." She avoided making eye contact with me as she added, "I can help Mom research that part."

"That's terrific." Caroline turned to me. "What do you think, Lauren?"

What did I think? A number of things: The murders had nothing to do with a book about Caroline's views on frugality. Since the alleged killer had committed suicide without providing any explanations, we didn't know many actual details about the crimes. And then there was the issue that throwing a "true crime" into this book seemed exploitive and downright tacky.

Nevertheless, accompanying Emily on her crime investigation would mean that I could, hopefully, keep her out of trouble.

"I think it's a great idea," I told Caroline. "After all, who doesn't love a good, gory murder mystery?"

★ ★ ★ ★ ★

There was just one problem with keeping Em out of trouble: I had to participate in activities that I normally wouldn't be caught dead doing. Tonight, for instance, we were going to a women's self-defense class—entirely, of course, Em's idea.

The minute we walked into the high school gymnasium I knew I was going to hate this. Jen, the middle-aged instructor, had the hard-body look of an exercise fanatic and the intensity of an army sergeant.

It was her mission to turn us—the roughly fifty females sitting on the bleachers—into "the kind of women no criminal will want to mess with." Her eyes swept over us. "For some of you," she said, looking directly at me, "this will require a major transformation."

I glanced around the room. My classmates ranged in age from perhaps eighteen to, I'd guess, the mid-sixties. I wasn't the oldest one in attendance; there were two gray-haired ladies sitting directly in front of us. Unfortunately, I was undoubtedly among the least fit. The skinny gray-hairs both wore T-shirts proclaiming "I Finished the Houston Marathon."

Jen said we had to stop thinking that violence happens to other people. "That's what those other people thought, too, until a mugger walked up to them in the parking garage." Self-defense, she said, was all about prevention. Avoid dangerous situations and steer clear of potential attackers. "When you have the choice between fight or flight, always pick flight. Fighting is a last resort."

I sent my daughter a look: *See, your old Mom is right—stay away from scary people and dangerous places.*

"But sometimes you have no choice," Jen said. "There's no one around to hear you scream, no way to get away, so you have to know how to fight the attacker off."

She looked around the class. "After a lot of practice, you

might even convince yourself that you're a lot tougher than you thought. You're a fighter, a bad-ass."

Yeah, I thought, that's really going to happen.

The instructor pointed at Em and me. "You two, come on up here to give the class a little demonstration."

I hate this, I thought, as Jen showed us some hand strikes and then made Em and me do them. I had to pretend-slam my palm into Em's chin when she grabbed me from the front, then she had to pretend-gouge and claw at my eyes when I grabbed her. After that we practiced elbow strikes and some kicks. Em did a nice job of landing her front kick at my mid-section, while I did a not-so-great job of landing my side kick on her knee.

By the time the next team of volunteers was called up to demonstrate, I was panting and sweaty.

"Good job, Emily," Jen said as we headed back to the bleachers. "You, Lauren, gotta keep practicing."

One very long hour later we were all allowed to leave.

"I learned a lot tonight," Em said as we walked to the car. "Didn't you?"

I nodded. "I learned to stay aware of my surroundings and avoid dangerous people and situations." In other words, no more Jen and no more self-defense classes.

CHAPTER TWENTY-THREE

Em had arranged to interview Nathan's coworkers at the university science lab. Telling her that I needed more background information for the new "true-crime focus" of Caroline's book, I accompanied her.

Em had lined up interviews with two of Nathan's colleagues. Tonight we'd meet with the night janitor who'd found his body.

The first person we talked to was a tall, gaunt young man named Alex. Nathan, he said, was a friend and fellow grad student, though they didn't see each other much because Nathan had liked to work at night. He'd last seen Nathan on the night he died. Alex was leaving the lab as Nathan was coming in. Nathan, he said, seemed "pretty happy because he just heard that he'd received a research grant."

"So it doesn't make sense that he would commit suicide only a few hours later," Em said.

Alex had to think about that. "Well, he was kind of a strange dude . . ."

"Strange in what way?" Em asked.

"Hard to read. Sort of quiet and always off somewhere in his thoughts—like a lot of scientists."

"Did it surprise you to hear that he'd confessed to poisoning two people?" I asked.

"Yes. Though I guess it would surprise me to hear that *anyone* I knew had killed someone."

"Did you ever see Nathan act aggressively?" Em asked.

Alex cocked his head, considering. "Never."

Em thanked him for his help and said he should call her if he thought of anything else. He said he would.

The next person we spoke to was a tense young woman with long, center-parted, black hair who introduced herself as "Dr. Allison Edmonds." Dr. Allison said Nathan was a "colleague" who worked in the same lab.

"Did you think that Nathan was acting differently lately?" Em asked.

"In what way?" Dr. Allison inquired.

"In any way," Em said. "More edgy, more aggressive, more depressed."

"Not really," Dr. A said.

"Were you surprised that he'd committed suicide? And what was your reaction when you heard he'd admitted to poisoning two people?" Em said.

"I wasn't really surprised about the suicide. He was very moody; he told me once that he was bipolar, but taking medication for it."

Em leaned forward. "So you *do* think Nathan killed himself?"

Dr. Allison looked annoyed. "I didn't say that; I said that it wouldn't *surprise* me if he'd committed suicide. What I *know* is that Nathan wouldn't kill anyone else. He was a pacifist, really anti-war, anti-violence. It even bothered him when people got angry."

Emily's eyes gleamed with excitement. "Did you ever hear him talk about Caroline Marshall or his mother's long-time argument with her?"

The scientist nodded. "He took a workshop with Caroline in order to see if he could patch things up between her and his mother. He said his mother was wasting valuable energy with her animosity toward Caroline."

"Did he also have animosity toward Caroline?"

She shook her head. "He said she was a blow-hard, but that was it. The only reason he had anything to do with her was to get back some journal his great-great grandmother wrote and that his mother claimed Caroline stole. He thought if he got it back, his mother might move on with her life."

"Did she? Move on with her life, I mean? I know that Caroline returned the journal."

"I don't know about that. I hadn't seen much of Nathan lately."

Dr. A looked as if she was getting impatient to leave but Em had more questions. "So if you're convinced Nathan didn't poison those women, why would he confess he did?"

For a brief moment the woman's eyes reflected her grief, but then her face became expressionless again. "Without more evidence, it's hard to speculate. Someone could have forced him to write the note or written it themselves after they killed Nathan. It's even possible—though rather unlikely—that someone managed to convince Nathan that he *had* killed those women."

"How could they do that?" I asked.

She shrugged. "Hypnosis, hallucinogenic drugs, mind-control techniques. As I said, it's not probable."

"Can you think of anyone who might have wanted to kill Nathan?" Em asked.

Dr. Allison thought about it. "No," she finally said. Before we could ask anything else, she added, "I can't give you any more time. Clearly more information is needed before anyone can formulate a hypothesis."

Em sighed as we watched Dr. Allison stride away. "I think she's hiding something, but I have no idea whether it has anything to do with Nathan's death."

"She feels upset that he died," I said.

"Yeah, she's upset about something," Em said, "but I thought she might be feeling guilty, too."

"What makes you think that?"

She smiled. "Call it investigator's intuition."

We left then but returned that night to talk to the janitor who'd found Nathan's body.

Clement Jones was a wiry man, probably in his fifties, with dull, resigned eyes. "You aren't reporters, are you?"

"No," Em said. "I'm just trying to find out what happened on the night Nathan Evans died."

"You a cop?"

"Nope, private investigator," she said, sending me a it's-not-really-a-lie look.

The man turned to me. "You a PI, too?"

"No, I'm the PI's mother."

He snickered.

"Why don't you tell us what you saw the night Mr. Evans died," Em said.

"I came into the lab around midnight, the time I normally come, and I saw Nathan kind of slumped over a table. I thought he might have been taking a nap."

"Did you see anyone else near the lab?" Em said.

"Didn't see nobody at all that night. Sometimes other people were there working, but not that night."

"So what happened once you saw Nathan?" Em asked.

"I thought I'd let him sleep, so I emptied the trash and did my work. When I got closer I could see he wasn't sleeping and, more than that, I could smell it. He'd puked all over the table, all over his salad." His nose wrinkled, as if remembering the smell.

"Was a salad the only food in front of him?" I said.

"Yeah, a vegetable salad in one of those restaurant plastic containers, and he had a bottle of water, too."

The janitor had called 9-1-1 and the campus police. "Then

they came and asked me a million questions." He sent us a look indicating his opinion of people who asked too many questions.

"Is there anything else you want to tell us?" I said. "Anything you think is important?"

He narrowed his eyes. "Don't know if it's important, but I just remembered something. When I emptied the trash in the lab that night there was another plastic container there with some lettuce in it. Looked like the same kind of salad Nathan had."

"So Nathan could have been eating with someone else," Em said, her voice full of excitement.

Mr. Jones shrugged. "That or someone else ate the salad before Nathan arrived. The container could have been there since lunchtime. I just thought it was strange that two people seemed to be eating the same thing, but only one of them got sick."

Very strange indeed.

We went back to the lab the next morning in hopes of finding someone who might be able to tell us more about the origin of Nathan's toxic salad, but no one seemed to know where it had come from. Usually, we were told, Nathan brought food from home, often a peanut butter sandwich.

"Somebody must have brought Nathan a take-out salad," a lab assistant said. "He'd never go to the bother of making himself a salad, and he wouldn't have bought it either. He always said restaurant food was a rip-off."

"Did people often bring him food?" Em asked.

She considered it. "Not really, though some of us saved any leftovers from our lunch, knowing Nathan would eat them."

Alex, the grad student we'd spoken to before, said Nathan had been carrying his usual paper sack with him when they'd encountered each other. "I just figured it was another peanut butter sandwich, though I guess it could have been something else."

So, conceivably, Nathan could have brought the salad to work with him. Perhaps he reasoned that Barbados nuts would go down easier in a crunchy salad than in a sandwich. Maybe he decided to make his last meal extravagant take-out. After all, he wasn't going to have to pinch his pennies for much longer. It was too many maybes, too much conjecture, and not enough facts, I thought as we left the lab.

"Wait!" called a voice from behind us.

We turned to see a petite young woman with a halo of curly brown hair. She'd been introduced to us earlier: Meredith, a student who worked part-time at the lab.

"I just thought of something I forgot to tell you before. That suicide note couldn't have come from the printer in the lab. At least not that night."

"How come?" Em asked.

"I was printing some documents late that afternoon and the printer ran out of ink. I couldn't find any extra cartridges so it wasn't until the next morning that I installed a new cartridge."

Em whistled softly.

"I guess Nathan could have printed the note at home and brought it to work with him," Meredith said uncertainly. "But I don't know why he'd bother because he would have assumed that our printer was working."

And his note had only been two short sentences, easy enough to scrawl on a sheet of paper. And wouldn't a scientist have reasoned that a handwritten confession with his signature would have been more convincing evidence?

A murderer, on the other hand, would more likely have reasoned that a typed note was less risky than a handwritten one—particularly if he wasn't sure what Nathan's handwriting looked like. So had someone other than Nathan brought the "confession" to the lab along with a toxic salad?

"Thanks very much, Meredith," Em said. "You've been really helpful."

The girl blushed, looking pleased. "One more thing. This might not be important, but I started thinking about a phone call we got at the lab. It was someone looking for Nathan. I told them he usually worked at night, but I'd leave him a note to return the call. The caller said that wasn't necessary and hung up."

"The caller didn't identify himself?" I asked.

She shook her head. "And I really wasn't sure if it was a man or woman. The voice was soft but kind of fake sounding—like the deep voices kids use in prank calls."

"Do you remember what day that call was?"

She nodded. "It was the morning of the day Nathan died."

CHAPTER TWENTY-FOUR

To celebrate her husband's homecoming, Katie cooked an elaborate dinner. Besides my son-in-law, Matt, Em, and me, she'd also invited Paul.

I was delighted to see how much more comfortable with Paul my girls were. They were no longer the polite strangers who only a month ago had made strained conversation when they'd been forced to dine together.

Most of all, though, I was touched and immensely relieved that Matt and Katie seemed so delighted to be in each other's company again. I'd even heard them whispering in the kitchen about how much they'd missed each other. It looked—dare I say it?—as if their marriage was back on track, now that Matt was no longer going to be spending six months a year thousands of miles away from Katie.

While most of the time I'd enjoyed my daughters' extended visit, I had to admit I was also glad that Katie was moving out of my apartment. Em, too, might be leaving soon. She'd started talking about returning to college next semester, moving back to Austin. She wasn't entirely sure if she wanted to become a private investigator, an FBI agent, or a lawyer, she said, but she guessed she could decide that while she was in school.

But now, as Katie returned to her own household with her handsome young husband and Em made her own plans, it felt as if all of us might be able to get on with our lives and move forward. Something, somehow, had shifted, and shifted for the better.

I made a conscious effort to return my attention to the dinner table, where Katie was attempting to shoot down her younger sister's theories on what had happened to Nathan. "Probably his mysterious caller at the lab was just a phone solicitor," she said. "They never leave a message because they know no on will call them back."

"That's a possibility," Em said. "But what about the fact that the lab's printer was out of ink the night Nathan died? He couldn't have printed his suicide note there."

"Maybe he printed it days before and kept it in his desk drawer until he mustered the nerve to kill himself," Matt said. "Or he could have found another working printer in the building that night."

Em tried another tack. "Well, everyone said Nathan only ate leftovers from the lab refrigerator or peanut butter sandwiches he brought from home. No one saw that salad in the refrigerator, so where did it come from?"

"I doubt where he got the salad is all that significant," Paul said. "What seems important to me is the Barbados nuts that were in the salad. Did Nathan know what he was eating? Did he purposely eat the nuts to kill himself? Or was he tricked into it or forced to eat them by someone who wanted to blame him for the other poisonings?"

"But why would someone pick Nathan to blame for the poisonings?" I said. "Why set him up?"

Paul shrugged. "To get the police to close the case? Or maybe the real killer believed Nathan knew his identity and wanted to get rid of him."

I wondered if Nathan actually had figured out who the murderer was. Maybe he knew someone at the university who was an expert on Barbados nuts or plant poisons, and Nathan had begun to wonder if his colleague had decided to put his knowledge of poisons to use. Or maybe he was personally acquainted in some other way with the killer. Perhaps his mother, who happened to have an intense, irrational dislike of Caroline? But surely his mother wouldn't have murdered her own son to get herself off the hook—would she?

I made a mental note to ask Nathan's colleagues if he'd ever expressed any interest in anybody at the university who specialized in toxic plants.

Paul said, "Maybe the reason Nathan was killed is that the real murderer wants his intended victim to put down her guard, to feel safe again."

"Caroline," I whispered. "He could have killed Nathan to lure Caroline out of hiding."

I reminded myself this was all conjecture. After all, there was a better than average chance that Nathan *had* committed the crimes he'd confessed to. Perhaps he was mentally ill, killing at the command of voices in his head. Hadn't one of his colleagues said he was bipolar?

But on the off chance that Nathan had *not* killed Mary Alice, Ophelia, or himself, I needed to warn Caroline that the poisoner might still be out there. I'd never forgive myself if the murderer showed up at Caroline's home tomorrow, bringing her some home-baked goodies filled with poisonous nuts or some equally deadly gift.

Caroline wouldn't appreciate my warning. She wanted to believe she was out of danger, that everything was back to normal. I phoned her anyway.

As the phone rang, I braced myself for her probable reactions: incredulity, fear, anger; maybe—God forbid—another plea to return with her to her Colorado hideaway?

Caroline didn't answer. I left a message for her to call me.

She didn't. I phoned again half an hour later. Still no answer.

"Maybe she turned off her phone, Mom. Or she's taking a nap," Katie said. "That happens to me all the time."

"Maybe," I said. But I had a bad feeling that the reason Caroline wasn't answering was more sinister.

The next morning I phoned her again.

"I think I should go to her house," I told Emily, who was sitting at the kitchen table eating a bagel.

"I'll come with you," she said.

As we drove to Caroline's house I realized I was babbling— what I always did when I was nervous. "I thought the dinner last night was a great success, didn't you? It was wonderful to see Katie and Matt looking so happy."

"Yeah, and it's also wonderful she's moving back to her own house."

I shot her a look. "I just hope they're more patient with each other this time. They've been living apart so much and they need to give themselves time to adjust."

Em leaned over to pat my hand. "Stop worrying. Katie and Matt are going to be fine."

I took a deep breath. "I hope so."

Neither of us said anything about what we might find at Caroline's house. Maybe if we didn't say it everything would be boringly normal. Caroline, her old, obnoxious self, would roll her eyes at our over-active imaginations.

But at least nothing looked amiss when we pulled into her driveway. I didn't see Caroline's car, but, if she hadn't gone out yet, it could be in the garage.

Em rang the doorbell. Nothing. I knocked loudly on the door, but no one responded. Could Caroline be out running errands? Had she gone out of town? Still, no matter where she was, you'd think she'd answer her cell phone.

Emily was looking in the living-room window. "Can you see

anything?" I asked.

"Nothing unusual. Too bad she locks her windows or we could just crawl in like we did at that cabin last year."

I shuddered. During the incident Em was referring to, Katie, with her younger sister's help, had crawled into the window of a locked cabin—and found a dead body.

We walked to the back of the house. I peered into the garage window. Caroline's car was sitting there. Now what?

Emily was at the kitchen window. "The lights are on," she said excitedly.

"Knock on the back door," I said. Maybe Caroline had been in the shower and hadn't heard our pounding.

She knocked, but nobody appeared. Then Em twisted the handle.

"Holy crap." Her face was ashen when she turned back to me. "The door's not locked!"

CHAPTER TWENTY-FIVE

We didn't find Caroline. She wasn't asleep in her bed, showering in her bathroom, or sitting at the computer with headphones on: all scenarios that might have explained why she hadn't heard us knocking. She wasn't anywhere else in the house either. We checked each room to make sure.

It didn't make sense. Caroline was not the kind of person who'd leave her door unlocked. She wasn't careless or forgetful, and she certainly wasn't trusting. She was well aware that bad people were roaming about, and she'd do everything she could to stop them from entering her house.

"I think we should call the police," I told Em.

"And say what? 'She left her back door open, officer. You must come investigate.' "

"I think something has happened to her, Em. Did you see those black marks on the kitchen floor? They weren't there the last time I was here. It looks like someone dragged her out the door and her shoes left skid marks."

Em looked dubiously at the double black lines on the floor. "They also could have come from some equipment scraping across the floor. I'm just telling you that the police are probably going to say there's no proof that anything criminal happened."

"Well, then I'm just going to have to convince them." I dug in my purse and phoned the police.

Fortunately Sergeant Martinez was in. "Are you saying you think Ms. Marshall's house has been broken into?" he asked.

174

"Well, I don't know. Maybe. The door's unlocked and there's no sign of Caroline. She's not answering her phone, and her car is still in the garage."

"Has the house been robbed?"

"Uh, I'm not sure about that either." Except for her computer and TV, I wasn't sure that Caroline had much that a robber would be interested in. "I'm worried that something has happened to her." When he didn't immediately respond, I added, "You do remember that someone already has tried to poison her twice?"

"Nathan Evans confessed to those murders in his suicide note. I appreciate your concern, Ms. Prescott, but at this point there's nothing we can do. It's too early to file a missing persons report."

I sighed as I hung up the phone. "He says if Caroline doesn't show up in a few days, I should call back."

"By which time, it could be too late to help Caroline," Em said. "Why don't we go talk to the neighbors? Somebody might have seen something."

No one was home at the two houses across the street, but at the stone cottage on the driveway side of Caroline's house a scowling, white-haired woman opened the door. "If you're selling something, I don't want it."

"We're not," I said with what I hoped was a trustworthy smile. "We're just trying to find out what happened to my friend, your neighbor Caroline Marshall. Have you seen her in the last two days?"

To my surprise, the old lady nodded and motioned for us to come inside. She led us to a small, over-crowded living room and indicated we should sit on a faded chintz couch while she took a facing chair, also chintz.

Mrs. Bradley introduced herself. "You're the woman who comes all the time to Caroline's house. She told me you're her assistant who's helping her with her book."

Her *assistant*? "That's right," I said, not wanting to explain the vast difference between an assistant and a ghostwriter. "I've been trying to contact Caroline, but she doesn't answer her phone. She's not at her house either, though her car is still in the garage."

"And she left her back door unlocked," Em added.

"She's a strange woman," the old lady said.

Well, yes. "I'm concerned that something could have happened to her. That's why I'm asking her neighbors if they saw anything out of the ordinary yesterday or today."

Mrs. Bradley thought about it. "A woman came to visit her yesterday afternoon. Caroline must have known her because she let her inside."

I tried to tamp down my excitement. "Do you remember what time that was?"

"After lunch, maybe 1:30. I was washing my dishes, and I could see Caroline's front door from the kitchen window."

"Did you see the woman leave?" Em asked.

Mrs. Bradley shook her head. "But I noticed her car was gone when I came back from my walk an hour later. I didn't see anyone else going in or out of her house."

I felt a stab of disappointment. "Did you get a good look at the woman?" Em asked. "Can you describe her?"

The old lady bristled. "I don't just sit at my window watching my neighbors, young lady."

"Of course you don't," Em said quickly. "It's just that you're such an excellent observer, I thought you might notice details that other people would likely miss."

Mrs. Bradley smiled, her ruffled feathers smoothed. "I've always prided myself on keeping an eye on things. I like to think of myself as the neighborhood crime watch."

As if to show off her skills, Mrs. Bradley proceeded to

describe Caroline's visitor: about five feet one, wearing slacks and a windbreaker with a pulled-up hood "so I couldn't see much of her face," and carrying a big tote bag. She'd talked to Caroline on the front porch for maybe thirty seconds before coming inside.

The FBI, I thought, should hire this woman. "You really do notice everything, Mrs. Bradley."

She preened. "I would have called the police when I saw you and your daughter looking in the windows if I hadn't known that you worked for Caroline."

Em and I thanked her for talking to us, and I gave her my cell-phone number in case she spotted Caroline.

"You know I just thought of something else," Mrs. Bradley said. "Probably it doesn't mean anything, but last night a car pulled into Caroline's driveway—late, around ten-thirty. The noise woke me. I figured at first it was just Caroline coming home from somewhere, but then about fifteen or twenty minutes later, I heard a car door slam. I got up to see what was going on, but by that time the car was backing out of the driveway."

"Did you see who was inside or what kind of car it was?" Em asked excitedly.

Mrs. Bradley shook her head. "I didn't have my glasses on, so I couldn't really see much. But I thought it was odd that the car didn't have its headlights on. It backed up fast and then drove away without the lights on."

Em and I looked at each other. Very odd indeed.

I was tempted to phone Officer Martinez to relay Mrs. Bradley's account of the recent activities at Caroline's house, but I figured he'd require more conclusive evidence.

"All we really know is that some woman visited Caroline yesterday at one thirty, and a car drove into Caroline's driveway around ten-thirty, leaving ten minutes later," Em said. "It could mean almost anything."

To make sure we hadn't missed something the first time, Em and I returned to Caroline's place and again walked through the house looking for clues. Aside from the marks on the kitchen floor, we saw nothing unusual—no overturned furniture or other signs of struggle, no open drawers or scattered possessions, and no calendar notations indicating where Caroline might be.

Feeling frustrated, I punched in Caroline's cell-phone number one more time. Caroline didn't answer, but what did happen sent a shiver down my spine. We could clearly hear a phone ringing somewhere in the house.

We followed the sound to the bedroom Caroline used as a study. We found her cell under some papers on her desk. This was most definitely not good.

We checked Caroline's phone to see if she had any messages that might tell us her whereabouts. There were three of them, all from me—two last night and one this morning.

"We can see who Caroline called," Em said. She took the phone and punched some buttons. "This shows Caroline's call history. Her last call—a short one to the public library—was made at eleven-thirty yesterday morning."

"I wonder if her phone wasn't working," I said. "That way she could have been at home but wouldn't have heard my messages."

Or she might have been dead by the time I phoned. I thought again of the marks on the kitchen floor. Had the killer dragged Caroline's body out her kitchen door to the car Mrs. Bradley had seen in the driveway last night? A car whose driver never bothered to turn on its headlights.

"Something isn't right," I said. "I wish the police would get on this before it's too late."

Em rolled her eyes. "That means they'd have to admit that something violent might have happened to Caroline, that she's just not taking a vacation and forgotten to tell anyone."

★ ★ ★ ★ ★

Regrettably, only a few hours later the police admitted just that.

I was half-watching the ten o'clock TV news when the announcer said, "The body of a local woman was discovered in a dumpster late this afternoon. Police have confirmed that she is Caroline Marshall, a well-known proponent of dumpster diving and frugal living."

My shriek brought Em running.

"What happened, Mom? What's wrong?"

"It's Caroline. They found her body in a dumpster this afternoon."

Wide-eyed, the two of us clutched each other, rocking silently, too shocked to say anything more.

CHAPTER TWENTY-SIX

Loud knocking on the door of my apartment jolted me from a pre-caffeinated stupor. I require a minimum of two cups of coffee in the morning before my brain joins the land of the living; so far I'd only consumed one.

I pulled on a robe and trudged to the living room. After checking through the peephole, I opened the door to Sergeant Martinez.

"I need to talk to you," he said, stepping inside.

Now, when it was too late to help Caroline, he wanted to talk? "You want coffee?"

"Sure." He followed me to the kitchen. "You heard about Caroline Marshall?"

"I heard it on TV last night. They said a grocery store worker discovered her body, but didn't say how or when Caroline died.

"We'll know more after the autopsy," he said with a tight-lipped expression that clearly said, Not that I intend to tell you anything.

Blame it on my inadequate level of caffeine, but I blurted out what I'd been thinking. "I can't keep wondering if Caroline was still alive when I phoned you. You remember that conversation—when you dismissed my concerns and told me to phone back in forty-eight hours?"

"Oh, I remember. You'd broken into her house, right?"

"We didn't *break in*. Her back door was unlocked and we just walked in."

"And what time was that again, when you *entered* her house?"

"Around ten or ten-thirty yesterday morning."

He wrote something on a little notepad. "And aside from phoning me, what else did you do in the house?"

I described how we'd walked through the place looking for Caroline or any signs of what could have happened to her. "The only suspicious thing we found was a double line of dark marks on the kitchen floor—the kind of skid marks shoes might make if someone was dragged across the floor."

Sergeant Martinez wrote that down. "That was the only evidence that an altercation might have occurred there?"

I nodded. "After that we went to talk to the neighbors to see if they'd seen anything."

He looked up, interested. "Had they?"

I told her what Mrs. Bradley had said about the woman visiting Caroline in the early afternoon and the car that had driven into the driveway that night.

"Did she say that she *saw* Caroline let the woman into the house?"

I tried to remember. "I think so, but maybe she only saw *someone* open the door. From her kitchen window she'd really only have a view of Caroline's porch—of the visitor—but not of the front of the house."

The officer made another note, then stood up. "If you think of anything else, please call me."

I held up a palm. "Wait! Can't you tell me something about how she died?"

He hesitated, obviously debating what to tell me. "I guess I can disclose that, according to the medical examiner's preliminary findings, Ms. Marshall was already dead by the time you phoned me."

"Caroline died a day earlier?"

"Yes." He turned to leave.

"In the afternoon?" I said quickly. Shortly after letting the mysterious woman visitor into her house? "Or in the evening?" Perhaps around ten or ten-thirty when the vehicle pulled into her driveway?

"I've already told you more than I probably should. We'll know more after the autopsy is complete."

I followed him to the front door. "Won't you at least tell me how Caroline died?" Somehow it would be better to know what had really happened to her than to let my imagination scroll through all the gruesome possibilities of how her lifeless body could have ended up in a dumpster.

"We aren't releasing that information yet." Without a backward glance he left.

"And you're welcome, officer, for all the useful information I provided you," I muttered as I closed the door.

Em appeared from her bedroom—the room previously known as my office—the minute she heard the officer leave. "I opened my door a crack and heard everything he said. It's really silly for the police to be so secretive about their investigation when the media is going to get the information out anyway. I was just reading the newspaper online and their crime reporter's blog. She interviewed the grocery-store worker who found Caroline. The guy said that her body was at the top of the bin and in a white body bag. And—get this—the killer wrote her name on the bag in marker, for easy identification."

I stared at her. "Wow. That's not just disposing of a dead body. It's making a statement."

"We just need to figure out what that statement says," Em said.

We? I was just about to interject that maybe we could now let the police do the figuring out when Em's cell rang. It was becoming even more clear to me that whoever was doing these killings was determined, probably insane, and very definitely someone I didn't want to mess with. As soon as Em got off the phone, I'd make that point. Forcefully.

"Great, I'll talk to you soon," Em told her caller. Then she transferred her attention to me. "That was Nathan's mother. She says that Caroline's death is incontrovertible proof that Nathan didn't kill those women and that whoever killed Caroline also killed Nathan."

Em smiled. "And guess what, Mom? She thinks the police have been bungling this investigation every step of the way. And she's hiring me to do more investigating. She wants me to find out who killed Nathan, and she said she didn't care how long my investigation takes or how much it costs as long as I give her some answers. Isn't that great?"

"Great" was not the word I'd use. Other more apt adjectives came to mind: dangerous, reckless, ludicrous, to name a few. An untrained amateur private eye attempting to find a psychopathic killer was insane, the gold standard for the term "hazardous to one's health." What it was *not* was a stellar career opportunity— the way Em apparently viewed the situation.

Four people had been murdered so far: Mary Alice, Ophelia, Nathan, and Caroline. Even if, by some remote possibility, all of those deaths were not connected, there was at least one ruthless killer at large—a killer who had gone to a great deal of effort to get to Caroline. If one believed, as I did, that Mary Alice and Ophelia's deaths had been failed attempts to kill Caroline, it had taken this persistent assassin months to finally eliminate her.

And Emily wanted to corner such a person! "Maybe you should leave this one to the police, honey," I said.

"Don't worry, Mom. I won't do anything that puts me in jeopardy."

I knew Em believed what she said, that she wouldn't knowingly do anything reckless. She'd always been a relentlessly hon-

est girl. The only problem, of course, was that the killer might
very well take a less charitable view of her meddling. After all,
Mary Alice, Ophelia, Nathan, and Caroline were not doing
anything risky, provocative, or dangerous either when they'd
died.

My mind reeled with that little insight. Maybe Em stopping
her investigation into this monster's business wasn't enough to
protect my daughter. Maybe she had *already* provoked him.

"You know I think we should take a little vacation, Em, get
out of town for a while."

My daughter looked at me as if I was losing my mind. "Go
where?"

Anywhere other than here. The one clear thing that all four
victims had in common was that each one of them had died
within the Houston city limits. Which was the biggest recom-
mendation I could think of for getting out of town.

"We could go anywhere you'd like," I said. "Austin, San
Antonio, the Hill Country. Or how about Big Bend? Remember
how much you and Katie loved hiking in the desert that time
we went there for middle-school spring break? We always said
we had to go back there, but we never did."

"Mom, we can't leave now," she said in the firm but patient
voice one used with a cranky toddler.

"Why not?"

"I have a job I need to finish."

"No," I said, "you do not. It's the police's job. Let them, the
trained professionals, do it." *They* were used to dealing with
dangerous criminals.

Em's eyes narrowed, her lips pursed. Without a word, she
swiveled and marched to her bedroom. Then she loudly
slammed the door.

I left the apartment a minute later. A long walk, that was
what I needed. I had taken many, many long walks during my

girls' turbulent teen years.

I paced and seethed, just the way I always had. The only things that were different: I no longer walked in a tree-lined suburban neighborhood and I couldn't tell myself that the Terrible Teens would soon pass.

Weren't we supposed to be through this phase by now? I fumed. What had happened to that wonderful stage of young adulthood when the child pulled away from her parents, started supporting herself in some satisfying (and not dangerous) career, moved out of the parental house, and began building an independent life?

Yes, I was aware that Em was hardly alone in postponing those traditional rites of maturity. Twenty-somethings by the thousands were moving back into their parents' homes after college graduation. A new word, "adultescence," had even been coined to describe the phenomenon. But was it too much to expect this gently nurtured generation to grow up already?

At my girls' ages, I wouldn't have been caught dead living with my parents. Holiday visits and occasional weekends were fine, but I'd never considered moving back into their house when I could be out on my own. My parents didn't spend endless hours worrying about me the way I'd worried—and, yes, still did—about my girls. Mom and Dad assumed that I was fine because I never told them any differently.

But was that the kind of relationship I wanted with my girls—not worrying about them because I was blissfully ignorant about their lives? Would I really feel any better if Em was living on her own and keeping it a secret that she was about to venture into the world of a serial killer?

Get a grip, Lauren, I scolded myself. It was time to stop being angry about my daughter's mule-headed refusal to follow her mother's eminently sensible advice. Time to think of Plan B.

I stopped walking and pulled my cell phone out of my pocket. I punched in the number for Janice Evans.

Fortunately, she was not one of those people who only responded to text messages; she answered. "We need to talk," I told her, "one mother to another."

I returned to my apartment an hour later.

Emily was sitting in the living room. She didn't look like a happy camper. "Well, at least *you* should be happy, Mom. There's been a change of plans. My investigative services are no longer required."

"Oh? How did that happen?"

"Mrs. Evans called when you were out. She said it makes more sense to let the police handle the case—which was *not* what she was saying yesterday. Maybe the police contacted her this morning and, now that Caroline is dead, too, they're more open to the idea that Nathan could have been a murder victim rather than a killer."

"I guess that's a possibility," I said as I unpacked the groceries I'd bought after my conversation with Nathan's mother. I glanced up and caught the look of disdain on my daughter's face. Had she guessed my part in Mrs. Evans's withdrawing her job offer?

Fortunately, I was not the target of Emily's contempt. "Mrs. Evans said this was entirely a cost-cutting gesture, nothing to do with me, and to send her an invoice for the work I've done so far." She sighed dramatically. "Then she laughed and said maybe she'd inherited the family frugal genes after all."

I shook my head, trying my best to look sympathetic. Later tonight I'd send Janice Evans flowers.

I just prayed that the killer had gotten the memo that we'd given up poking our noses into his/her crimes.

CHAPTER TWENTY-SEVEN

I still thought it was a good idea for us to get out of town in case "Eliminate Emily Prescott" was on the murderer's to-do list. But before we could leave we still had Caroline's memorial service to attend.

I was about to attend my fourth funeral for too-young-to-die people, none of whom had expired from natural causes. Three of them had been poisoned by toxic plants, the fourth, Caroline, had apparently died of asphyxiation coupled with a skull fracture.

In my view, Emily still seemed much too interested in Caroline's death. She poured over the few lines in the newspaper mentioning the medical examiner's findings. "It sounds as if the killer knocked Caroline unconscious with a hard blow to her head, then stuck her in an airless body bag so she'd suffocate in case the skull fracture didn't do the job," she told me as she ate her breakfast.

"I'd guess the person Caroline invited into her house that afternoon clubbed her with something. What I can't figure out is how the killer got her to that dumpster. It's not as if you can carry a body bag out in broad daylight, particularly if you have an eagle-eyed neighbor like Mrs. Bradley watching the house."

"Maybe the car Mrs. Bradley heard that night in Caroline's driveway was someone coming to collect the body and transport it to the dumpster," I said, losing my appetite as I thought about that. Had Caroline lain in the body bag on the floor of her own house until the killer returned to dispose of her body?

Apparently Em was not experiencing any similar queasiness as she poured herself another generous serving of granola. "What I don't understand is why the murderer suddenly changed his M.O. He seemed to be entirely focused on toxic plants—Barbados nuts and the oleander whistle. Why change methods now?"

"Because Caroline refused to eat the nuts the killer offered her or said she'd rather not blow into any handmade whistle?" I suggested. "Because she'd become a lot more wary of people she encountered?" So why then had she invited that visitor—and possible killer—into her house?

Em shook her head. "But this is a very determined and persistent killer. If it was important to him that Caroline die from poison, he could have found a way, even if he had to hold a gun to her head and force her to eat the nuts."

"So, are you suggesting this was a different killer?" I said. "One who wasn't into poison?"

"I don't know. Could be a second person who was in cahoots with the poisoner. Or maybe the most important thing to the murderer now was for Caroline's body to end up in a dumpster—and he didn't care that much how she died."

I thought about that. "Certainly walking into her house and knocking her on the head would be a lot easier than tricking her into eating poisonous food."

Em chewed thoughtfully. "Maybe the killer was getting impatient and just wanted to be done with it already."

"That's certainly possible. If Mary Alice's poisoning was, as we presume, the first attempt to kill Caroline and Ophelia's was the second botched effort, the murderer likely would be feeling frustrated."

I took a tentative sip of coffee, testing how my stomach would respond. Encouragingly, my stomach was fine with it. I took a second sip.

Em leaned forward. "I have this fantasy of encountering the murderer and finally getting all my questions answered: why he did it, why use those poisons, how he managed the logistics of it all. Wouldn't that be awesome?"

My hitherto calm stomach suddenly gave a lurch. I set down my mug. "Actually, awesome is not the word I'd use."

Like the woman herself, Caroline's memorial service was both distinctive and, yes, strange. It took place in the same community college conference room where Caroline had taught her last frugal-living class.

About one hundred mourners were in the room, frankly more than I thought would be there. A significant number were sensible-looking, plainly dressed women who might have been Caroline's former students. A minority of the audience had the look of gawkers, come to see what kind of woman would teach dumpster diving and then end up dead in a dumpster. Maybe a few of them were journalists.

Most of the survivors from that ill-fated potluck at Caroline's were also there. Hard to believe that four of the ten people at that dinner party—almost half—were now dead.

As far as I could see, the only typical memorial props were an arrangement of red and white carnations on a table at the front of the room, sitting next to a framed photo of Caroline. It was the photograph Caroline had used for advertising brochures. In it she was smiling, empathetic-looking, leaning toward the camera in a I-just-want-to-help-make-your-life-better pose.

A tall man I didn't recognize walked up to the podium where Caroline used to give her lectures. "Hi," he said, "I'm Will Marshall, Caroline's brother."

Except for the one time she'd said her brother had thought

going to their grandmother's cabin was boring, Caroline hadn't spoken about her brother. I could see a vague family resemblance: the siblings both were tall and lean, with blue eyes. Caroline, though, had projected a kind of forceful energy that her brother, from first glance, did not seem to possess.

"My sister's death came as a complete shock to me and, undoubtedly, to all of you, too," he began, gazing earnestly around the audience. "Caroline was my big sister, the girl who throughout our childhood constantly bossed me around. But she was also the kid who beat up a school bully to protect me. After Caroline gave this hulking, ten-year-old delinquent a black eye, he never picked on me again."

He grinned. "Incidentally, although this guy was two years younger than she, he was a good twenty pounds heavier and a whole lot meaner. But there was something absolutely fierce and fearless about my sister. She was the kind of person you didn't want to cross."

There were a few nervous titters from the audience. Perhaps people who had personally experienced Caroline's fierceness or had had the poor sense to cross her? My own reaction was a bit different: If Caroline was such a scrapper, why hadn't she fought back against her attacker? Though, of course, if her assailant had hit her unexpectedly from behind, maybe she'd been knocked unconscious before she'd had a chance to fight.

"Even as a kid, Caroline was always a problem solver, always prepared," her brother said. "So I guess I shouldn't have been surprised to discover when I arrived at her house, after the police notified me of her death, a neatly labeled folder in her desk that contained her will and instructions on the kind of funeral she wanted."

He gave a small, rueful smile. "Not surprisingly, she didn't want anything elaborate and definitely NOT costly. Cremation, she informed us, was a much more frugal alternative to burial, and she definitely did not want us to pay for a coffin."

At that the audience did laugh. Even in death Caroline had tried to squeeze every penny.

"In lieu of a religious service, my sister asked that we share our memories of her. 'They might not be flattering, but at least there should be some good stories,' she wrote."

This got a big laugh, too. Perhaps, I thought, Caroline Marshall was more self-aware than I'd given her credit for.

There was a longish pause, during which I wondered if anyone was going to choose to share their stories. But finally a spry, white-haired woman walked to the podium.

"I'm Helena Cruise and I took one of Caroline's first dumpster-diving workshops. She hadn't worked out all the kinks yet, and there were some nasty accidents, some bad publicity, accusations of negligence and ignoring safety issues. People called her greedy, a trespasser, a scavenger who wanted to make a buck sifting through garbage.

"Despite all that, Caroline never faltered. She was the embodiment of the word 'persistence.' She dealt with the problems, instituted some safety rules, and got on with her business. What I remember was how much fun she made it all seem. Dumpster diving was a treasure hunt, being frugal was a game you could win. No matter what you thought about her personally, you had to applaud her passion."

A sharp-featured woman I remembered from Ophelia's memorial service stood up next. Hadn't she told me she'd been fired by Caroline?

"I hadn't planned on speaking at this event because Caroline and I didn't part on the best of terms, and my mother always taught me that you shouldn't speak ill of the dead," she began. "But, apparently, Caroline wanted us to share our stories about her, so I will. I worked for her when she was just starting her business. I thought she was a tyrannical bitch and total control freak, while sweet Ophelia tried to soothe all the employees' hurt feelings."

She looked around, her expression mocking. "Clearly I didn't like Caroline Marshall. You picked up on that, huh?"

She waited for the uneasy laughter to subside. "The woman fired me, unfairly, I thought. But now, after all these years, I can admire her vision, her ability to work hard and to grow a business. She was not a likeable person, but she certainly was a strong one."

Em and I looked at each other. "Can't remember the last time I heard the words tyrannical bitch, bossy, greedy, and total control freak used in a eulogy," I whispered.

Em nodded. "What I kept hearing was a bunch of motives for why people wanted to kill Caroline." She glanced around. "Maybe someone right in this room."

CHAPTER TWENTY-EIGHT

Caroline's brother Will sent me a look that reminded me of a salesman trying to sell a client something she really didn't want. Not a good sign, I thought, glancing uneasily around Caroline's living room.

It was the place where Caroline had probably been murdered. The skids marks made by her shoes as her body was dragged across the floor had started from the living room. I wondered if Will or his mother, sitting on Caroline's aging sofa, realized that when they requested I meet them here "to take care of some business."

Will cleared his throat. "I appreciate everything you did for my sister, Mrs. Prescott—all your work on her book. The last time I talked to Caroline, about a month ago, she seemed very excited about it."

"Thanks," I said. What I wanted to say was, Let's jump to the bottom line, Mr. Marshall; I can tell by your expression it's not going to be good news.

"As executor of Caroline's estate," he continued, "I'm proposing that in lieu of the money she owes you, you instead acquire all the educational materials from her classes and all rights to the book you're writing. I only ask that her name also be on the book's cover. You, of course," he added, with a forced smile, "will receive all the royalties."

All of *what* royalties? "Thanks anyways, but I think I'd rather have cash for the work I've already done." Particularly since it was likely to be the only money earned from Caroline's little vanity book.

"I think Will has made you a very generous offer," Caroline's mother said, her gaunt face growing red. If all that cosmetic surgery hadn't prevented it, I'm sure she would have been sneering, but only her mean little eyes conveyed her anger. "In fact, I told my son that I thought it was much *too* generous. If the book becomes a best seller, we won't be entitled to any of the proceeds, which strikes me as unfair. I personally think that we should get a cut of the royalties."

"That won't be happening, Mother," Will said. "Lauren will be doing all the actual writing. She deserves something for her work."

"But Caroline provided the content of the book," his mother protested. "All *she's* doing is typing it into coherent sentences. I'm sure your sister didn't intend for the writer to receive all the profits."

Did the woman really believe her own drivel? I wondered. Caroline had said her mother was greedy and extravagant. She'd also used the word "loathsome." After being around her mother for roughly ten minutes, I could see what she'd meant.

I told myself to stay calm. No matter what I said, I doubted I could ever make any inroads through Mrs. Marshall's total self-absorption, but Will at least seemed open to reason.

I directed my arguments to him. "What you don't seem to understand is there's no guarantee that Caroline's book will ever be published." In fact, knowing the current realities of the book business, I doubted that anyone would be particularly interested in publishing it.

"Caroline hired me as a freelance writer to complete a writing project. We had a signed contract, which I'll be happy to show you. When I finish the book, Caroline agreed to pay me an additional fifteen thousand dollars. I have every intention of completing it."

Will looked genuinely pained. "I realize what she agreed to, Lauren. I saw the contract when I went over her accounts. But unfortunately she seems, uh, very short on funds. In fact the only significant asset she possessed was this house. Until we sell the house there's not enough to pay you."

Was he saying Caroline was broke? While I'd never thought that Caroline was by any means affluent, I always assumed she was frugal by choice, not by necessity.

Involuntarily, my eyes shifted towards the dining room. Mary Alice had died there. Ophelia had died sitting with Caroline at the little breakfast table in the kitchen.

"*If* we sell the house, you mean," Mrs. Marshall snapped, echoing my own thoughts. "It's going to be damned hard to unload it when potential buyers learn that three people were murdered here." She shuddered. "I refuse to spend even one night in the place."

Somehow she made it sound as if turning the house into a crime scene was her daughter's final affront: inconveniencing her mother by dying in a scandalous manner and, in the process, lowering the price of the property.

Mrs. Marshall sighed. "I could never understand why my daughter—personable, college-educated, with a degree in marketing, a girl who'd had *every* advantage—got into this work. Basically all she did was teach blue-collar housewives how to save a few pennies! I told her it was demeaning, but of course she wouldn't listen to me. Now it turns out that her so-called business wasn't even profitable."

I stared at her, feeling sorry for the little girl who'd had had to grow up with such a monstrous mother. "I believe Caroline felt that she was genuinely helping people—of all income levels—to gain financial control of their lives."

She waved her hand dismissively. "She always was an enigma

to me. A willful child who turned into an even more eccentric adult who would do anything to get attention. The final indignity for me is her stipulating that her remains are to be scattered on an abandoned mountaintop in Colorado. She used to go there to visit my mother—a woman just as peculiar as Caroline. Who in their right mind would want such a thing?"

"I went to that cabin with Caroline a few weeks ago," I said. "A retreat to write the book." And to escape—unfortunately, only temporarily—from a determined killer who was stalking her. "Caroline loved the place, said she'd spent the happiest summers of her life there with her grandmother."

"*I* certainly never enjoyed being out in the middle of nowhere, though I really couldn't stand spending time with my mother anywhere else either," Mrs. Marshall said.

No one said a word. Will and I looked at each other. "My wife and I go to Grandmother's place at least once a year," he told me. "It's very peaceful. We'll scatter Caroline's ashes there, as she requested."

Mrs. Marshall rolled her eyes. "Cremation is so vulgar," she began.

"I need to go," I said, standing up.

Will rose too. "I understand that you might want to consult an attorney about what we talked about," he said. "But why don't you at least take Caroline's notes for her book and copies of the handouts she used in her classes? I've packed all of it into a cardboard box."

I hesitated. If I took the materials was I agreeing to accept the papers in lieu of the money Caroline contracted to pay me?

Caroline's brother seemed to sense what I was thinking. In a gentler voice, he said, "Please, take it. No obligations. Mother and I are leaving tomorrow. You can let me know later what you decide. I'd like to think that someone was putting all of Caroline's work to good use."

I nodded. In the entry hall he gave me the box, which seemed to contain a pile of manila folders and notebooks. "I'm sorry for your loss," I told him as I left.

"Thank you," he said. Both of us, I noticed, pointedly ignored his mother.

"Really, Mom, we're not in any danger at all," Em told me in the patient voice I used to employ when assuring her toddler self that there were no monsters under her bed.

We were sitting at the kitchen table eating a take-out pizza. "I'm sure that's what Nathan thought, too," I said. "Up until the day somebody poisoned him."

"But the killer had a *reason* to poison him. There's no reason to get rid of us."

So she'd had a chat with the killer to clarify his motives? I took a deep breath, then another. It didn't help much. I still wanted to scream in frustration. Why was my otherwise astute daughter so oblivious to the very real threats to her life?

"I'm assuming that Nathan was murdered because the poisoner believed Nathan had guessed his identity," I explained. "Some of his friends said Nathan talked a lot about the murders, trying to solve the case. Maybe he questioned the wrong person." I sent my daughter a stern look. "Since *you've* also been doing some very public digging into these deaths, it's not inconceivable that this psychopath might want you off the case, too."

Em, unfortunately, did not look the least bit frightened. "But I don't think that's why Nathan was killed, Mom. I've been rereading all my notes, and the only thing that makes sense is that he was murdered as a way to lure Caroline back into town, to make her feel safe enough to come out of hiding. And it worked. As soon as Caroline thought the killer was dead, she moved back into her home."

"Where, within a matter of days, she was murdered," I muttered. Her theory made a warped kind of sense.

She nodded. "I think the killer picked Nathan because he seemed a plausible murderer. He was at the potluck dinner where Mary Alice died, he was knowledgeable about toxic plants, and his family had a feud with Caroline—in other words, he had motive, means, and opportunity."

"What a terrible reason to die—because you happened to be at a dinner, knew something about poisons, and your mom resented Caroline for stealing her mother's affection decades ago." And even more frightening was a killer so cold-blooded and amoral that he apparently had no qualms about ending the lives of three innocent bystanders.

Em, I noticed, was eyeing the last piece of pizza in the takeout box. I waved my hand magnanimously. "What you're saying is reasonable, but this killer's behavior is anything but rational. What if instead of deciding 'goal accomplished, intended victim dead,' he's discovered that he enjoys killing? Or maybe all along he was a serial killer who intended to murder all four of those people, in which case Mary Alice, Ophelia, and Nathan were not random casualties in the war against Caroline, but were merely a few on a long list of the killer's victims."

Emily swallowed her pizza and opened her mouth to reply.

I didn't let her. "Since we can't know what this assassin's motives are and who else is on his hit list, I still say we need to get out of town for a while."

"Until the killer is arrested?" Em said, her voice rising rapidly. "What if he's never caught? Are we going to be in hiding forever?"

She made it sound as if I was suggesting we enter the Witness Protection Program. All of this love of melodrama, I thought, had to come from her father's side of the family. The Prescott family tree boasted more than its share of drama kings and queens.

"We deserve a vacation, and we're just going to be gone for a few days." At least no more than a week or two. Hopefully, within that time the police would make some progress. According to Paul's police sources, this string of widely-publicized homicides had embarrassed the HPD into putting more resources into the investigation.

I had no clue where we would go; all I knew was that it was going to be someplace cheap. "Staying here makes me feel too much as if we're sitting ducks, honey." Like unsuspecting Caroline opening her door to her killer.

"Sometimes it kind of freaks me out, too," Em admitted. "If it makes you feel better, maybe we should leave."

I smiled with relief. "Great!" At least the child had also inherited my family's strong strain of common sense.

"If you lend me your car, I'll go visit my friend Stacy in Austin. She said I can sleep on her couch."

"Uh, if you take my car, I won't have any means of transportation."

"Oh, you'll be on vacation with Paul," she said. "You won't need your car."

"And you know this how?" While Paul and I had discussed taking a trip, we'd never decided on dates or destination.

"Oh, we talked this morning when you were at Caroline's house. He said if I had someplace else to go, the two of you can go to Santa Fe and Taos. I told him you'd love that, then I called Stacy to make arrangements."

"Nice to know that everything's all worked out," I said sarcastically. Without consulting me at all.

"While I'm in Austin, I'm going to see what I have to do to return to UT next semester. I've been thinking that getting a law degree might be a good idea after all. I could use it in a lot of careers—joining the FBI, becoming a private detective or maybe even a judge."

I smiled. It was probably better not to dwell too much on the image of Judge Emily on the bench. "I'm so glad you've decided to go back to school. That's wonderful news."

"I knew you'd be happy," she said with a grin. "By the way, Paul said you should call him. I think he's making plane and hotel reservations for tomorrow." She took a last sip of her diet soda. "I'm going to start packing."

I sat there in stunned silence. Sure, I'd probably been outmaneuvered by my plotting daughter and boyfriend, but in this case, that was not necessarily a bad thing.

I picked up the phone to call Paul. I wanted to hear all about our trip.

CHAPTER TWENTY-NINE

Paul, it turned out, was a remarkably easy person to travel with. That shouldn't have been surprising, since he was, in general, an exceedingly easy person to be around, but sometimes, in my experience, otherwise compatible people made difficult traveling companions. One person, for instance, likes to sightsee from dawn to dusk, lingering over every exhibit in every museum, while the other thinks vacations are specifically designed to nap by the side of the hotel pool. Fortunately, both Paul and I were eccentric explorers, meticulously perusing exhibits we found interesting and ignoring the others. We were both flexible about schedules.

Our first day in Santa Fe we spent the morning strolling around the downtown Plaza, sticking our heads in an occasional shop, and talking nonstop. Paul told me I should turn my half-finished Caroline book into several magazine articles, which seemed a good idea and less daunting than trying to finish the book now. The articles, we agreed, could bring in some much-needed cash as well as possibly interest a book publisher.

Over a delicious lunch of New Mexican blue-corn enchiladas and green-chile tamales, we shared stories of our childhoods, our families, and even our exs. Paul told me his ex-wife, happily remarried, sent him a chatty yearly birthday note. "We're friendlier now than when we were married." I told him about my girls' recent visit with their father. My ex-husband was now doing dental work on fellow inmates and, according to our daughters, finally seemed to be adjusting to life behind bars.

We spent our afternoon savoring the breathtaking paintings at the Georgia O'Keeffe Museum and the inventive handmade pieces at the Museum of International Folk Art. The next day we drove out of town to explore the awesome Puye' cliff dwellings, which were believed to have been built in the thirteenth or fourteenth century. After all that walking, we returned to town to waste the rest of the day lying by the hotel pool, reading novels and drinking frozen margaritas.

"I'd forgotten how much I love Santa Fe," I said from my lounge chair as Paul emerged, dripping, from the pool.

He smiled lazily at me. "One of my favorite places on earth."

"Mine, too." I wondered if all that swimming laps was what kept his body so well toned and muscular. Suddenly realizing that he was aware of my perusal, I stammered, "Love the desert. Certainly understand why Georgia O'Keeffe was so drawn to it."

"Uh-huh." His eyes narrowed and his smile turned less lazy. "Turn over and let me rub some more sunscreen on your back. I'm afraid you're getting sunburned."

I turned as ordered and was delighted at his thorough job of applying lotion to every inch of my exposed skin.

Not wanting to appear ungrateful, I baked in the sun for a good fifteen minutes before saying, "I really am getting too warm. Think I'll go back to the room to shower."

He glanced up from his lounge chair, his expression unreadable. "Actually, I'm getting kind of hot myself."

I smiled brightly. "So you're coming in with me?"

He practically leapt from his chair. "I am," he said with a look I had no problem at all reading.

We had another lovely dinner that night at an intimate, candlelit restaurant off the Plaza. I took a sip of my Riesling, trying to remember when I'd last felt so content.

"Right before we left the hotel I got texts from both Katie and Em," I told Paul. "Katie sounds really happy to have Matt back home. Em went to the registrar's office and got everything set up for going back next semester."

"Excellent," Paul said. "Is she scouting out places to live in Austin? From what she said, I gather she wasn't thrilled with living in a dorm."

"As a matter of fact, she and Stacy are talking about sharing an apartment in the same building where Stacy's living now. The apartments there are small but close to campus and reasonably priced. And Stacy even loves to cook."

"Great. But don't underestimate Emily. She told me she was watching TV cooking shows to learn the basics."

"She is?" It was the first I'd heard of it. One of Paul's many exceptional qualities, I reflected, was his ability to listen and be genuinely interested in even the most mundane subjects. I valued that almost as much as his affectionate tolerance of my sometimes high-strung girls.

Paul nodded. "I think she didn't mention it because she didn't want to risk having her culinary efforts compared with Katie's."

I took a bite of my spicy risotto. "Emily never wanted to try anything that Katie excelled in." Fortunately, for Em at least, Katie had never been very scholarly, so Em was free to achieve in all things academic.

He grinned. "Yeah, I felt that way about my older brother, too. It's a good thing that I had no aptitude for mechanical engineering and he wasn't remotely interested in journalism."

We ate for a few minutes in companionable silence. Then Paul said, "There's something I have to tell you, Lauren."

Somehow I knew that whatever he had to say was not good news.

"Do you remember me telling you about my friend in Seattle

who wanted to start a new magazine?" When I nodded, he said, "Against all odds he's managed to find funding and coax some very talented writers to get on board."

I couldn't bear to hear any more. "And he's coaxed you into becoming editor-in-chief?"

He looked solemn, even apologetic. "This is an opportunity I just can't pass up. Unfortunately, living in Seattle is a non-negotiable part of the job."

I swallowed. "I understand." I studied my plate, praying that I could make the tears welling in my eyes disappear.

He took my cold hand in his large, warm one. "I want you to come with me."

My head jerked up. "What do you—?"

"I'm asking you to marry me, Lauren. This isn't the eloquent proposal I intended, but I love you with all my heart and want to spend the rest of my life with you."

I stared at him. For one of the few times in my life, I was genuinely speechless. I knew I should be ecstatic, but instead all I was feeling was confused. Yes, I loved Paul, and the idea of never seeing him again was almost too painful to contemplate. But I didn't know if I wanted to marry him. I wasn't sure if I wanted to marry anyone again.

After the disastrous conclusion to my twenty-plus-year marriage to a man I'd hardly known at all, I told myself, Never again. Marriage—or perhaps my idea of what being a wife entailed—had turned me into an invisible woman, a family nurturer who saw to everyone's needs except my own.

In fairness, no one, including my weasel of a husband, had demanded I sacrifice myself on the altar of marriage and motherhood. It was just what I'd done. For years, especially when the girls were young, I'd enjoyed doing it.

Only in the waning days of my marriage did I realize how much I'd missed, how underdeveloped significant parts of me had become after years of neglect. Stan, of course, helped me to these realizations by confiscating all our valuables and leaving town with his girlfriend. But even before that dreadful day when I'd stood, stunned, in my suddenly-empty living room, I had sensed that I was only half living my life.

Stan's betrayal taught me that I was stronger than I'd thought. My rusty journalism skills were, thank God, still marketable and I suddenly remembered how much I loved to write and to interview people. After a shaky start, I even began to enjoy my solitude. It was a tough transition, but in the end I felt proud of myself and my growing self-sufficiency.

Which was one of the reasons I wasn't sure if I was ready to give up that hard-won independence. I was just getting used to this new freedom to do what I wanted and be responsible only for me. Maybe in a few years, when this feeling of finally being comfortable in my own skin was more familiar, I would be happy to share my life with a loving partner, but right now it seemed too soon.

I tried to explain this to Paul.

"You're saying you love me, but you don't want to marry me? Or you *might* want to marry me, just not now?"

I searched his face, trying, unsuccessfully, to read what he was feeling. "I don't know what I'm saying," I said, feeling simultaneously miserable, cruel, foolish, and conflicted. "I love you, but I need time to think about the rest of it."

"The rest of it?" Paul said. "Is the idea of marriage so repugnant to you that you can't even say the word?"

I suddenly felt an urge to kick him in the shins. Couldn't he understand that I didn't want to discuss this before I had time to sort out my feelings? This trip had been so perfect, so romantic, until he'd spoiled everything by telling me he was going to move two thousand miles away and wanted me to go with him. Never mind that I'd be on the opposite side of the country from my children and friends, that I'd be leaving a city I'd lived in more than half my life, that I knew no one in Seattle. And now he was trying to pressure me into making a quick decision?

"No," I said quite testily, "the idea of our *marriage* is so unexpected that I need time to think about it."

Something seemed to shift in Paul's eyes. Was it relief I saw there? Disappointment? Whatever it was, it was gone in a second. "Of course," he said quietly. "Take as much time as you need."

I nodded, trying to smile as I wondered how this all was going to end.

Chapter Thirty

As soon as I got back from the trip, I threw myself into my writing. I needed to do *something* to distract myself from my nonstop obsessing about Paul and his marriage proposal and, with the loss of the expected payment from Caroline, I also needed to make some money.

I planned to turn the now-abandoned manuscript of Caroline's memoir into several articles. Before I left on our trip, I'd queried several magazines to see if they'd be interested in a piece on Caroline's frugal-living tips. I had an e-mail reply now from an editor of a regional monthly, saying he'd consider an article, but only if it had a different slant.

What he wanted was a profile of Caroline that included an account of her murder and the poisonings that took place in her home. He wasn't interested in the penny-pinching tips I'd proposed except for a description of dumpster diving, which he thought his readers would probably find "equal parts intriguing and repellent."

In other words, he was interested in the sensational, true-crime version of the story rather than the good-housekeeping tips. And he wanted it soon "while the story is fresh in the public's mind."

It was not the article I wanted to write, but right now it was the only one that anyone was interested in publishing. The money was good, and if I sold a few more pieces to other magazines, I might be able to make up the remainder of the money Caroline had promised me for writing her book.

Writing was also a good way to avoid thinking about Paul and his proposal.

I spent most of the morning outlining the article, seeing what information I already had and what I needed to get. I quickly determined that what I had was a lot of dry facts: biographical information on Caroline, the basics of dumpster diving, and the who-what-where-when of the murders—minus, of course, the identity or motive of the killer.

I needed to find a way to somehow convey a sense of the complex, prickly, ambitious woman who'd so infuriated somebody that he or she had butchered two other people in botched attempts to murder Caroline and then killed a third, Nathan, in order to lure her out of hiding. While I certainly didn't want to imply that Caroline deserved this—even sweet, saintly people, after all, could become victims of a murderer—I nevertheless wanted my piece to convey the strong feelings, both positive and negative, that the charismatic Queen of Dumpster Diving seemed to evoke.

The question, of course, was how was I going to accomplish this. I scanned the notes I'd made when I'd accompanied Caroline on a dumpster-diving expedition. "Scavenging for treasures in the trash," Caroline had called it. Of the four people on that outing, only two of us—Ellen and I—were still alive. The other two—Ellen's sister, Mary Alice, and Caroline—had both been murdered.

Ophelia had led a second dumpster-diving expedition the same day. I'd met the members of that group at the potluck dinner: Nathan, the grad student; Ethan and Margaret, the earnest homeschoolers; and Josie, the friendly, gray-haired hippy, and Ed, her grumpy husband. Two of that group, Nathan and Ophelia, were also now dead.

I shivered, suddenly cold. Four people who'd been alive and

vital just a few months ago had met violent, senseless deaths. Undoubtedly all of them expected to have many years ahead of them—and would still be alive today if they had not encountered a vicious and relentless murderer.

Did I really want to write this article, possibly endangering myself? I certainly needed the money. It was also an intriguing story for which I already had a lot of the necessary background information. But revisiting those murders seemed too much like poking a stick into an angry hornets' nest. I'd already cautioned my daughter to stop investigating these crimes, to not provoke a volatile psychopath. Was I being a reckless fool to not heed my own sensible advice?

Perhaps I could make the article more about Caroline and dumpster diving and less about her killer. I had to describe the crimes, of course, but I wouldn't speculate on who had perpetrated them. The four deaths were a terrible tragedy, but I would make clear that I had no knowledge or desire to solve this particular murder mystery.

Dumpster diving, the editor said, would intrigue and repel his readers. I'd give them accounts of rummaging through stores' smelly garbage bins to find dinner and dodging angry apartment-complex managers while you sorted through their tenants' discards.

Josie and Ed, I remembered, had been quite enthusiastic about the "treasures" they'd discovered in a deli's trash can—wrapped luncheon meats, assorted day-old breads. The night of the potluck dinner they'd said they intended to continue dumpster diving. I wondered if they were still doing it.

Yes, I'd talk to Josie and Ed again. Maybe I'd call Ellen, Margaret, and Ethan, too, to talk about dumpster diving and their memories of Caroline. Then I could check in with the police to get a quote about the murder investigation. I jotted down a list of everyone I needed to call.

Emily appeared in the doorway. "Are you hungry, Mom? You've been working for hours." When I nodded absently, she surprised me by offering to cook dinner.

My daughter, I was happy to see, seemed to have acquired new resolve since her trip to Austin. Today she'd registered for summer school at the community college and had found a job waitressing at a neighborhood Tex-Mex restaurant. She also appeared to have given up her private-investigation inquiries into Caroline's murder that had made me so nervous.

"Did you and Paul have a good time in Santa Fe?" Em asked as she placed a feta cheese omelet, baked tomatoes, and green salad on the kitchen table.

I took a few bites of what turned out to be a surprisingly delectable omelet. "The trip was great. I've always loved Santa Fe." Which was only a bit of an untruth. I had had a great time until Paul ruined everything by proposing.

Em looked as if she was about to ask some follow-up questions, but I didn't give her a chance. Pointing at the food on my plate, I said, "This is absolutely delicious. Paul told me you'd started watching cooking shows. How come I didn't know that?"

Looking pleased, my daughter obligingly launched into a description of her newfound interest in cooking. "And the reason Paul knew this is because he pays attention and is genuinely interested in what I'm doing."

I felt a stab of an emotion I couldn't identify. "You think I'm not attentive?"

"No, you are," she said quickly. "I guess I was comparing him more with Daddy. I mean I know Dad loves me, but he never was really interested in what I thought or felt about things."

In truth, Stan had not been interested in what anybody other than himself felt, though he'd tried to be a good father. "Your dad does care about you and Katie; it's just that he's never been, uh, a very curious person."

"Yeah," Em said. "And Paul is." She paused. "Though certainly he's more interested in Katie and me because he loves you. He knows we're important to you." She sent me what she undoubtedly thought was a guileless look. "Don't you think?"

This was not a discussion I intended to have with her right now. "I'm sure he finds you and Katie fascinating young women in your own right."

Em rolled her eyes. "Undoubtedly." She waited a beat then said, "Surely you know me well enough to realize I won't give up that easily. So just tell me. What's up with you and Paul? There was some weird undercurrent between you when he dropped you off last night."

Emily had always been as tenacious as a pit bull—very much like her mother, Stan used to say. She wouldn't stop probing until I told her at least a little. "He's moving to Seattle. Soon. Got a job as editor-in-chief of a new magazine there."

Em nodded. "Paul must be really excited. It sounds like just the kind of challenge he was looking for."

"Except it's in *Seattle,*" I spit out.

She looked puzzled. "Lots of people have long-distance relationships these days, Mom. My English professor teaches in Austin while her husband works in Boston. She says living apart keeps their relationship from getting boring."

She sounded, I thought irritably, like one of those people who used to talk about how great "open marriages" were. "Paul wants me to move to Seattle with him."

"Oh," Em said.

"You can write that our investigation into all the deaths is ongoing," Officer Thomas Smith, official police spokesman, told me over the phone.

"Is that one investigation? Are you assuming now that one

person murdered Caroline Marshall and the two women who died at her house? Because, obviously, Nathan Evans didn't kill Caroline, and it seems questionable that he killed Mary Alice or Ophelia, despite that weird typed confession. Don't you agree?"

"I can't comment on any of that at this time. Our investigators like to keep all their options open."

I rolled my eyes. So much for keeping the public informed. "So I can quote you as saying you have no leads?"

"No, you cannot," he snapped. "I did not say anything like that."

"In point of fact, Officer Smith, you haven't said anything at all. You wouldn't want our readers to assume the police are unable to solve these grisly and very high-profile cases, would you?"

"What you can say is that the police department is doing everything in its power to find the perpetrator of these vicious homicides. To that purpose, additional resources have been assigned to the case."

Well, at least he'd told me they were looking for a single killer—though, considering Officer Smith's wariness, it was possible the use of the singular was merely a slip of the tongue.

"Is there anything more specific you can tell me about the investigation?" I asked. It wasn't as if I'd thought he would offer me a list of suspects, but I'd still expected more than "we're working on it."

When he didn't respond, I added, "Can you at least tell me if Nathan Evans's death is still considered a suicide? Now that we know he wasn't the person trying to kill Caroline Marshall, it seems unlikely he was the one who wrote the letter confessing to the murders of Mary Alice and Ophelia. Someone must have been trying to set him up."

"His death is now classified as a homicide," the officer said.

"And I am afraid that is about as specific as I can get at this time."

I hung up the phone, hoping the police knew more about the murders than they were saying. Otherwise I was afraid that despite the extra police resources and ongoing inquiries, one diabolic killer was about to get away with murder. Four of them.

Unfortunately, the rest of my magazine article wasn't going much better. It wasn't bad exactly, it just wasn't exciting. Only the few paragraphs I'd included about Caroline's murder might qualify for the "provocative piece" the magazine editor had requested.

I glanced at the list of people I still wanted to call for quotes. I'd found an old newspaper article about a student from one of Caroline's early classes suing her after he was cut by broken glass during a class dumpster dive. The guy, one Ralph Johnston, sounded indignant that Caroline had refused to pay for his trip to the emergency room. The newspaper didn't say if he'd won the lawsuit.

I found the phone numbers for three Ralph Johnstons in Houston and dialed the first one. A very young child answered the phone. "Grandpa sleeping," she said.

"Then could you get your mom or another grownup for me to talk to?"

"Bye-bye," she said as she hung up.

Perhaps Grandpa was not the man I was looking for. I dialed Ralph number two. That number, I was informed, had been disconnected.

Ralph number three answered his phone, sounding irritable. Well, the guy in the article had sounded bad-tempered too. Feeling slightly more hopeful, I told this man who I was and inquired if he was the same Ralph Johnston who'd sued Caroline Marshall over a dumpster-diving injury.

"What if I am?"

I grinned. "I'm writing a magazine article about Caroline, Mr. Johnston. I hoped you'd tell me your experience with her. If you prefer, I won't use your name."

"I don't care if you say my name," he snapped. "That woman was a greedy bitch who didn't give a damn when a student got seriously hurt following her cockamamie advice. When I was cut by broken glass in the first dumpster she took us to, she said it wasn't her fault. Whose fault was it, I ask you. She said I should have been more careful or worn gloves—even though she didn't mention these profound warnings until *after* I was cut. Somebody else in the class got food poisoning after eating honey from the dumpster. Of course that wasn't Caroline's fault either. Apparently that woman should have known enough not to eat discarded food."

"You sued Caroline for damages for your injuries?"

He grunted. "We ended up settling out of court. No damages, but she paid all the doctor bills—after first complaining that I shouldn't have gone to an 'extravagant' hospital emergency room. She probably thought I should have gone home and had my wife stitch up the cut with her needle and darning cotton."

"What about the other person in your class who got sick? Did Caroline pay for her medical expenses, too?"

"Don't really know. I only heard about her later."

I told him Caroline had added a discussion of safety precautions to her later classes. "She had everyone wear gloves for our dumpster diving, and we dug with sticks, not our hands. She also gave a talk on not eating risky food."

Ralph made a derisive snort. "Yeah, she wanted to make sure that nobody else sued her. Didn't want anything reducing her profits."

I would have liked to believe Caroline had changed because of concern for her students' well-being, but Ralph's explanation sounded more probable. "One last question," I said. "Do you ever use any of the frugality tips you learned in the class?"

"Oh, sure, all the time," he said. "The woman was a selfish jerk, but she knew her penny-pinching."

Apparently Caroline had been good at inspiring other former students to embrace cost cutting. Looking for some more quotes, I phoned some of the people I knew from the infamous potluck dinner. Josie Stone, the woman who reminded me of an aging hippy, said she and her husband, Ed, the laid-off geologist, were still regularly checking out deli dumpsters for sandwich meat and only slightly stale bagels. Margaret and Ethan Galen, the frugal homeschoolers whose house I'd visited, said her family was living on "next to nothing," though, as she pointed out, they'd been doing that long before they'd taken Caroline's class.

Had she and her husband learned any new skills from the class? I asked.

She had to think about it. "Well, I'd never been dumpster diving before."

"Have you gone again?"

"Only once," she said. "It's not really my thing; my family is more into growing our own food. But Josie and Ed get a lot of their meals from dumpsters behind delicatessens. They've brought some tasty deli discards to our communal dinners."

I would have thought that after that first disastrous dinner at Caroline's, no one would willingly attend another. "Have you had a lot of these group dinners?"

"We're going to have our third one this week. Why don't you join us? You'll know everybody there: my family, Ed and Josie, Ellen—everybody from our class."

The *surviving* members. Four of the ten people at the original potluck wouldn't be able to attend, even if they wanted to. "I'm surprised Ellen is coming."

"You mean because of trauma from her sister's death? That's

why Josie and I were so insistent that she attend our first dinner—to help obliterate those terrible images. I think Ellen
enjoyed it. She misses her sister and appreciates the company."

"It sounds almost like a survivors' support group," I said.

She laughed. "You might say that. See what you think."

"Thanks, I'll be there." Even if I didn't want to be.

But surely my reluctance to attend was just an irrational fear.
After all, no one had been poisoned at the most recent potluck
dinners. If Mary Alice's twin sister could brave another
dumpster meal, so could I.

I hesitated for a moment and then phoned Paul. We were
making an effort to spend more time together before he moved.
While this was not exactly a fun outing, I would be glad for his
company. "Want to be my date at another dumpster-diving dinner?" I asked when he answered.

He laughed. "Now how could I pass up an irresistible invitation like that?"

CHAPTER THIRTY-ONE

"Do you think we should have brought a food taster with us?" Paul whispered as I knocked on the front door of Margaret and Ethan's unassuming brick ranch house.

"Behave yourself!" I hissed as the door opened and brisk, no-nonsense Margaret ushered us inside. Her blond hair was still cropped short as a boy's, but despite the fact that she'd undoubtedly chosen the hairstyle for its low-maintenance, the style suited her small bones and willowy body.

Margaret seemed more interested in what we'd brought to the dinner than in either of us. Paul had contributed two bottles of white wine and I'd brought my chicken fruit salad. Margaret nodded her approval.

Only then did she shift her attention to Paul. I introduced him, and Margaret said she was glad he could join us. She motioned for us to follow her.

"Look who's here," she called in the direction of the living room, where, from the sounds of it, at least some of the group were already gathered.

Had she not told the others that Paul and I were coming? But Margaret's husband, Ethan, and Josie both turned to smile at us, and cranky Ed nodded, none of them appearing surprised.

From her seat on the couch, Ellen, for some reason, looked annoyed. I remembered that she'd also been peevish at that first potluck dinner at Caroline's house, but I'd attributed her bad temper then to the argument she was having with her sister,

Mary Alice. Who, I wondered, had provoked her temper tonight?

I greeted everyone and then introduced "my friend Paul." He raised an eyebrow at my description. "And here I'd hoped we were so much more," he said under his breath.

Maybe, I thought, it would have been better to leave him home.

Ellen, glowering, marched up to me. "Why are you writing an article about that reprehensible woman?"

I blinked, not sure how to respond. Did she think that only nice people deserved magazine coverage? "The short answer is I have to pay my rent."

Ellen started to respond, but I cut her off. "The long answer is I've already spent a lot of time helping Caroline write her book, and I want to make use of my notes. I need to get some compensation for all that work, and this article seemed the fastest way to get it. Fortunately, Caroline is still considered a newsworthy topic."

Ellen's sneer indicated that she wasn't sympathetic to my argument. "Caroline is only *newsworthy* because she was murdered."

So? "Of course the media is always interested in bizarre murders, but, if you recall, I was doing an article about Caroline's frugality tips when you and I met." Before any murders were involved.

Like a nippy terrier, Ellen was not about to let go of the topic. "I find it hard to believe that your article is only about saving money."

"It's not only about that," I admitted, "but that's part of it."

"As well as lots of sordid details about my sister's murder, I'll bet." Ellen's face now sported furious red blotches. "No doubt you'll be reliving every gory second of her death, every spasm of agony, for your readers' enjoyment."

Now I was getting angry. "That is *not* what I'm writing. And it's not about Mary Alice at all. It's a profile of Caroline." And, if the editor had his way, also a lengthy discussion of her murder. But I had no intention of describing Mary Alice's death.

Ellen did not look appeased. "It's not just reliving Mary Alice's murder that bothers me. I have a basic problem with giving that publicity slut any more media attention. The way I see it, if Caroline hadn't been such a generally loathsome human being, someone wouldn't have kept murdering innocent people to get to her. And my sister would still be alive today."

Paul took a step forward, sending her a cold stare. "That sounds very much like blaming the victim for the crime. Just because a psychopath wants to kill you doesn't mean that you've done something to deserve to die. And, frankly, it's hard for me to see how Caroline was in any way responsible for your sister's tragic death."

Ellen's eyes narrowed. "If she hadn't been at that dinner at Caroline's house, Mary Alice would still be with us."

Ed joined the argument. "The guy has a point, Ellen. No one could have foreseen that attending a dinner party would result in murder. It's only in hindsight that people say, 'She shouldn't have gotten on that plane that crashed' or 'They shouldn't have walked down that street where a mugger was waiting' or—"

Josie shoved a tray into her husband's hands, interrupting his monologue. "Why don't you tell everyone where our hors d'oeuvres came from, Ed?"

Ed smiled, apparently more than willing to switch topics. "Josie and I just discovered these dumpsters behind a posh little grocery store. They have a spectacular deli department with all kinds of cheese we'd never even heard of." He glanced down at the assortment of cheeses on his tray, all perched on crackers. "So, have a taste. It's a regular gourmet smorgasbord, if I say so myself."

Paul glanced at the unappetizing looking morsels with the

expression of someone who has just been asked to eat a cockroach. I bit my lip to keep from snickering.

Unfortunately, Paul was an observant man who apparently didn't appreciate being snickered at. "I'm afraid my doctor won't let me eat cheese," he lied, "but Lauren here loves it. Why don't you try some of those unusual-looking ones over there, sweetheart? I know what an adventurous palate you have."

I was going to kill him. Slowly and painfully. In the meantime I was going to eat some of this smelly cheese. I popped a cracker into my mouth. "Delicious!"

"Just wait," I whispered to Paul as Ed moved on to tempt another guest.

He smiled. "One of us has to be able to drive you to the emergency room."

Margaret and Ethan both politely accepted a cracker from the gourmet smorgasbord, looking about as enthusiastic as I. But it was their children who expressed what the others of us wouldn't.

All three of them had just arrived in the living room. Red-haired Lucy, the eleven-year-old baker, took one bite and made a face. The second child, Lucy's seven-year-old brother who hated vegetables, popped a cracker into his mouth and declared, "Yuck!"

"Don't be rude," his mother told him while pulling her youngest daughter, a toddler, away from the tray.

"But it's gross, Mom," he protested.

"It's probably an acquired taste," Josie, ever the diplomat, said.

Fortunately we were saved from more gourmet cheeses by Margaret's announcement that we should all come to the table.

Lucy walked over to me, a big grin on her freckled face. "When I heard you were coming, Mrs. Prescott, I made sure Mom put out some of my zucchini bread."

I smiled back. "I appreciate that. I bet it's going to be my favorite part of the dinner." And definitely a big improvement over the hors d'oeuvres.

I introduced her to Paul, telling him how much Em and I had loved Lucy's homemade zucchini bread when we'd come here to interview her mother.

"Now that's something I look forward to trying," Paul said.

"There's no cheese in it," Lucy said.

When he looked puzzled, I added helpfully, "She means you won't have to worry about your food allergies, dear."

"That's a relief," Paul said, looking only slightly sheepish.

Lucy studied him. "Is he your husband?" she asked me in a whisper.

Paul leaned down, whispering into her ear. "Not yet, but I'm working on it."

Margaret and Josie were bringing plates of food into the dining room. Besides my salad, there was a green salad, several different types of casserole, an assortment of cold meats, and Lucy's zucchini bread.

Ed pointed at the meat. "That comes from the same deli as the cheese. What a find, huh?"

Margaret told us to take whatever seats we wanted. Lucy asked if she could sit with me and I told her I'd be delighted.

Unfortunately, Ellen-The-Curmudgeon waited to see where I was sitting, Paul and Lucy on either side of me, then found a chair directly across from me. "So, Lauren," she said, "tell us everything about the police investigation. Have they found the killer yet?"

Everyone at the table suddenly seemed to stop what they were doing and focus their attention on me.

"The only thing the police spokesman would tell me is that their investigation is ongoing," I said.

"You didn't press him?" Ellen asked.

"I *did* press him," I said a tad too defensively. "That's all he'd tell me."

"Bunch of incompetents," Ellen muttered.

"Maybe they don't want to make any announcement until the perpetrator is arrested," Ed said.

Ellen glared at him. "Or maybe they just think it sounds better to say 'We're still investigating' than 'We're giving up on this because we're no match for this killer.' "

Ed raised his eyebrows. "You make it sound like a TV detective show, Ellen. This killer is probably insane, not a diabolically clever villain."

Ellen snorted. "I was giving my assessment of police stupidity, not praising the murderer's brilliance. And given all that I know about Caroline, you wouldn't have to be crazy to want to get rid of her."

Paul and I exchanged a look. What had Caroline done to earn this woman's enmity? Ellen's intense animosity seemed much more than a sister's understandable bitterness about Mary Alice's death taking place at Caroline house. I'd thought that Ellen had had only minimal contact with Caroline before her sister's death.

Margaret clearly thought a change of subject was in order. "I think all of our cooks are to be commended. Everything is delicious."

Paul held up what remained of his piece of zucchini bread. "You could sell this bread to a restaurant, Lucy."

The girl blushed, looking proud. "I helped Mom make the lasagna, too," she said. "All the vegetables came from our garden."

"I helped pick the vegetables," her brother said, clearly wanting in on the praise. "And I help Dad build things."

"What kind of things do the two of you build?" Paul asked.

"Everything," the boy said airily. "My dad is a master

carpenter. Right now he's fixing up Miss Ellen's house."

Ellen said, "Speaking of that, Ethan, I wanted to make sure that you're almost finished with the renovations. I want to put that house on the market ASAP."

Ethan had the look of a man who'd heard it all many times before. "As I said, I'll be done by the end of next week."

"You're selling your house, Ellen?" I asked.

"I'm selling my parents' house. Ethan has been making much-needed repairs on the place: things that should have been done years ago except my stubborn sister wanted to hold on to the house but didn't want to lay out the cash to fix it up."

Actually now that she'd mentioned it, I remembered how she and Mary Alice had been arguing about that very topic at Caroline's potluck dinner. Mary Alice said she wanted to keep the house for her daughters while Ellen wanted to sell. Wasn't it convenient that her sister's death allowed Ellen to get exactly what she'd wanted?

"So, Mary Alice's daughters don't want to live in the house anymore?" I asked.

"The girls never wanted to live in that dump," Ellen said. "That was just Mary Alice's lame excuse for not selling. The real reason she refused to put the house on the market was that she knew I wanted to. If I'd suggested keeping it, she would have said, 'Sell.' Fortunately her daughters are happy to get rid of the place and pocket their profits. Unlike their dear mother, they're more interested in making a buck than in torturing me."

This was the same woman who'd started the evening proclaiming how distraught she was over her twin's death?

Before Ellen had a chance to launch into another tirade, Josie pointedly asked Ethan and Margaret about their garden. Another change of topic to shut Ellen up.

Looking grateful, Margaret began to list the many vegetables and fruits the family grew. The garden, Margaret had told me, provided the majority of their meals.

"If this meal is any indication of the way your family eats, I'd say they're lucky to have such talented vegetarian cooks feeding them," Paul said.

"Mom and I can our vegetables and fruit so we can eat them all year round," Lucy said. "That man at our last dinner, Mr. Evans, said that home canning could cause botulism, but my mom said it isn't dangerous if you know what you're doing."

"Nathan Evans was a paranoid nutcase," Ellen muttered. "Once again he refused to eat our food. Why come to a dinner if you're afraid to eat the meal?"

I could see from the expression on Lucy's freckled face that she felt her little lecture on canning safety had been rudely interrupted. She turned to me. "The trick, my mom says, is to seal the glass bottles properly and then no one gets botulism. My aunt's baby died from botulism from honey, but it wasn't because of improper canning. Babies just aren't supposed to eat honey."

I smiled at Lucy. "I would have no hesitation at all in eating any food you and your mother canned." Then what Ellen had just said struck me. "Nathan came to your last group dinner?" Considering his squeamish behavior at the dinner at Caroline's house, I was astonished he would willingly attend another potluck.

"I think he just wanted to question everybody," Ed said, rolling his eyes. "He saw himself as some kind of brilliant amateur detective who was going to single-handedly solve the crime."

"Yeah, a regular Sherlock Holmes," Ellen said. "Except Nathan was such a suspicious weirdo, it wouldn't have surprised me if he actually did poison Mary Alice and Ophelia. Maybe voices in his head told him to kill them."

"But he was already dead by the time Caroline Marshall was killed," Paul said.

"There could have been two killers," Ed said. "Or even three, one for each victim, if, say, Ophelia's killer was a copycat murderer who tried to make her death look like Mary Alice's in order to make the two crimes seem connected. It's also possible that Nathan committed the first two murders—the ones he admitted to—and another person killed Caroline. After all, the first two involved poisoned food, while the last one was entirely different. Caroline was strangled or bludgeoned to death—I don't think the newspaper was clear on that—before she ended up in the dumpster."

I saw the little boy's eyes widen and, beside me, Lucy visibly shuddered.

Margaret took in her children's frightened expressions. "Lucy, why don't you kids go to the kitchen for dessert and then you can play for a while before bedtime." She pulled her youngest from the high chair and started towards the kitchen, Lucy obediently following her.

Her brother, however, didn't budge. Clearly the boy didn't want to miss a second of any blood-and-guts talk.

"Now, son," his father said sternly.

As the boy reluctantly got up I saw Josie jab her husband with her elbow.

"What did I do?" Ed asked her as he rubbed his side.

"Scared the children with all your grisly murder talk."

"I'm probably not telling them anything they don't already know."

"Don't worry about it," Ethan said.

Ed opened his mouth, then abruptly closed it. "I'm going to be sick," he said as he ran for the bathroom.

CHAPTER THIRTY-TWO

There was something about seeing a fellow guest, hand clasped over his mouth, run from the table that tended to put a damper on dinner conversation. Or at least that was the way Ed's departure affected us.

His wife registered our shocked expressions. "He gets sick when he eats too much dairy." Josie shook her head, appearing more annoyed than concerned by her husband's illness.

Paul sent me a look that clearly said, I *told* you not to eat the cheese.

Ellen smirked at me. "For a minute there, you thought he was poisoned, didn't you? Let me tell you Mary Alice was nothing like that. Horrible convulsions, agonizing retching . . ."

"I know," I said coldly. "I was there."

"I keep forgetting that," she said, looking irritated at having her story interrupted.

Josie stood. "I'm going to go check on Ed."

She returned a minute later. "He'll be okay, but he wants to go home to bed. The doctor told him yesterday that he's lactose intolerant, and I think Ed's starting to grasp that's not something he can ignore."

Ed himself appeared in the doorway, still looking queasy. "Sorry we have to leave early." He tried to laugh. "It wasn't the company."

Margaret walked them to the door. I could hear her telling

Ed she hoped he felt better and saying they'd plan another dinner soon.

I glanced around the diners still at the table. I found it hard to imagine why they'd want to continue having these strange dinners. The food wasn't great and the guests didn't seem to have much in common other than their brief attendance at Caroline's frugal-living workshop. None of them even seemed to have liked Caroline. As far as I could see, the only thing holding the group together was that they'd all witnessed one tragic death and had known the victims of the three other murders. They were all survivors—or at least they were so far.

I shivered, suddenly wishing that Paul and I had a good excuse to leave early, preferably something less painful than Ed's gastrointestinal problems.

It took a moment for me to realize that Ellen was talking to me. "So, Lauren, who do you think killed Caroline? Will you tell us in your magazine story?"

"I have no idea who killed her." I'd already said that the police wouldn't tell me anything. Did she think I had some secret knowledge that I was saving for my article? Hell, maybe this spiteful woman thought I'd murdered Caroline myself. "Who do *you* think killed her?"

Ellen cocked her head, apparently considering the matter. "For a long time I thought it was Nathan. He knew a lot about plant poisons, disliked Caroline, and at our last dinner he couldn't stop talking about the murders—it was like he memorized every detail of the crimes. But since he was already dead when Caroline was killed, that ruled him out."

When she didn't say any more, Paul said, "So you don't have any other suspects in mind?"

"No one specific. Undoubtedly it was one of her legion of enemies, but which one I couldn't say. Caroline had a real talent for pissing people off. She fired employees for no reason, stole other people's ideas and claimed they were her own, and basically didn't care how many people were hurt as long as she got ahead."

"Many CEOs are selfish, ruthless people," Paul said. "It's not as if a lot of them are being murdered."

Ellen shrugged. "Maybe she just antagonized the wrong person."

"I know about the employees she fired, how she used Nathan's grandmother's ideas to start her own business, and I read about the students who sued her after being injured in a class dumpster dive," I said. "But all of that was years ago, and frankly none of those incidents seems serious enough to provoke homicidal rage."

Margaret had her hostess-changing-the-subject look as she said mildly, "I guess some people just hold a grudge. I know a family like that at our church. Their daughter was killed by a drunk driver, and the parents are obsessed about making that driver pay for what he did. It's hard for those of us who haven't gone through that—losing a child—to understand their need for vengeance."

Ellen nodded. "Oh, I get that. An eye for an eye, as the Bible says." Then, incongruously, she smiled. "Is everyone ready for dessert? I made the cake. It's not from a dumpster, but I used an old cake mix and canned fruit I found in my pantry."

Paul sent me a look. I had a very strong suspicion he was going to pass on dessert.

When Ellen left to cut her cake, Ethan insisted on pouring us all some more wine. Maybe he wanted to get rid of it so Ellen couldn't imbibe any more. She'd been the only one who'd drunk much this evening, and she had become noticeably louder and more belligerent. I might have been imagining it, but her departure to the kitchen made the atmosphere in the dining room instantly calmer.

I took advantage of the sudden quiet by pulling out my mini tape recorder and asking Margaret and Ethan the questions I'd come here to ask: What lessons, if any, had they learned in Caroline's class? What was their opinion of her and her teaching? "I know your family was already living very frugally before you took the workshop," I added, "but anything you want to say about Caroline's philosophy or the class would be helpful for my article."

I wasn't about to print any of Ellen's ranting about how Caroline was responsible for Mary Alice's death, but I still needed some more comments for my article. Tomorrow I'd phone Josie to see if I could get something more from her.

"Her class didn't really tell us anything we didn't already know," Ethan said.

"Except the stuff about dumpster diving," Margaret said. "We'd never tried that before."

Ethan snorted. "And aren't likely to do it again, are we? Caroline could talk all she wanted about finding treasures and recovering perfectly good food, but basically what we were doing was just digging through garbage."

"It really was kind of gross," his wife agreed. "I know Ed and Josie love finding deli discards and everything, but who knows how old the food really is or if there's something wrong with it? There could have been rats and insects crawling around in those bins. Caroline didn't discuss how sick people can get from eating bad food."

"Caroline didn't want to talk about *anything* unpleasant," Ellen said, as she and Lucy brought plates of cake to the table. "Basically she didn't care if people got hurt—or died—because of her actions. As long as she got paid and got good publicity, she was fine with it all."

So much for the brief moment of quiet. Even the way Ellen slammed a large piece of her cake in front of Paul was belligerent. "You'll be happy to know there's absolutely no cheese in this, so you can eat up."

Before sitting down, she emptied the remains of the wine bottle into her own glass. "I hope you'll quote me in your article, Lauren, as saying the class was a waste of money and Caroline was a charlatan as well as a disgusting human being."

When I didn't respond, Ellen sneered at me. "I bet you're afraid to tell the truth about Caroline in your little article, aren't you? You think readers only want to hear about the 'tragic loss of this dynamic, successful woman.' "

She emptied her glass in one long gulp. "What you don't seem to realize, Lauren, is that a smart writer would avoid the subject of Caroline Marshall like the plague. Forget about your article, forget you ever met the woman. Because, strangely enough, everyone who gets too interested in Caroline seems to end up dead."

"That's enough, Ellen," Ethan said, glowering at her. "You've had too much to drink."

Paul and I exchanged a look. "I'm sorry, we have to get going," I said to Margaret. "Thanks for everything."

"But you didn't eat your cake," Ellen wailed, pointing at our untouched desserts.

"No," Paul said as we stood to leave, "we didn't."

CHAPTER THIRTY-THREE

My deadline was looming, an occurrence that usually prodded me to write faster, as my article and I surged toward the finish line. Unfortunately, this time that wasn't happening. The piece just wasn't gelling, and, for the life of me, I couldn't say why. Despite all the interviews I'd conducted, all the hours I'd spent in Caroline's company, I seemed unable to write a compelling portrait of the woman.

Part of the problem was that Caroline herself was so elusive. For a person who had chosen to become a public personality, Caroline Marshall was an intensely private and unrevealing woman, someone who'd offer only occasional tiny glimpses of herself. In fact, there were only a handful of things I knew for sure about Caroline: she was driven, intensely ambitious, and she genuinely believed that being frugal was the key to controlling one's own destiny. For all the hours we'd spent together, that wasn't much to know.

I scanned my assembled notes and various newspaper articles that had been written about her, searching for some inspiration. The press called Caroline "Queen of Dumpster Diving" and "a charismatic proponent of penny-pinching." The acquaintances I'd interviewed said she was a self-absorbed workaholic and a tyrannical boss uninterested in anyone's welfare except her own—a woman perhaps admirable from afar, but not very likeable up close.

I understood these assessments of Caroline but I still didn't get how she'd incited such intense dislike in so many of her seemingly casual acquaintances. Granted, Caroline was not a sensitive, caring person, but neither was she evil or sadistic or bilking money from her followers. In fact, her generally sensible advice had probably saved her students thousands of dollars.

Despite the accusations I'd heard at the dinner last night, I didn't believe Caroline had inflicted damage on numerous people. While Ellen had argued that Mary Alice and Ophelia would not have died if they hadn't been at Caroline's house, that did not mean Caroline was responsible for their murders. Nathan's death also might be somehow connected to his knowing Caroline, but that wasn't Caroline's fault, either. She had been hiding in Colorado when it happened.

I'd been surprised to find out that Nathan had gotten together again with the original potluck dinner guests. He'd seemed so acutely uncomfortable at the dinner at Caroline's, refusing to eat the communal food and not saying much aside from dire warnings about toxic plants. I couldn't believe he'd voluntarily reunite with the group. Had he come only to seek clues to Mary Alice's and Ophelia's deaths? His fellow guests said he'd seemed obsessed by the crimes. Did he suspect one of them was the killer? Or were they just a small part of the people he was questioning?

I spent several minutes thinking about that. Nathan's persistent questions could have alerted the killer that he or she was about to be discovered. Had the murderer then decided to eliminate the threat by getting rid of Nathan before he had a chance to tell the police what he suspected?

A sudden knocking on the door of my apartment startled me. I wasn't expecting anyone, and Paul, one of the few people I knew who might drop by, was out of town for a few days.

I peered out the peephole, then opened the door. "Mrs. Marshall?" I stared at Caroline's cold-eyed mother. What was she doing here?

"Sorry to show up without calling," she said, not sounding at all apologetic. "I needed to see you in person."

I invited her inside and pretended not to notice her look of disdain as she scanned my tiny living room. She'd had a similar reaction to Caroline's place, I remembered. Our subpar interior decorating was apparently a major faux pas.

"What can I do for you, Mrs. Marshall? I didn't know you were in town."

"Caroline's house has sold and I came back for the closing. I'm here"—she indicated my apartment with a wave of her hand—"because I've been reconsidering Caroline's financial arrangements with you."

"Reconsidering?" The last time I'd seen her, she and her son had made it clear that she wouldn't be honoring those "financial arrangements" with me because Caroline had not left enough money to cover them.

"When I thought about it, it didn't seem fair to you to not get the remaining money Caroline owed you. Fifteen thousand dollars, right?" When I nodded, she said, "Since we've sold the house, there are now funds available to pay you."

"Why, that's great." After our last meeting, I would have said that Mrs. Marshall couldn't have cared less about giving me a fair deal. But, apparently, Caroline's mother was more altruistic than she looked.

"I thought you'd be pleased." Smiling the slight lip movement of someone who didn't want to disturb her plastic surgeon's handiwork, Mrs. Marshall pulled an envelope from her bag. "I've brought some papers that I had my lawyer draft for you to sign. Essentially all they say is that when you accept my check you will turn over all the material you've already written on this book and agree not to publish anything more about Caroline."

I took the envelope from her, but didn't open it. "But your son already gave me all of Caroline's class handouts with the understanding I'd use them for magazine articles or books." It had seemed a very cheap move—Caroline's class handouts in lieu of the cash owed me—especially considering that I had grave doubts that any of it was publishable.

"As I said, I've had time to reconsider that decision. It's embarrassing to me to have to read Caroline's tips for blue-collar housewives. And, frankly, I think it would be a big relief to you to *not* have to write about digging through trash bins—and be well paid not to do it."

She was paying me *not* to write about Caroline? Previously I'd had the impression that Mrs. Marshall was only interested in holding on to every cent of Caroline's money. She hadn't seemed particularly concerned then about what I wrote or did not write. "Is it just the how-to pieces you don't want published?"

"I don't want you to write *anything* about her. Not one word," she added, as if I might be too slow to grasp the concept.

A sensible person would no doubt have said, "Fine, hand over the check and I'll sign whatever you want." But I wasn't all that sensible and I'd always hated people telling me what to do. So I took perverse pride in telling her, "Oh, that's really unfortunate, since I've already agreed to write a profile of Caroline for *Texas Magazine*. It's due next week. I'll send you a copy when it's published."

Mrs. Marshall looked as if she'd lunge for my throat if it wouldn't have disturbed her perfect hairdo. "Cancel the article. I'm sure even you can grasp the stupidity of giving up fifteen thousand dollars just for the thrill of seeing your byline in a little regional magazine."

Even you can grasp the stupidity? I was about to tell her to get out of my apartment, but she was already standing up to leave.

"I'll come back tomorrow afternoon with a cashier's check," she told me. "I'll expect the signed contract as well as written confirmation that the magazine will not be running any story on my daughter." She started toward the door, then turned back. "And, Mrs. Prescott, don't even think about taking my money and then going ahead and submitting your magazine profile. You'll find that when I'm crossed, I can be a very litigious woman."

Oh, my! I moved quickly to lock the door after her. I felt as if something was going on that I did not begin to grasp. What was the woman so afraid that I'd write? Was it really worth fifteen thousand to her not to be embarrassed by her daughter's money-saving tips?

Before I could contemplate those questions, my cell phone rang. I glanced at the ID, relieved to see my caller wasn't Mrs. Marshall.

"Hi, Josie," I said, "thanks for returning my call. I hope Ed is feeling better today."

"Oh, Ed's fine," she said. "He was just a little too enthusiastic about trying all those exotic cheeses. I think it's starting to sink in that when the doctor told him to give up dairy, it wasn't a casual suggestion."

I told her I was glad Ed was okay and said I'd phoned her to see if she had any comments on Caroline or her class for my article. "I asked everyone else after you and Ed had left the dinner."

"I'm surprised you managed to get any usable quotes," Josie said. "From what I heard, Ellen was drunk out of her mind. She's been drinking a lot since Mary Alice died, but this—this is so tragic."

Was I missing something here? "Everybody copes with their grief in different ways," I said, inanely.

"You don't know, do you? I assumed Margaret called you, too."

"Know what?"

"Ellen was in a car accident last night. Ethan offered to drive her home, but Ellen insisted on driving herself." Josie paused, sounding as if she was crying. "The police said her car veered off the road and hit a tree. She died before they got her to the hospital."

For long minutes after we hung up, I sat staring at my phone, remembering what Ellen had told me last night: "Everyone who gets too interested in Caroline seems to end up dead." Now, mere hours later, Ellen was dead. I'd thought she was threatening me, trying to scare me into not writing my article. But what if instead she had been trying to *warn* me?

I took deep breaths and told myself to get a grip. Surely I was leaping to conclusions, making connections that didn't exist. I'd seen with my own eyes how drunk and belligerent Ellen had been. I could picture her refusing Ethan's offer to drive her home, then speeding off recklessly, right into a tree. It made sense. And Ellen had hardly seemed "too interested" in Caroline. From what I'd observed, she didn't much care who'd killed Caroline; she was just glad Caroline was dead.

Still, no matter the causes, this was one hell of a lot of fatalities. Five of the ten attendees at the potluck dinner at Caroline's house were now dead—and I was one of the few remaining.

CHAPTER THIRTY-FOUR

Em glanced up from the contract Caroline's mother had left. "Have you read this? It's like those corporate nondisclosure agreements that new employees have to sign."

"Except I don't know any trade secrets or any other secrets, for that matter." I had read the legal papers, which basically said that once I was paid, my previous ghostwriting contract with Caroline was officially terminated. That was straightforward enough, but what didn't make sense was the demand that I never write anything about Caroline—no magazine, newspaper, or online article or any kind of book. Nor could I give out this information verbally so someone else could write it.

"Mrs. Marshall told me she didn't want to be embarrassed when her friends read her daughter's 'blue-collar advice,' " I said. "But a month ago, when she and her son told me Caroline's estate had no funds for paying me, they both seemed to be okay with me writing anything I wanted."

"Makes you wonder why all of a sudden she's so worried about being humiliated," Em said. "I can't imagine even her snobbiest friends sneering at Caroline's starting a successful business. They might even find some of her penny-pinching tips useful. I read somewhere that very rich people can be really cheap." She cocked her head, her contemplating position. "Of course it's possible that now they've got the money from the sale of Caroline's house, they just want to pay you off and fulfill their daughter's contract with you—tying up loose ends, so to speak."

"But it's not fulfilling their daughter's contract with me at all," I said. "It's the total opposite of Caroline's agreement, which gave me the final payment only when I completed the book. This contract pays out when I hand over an *unfinished* book, all my notes and interviews, and I agree to write nothing more about Caroline. Ever."

Em took a bite of her sandwich. Ever since she decided to return to college next fall, she'd shifted into high gear, working extra waitressing shifts to pay for school while taking an online college history course to get some degree requirements out of the way. As a result, she was usually too tired to do much of anything else, including—I was relieved to see—her private investigator activities.

Now, however, Em was once again wearing that excited I-can-solve-this-puzzle look. An expression that made me intensely nervous.

"Clearly there's part of this story we don't know," she said. "In the time since the Marshalls first talked to you, did something happen to make her fear public scrutiny? It could be, say, she's about to file for bankruptcy. In that case, it could be pretty embarrassing for everyone to read her daughter's money-saving tips."

Caroline had said that her parents were always in debt, living an extravagant lifestyle they couldn't afford. Maybe her mother *was* on the verge of bankruptcy. "But if she's broke, would she be willing to give away fifteen thousand dollars?"

"Maybe she found something when Caroline's house was being cleared out," Em said. "Like some shocking or potentially humiliating information that she's afraid you're going to publish."

Too bad I was unaware of this shocker. I tried to think what behavior of Caroline's Mrs. Marshall would not want the general public to know about. Stealing Eloise's ideas to start her own business? Firing her employees indiscriminately? Refusing to pay for her students' dumpster-diving injuries? Somehow I didn't think that any of that would particularly bother Caroline's mother. After all, wealthy business owners routinely did that sort of thing. "Whatever it was, it would have to be something that would appall her upper-class friends."

Em considered the various possibilities. "Illegal drugs? Child pornography? Blackmail, embezzlement, terrorist plots?"

I rolled my eyes. "Don't get too carried away. Caroline could be ruthless and indifferent to other people's suffering, but I never saw her do anything criminal."

Emily sighed. "We should have finished our background check on her."

"We were never going to do a background check."

Em shrugged. "You might not call it that, but that's what you were doing when you looked for biographical information for your article. Unfortunately, you only talked to people connected to her work—her students or employees. Whatever is setting off her mother could well be connected to Caroline's past, her personal life."

"Or it could be entirely connected to Caroline's mother's neurosis. The woman is too concerned about what her snooty friends think. Having her daughter repeatedly described in the press as 'the murdered Queen of Dumpster Diving' is not the kind of publicity to warm a social-climbing mother's heart."

The more I thought about it, the more likely that explanation was. It was not any scandalous secret that had made Caroline's mother try to stop any further publicity about her daughter. It was her horror of the tabloid-like coverage of her daughter's lurid murder. Mrs. Marshall's response was to try to stop *all* stories about her daughter. Out of sight, out of mind, and the scandal would die down, she probably reasoned.

Em was having none of it. "But that's not really the point, is it? Sure, it could be that Mrs. Marshall simply didn't want her friends reading any more about Caroline's dumpster diving. But most people wouldn't shell out that much money to stop stories about their daughter unless they had a very good reason And, if you're still planning to go ahead with the profile of Caroline, Mom, don't you want to know more about her? Maybe you won't find out where the skeletons are buried, but you might get a picture of what her life was like before she became a famous frugalista."

"You sound as if I've been ignoring people who are eager to tell me all about Caroline's past. I don't know anyone like that or have any way to contact them."

She nodded, finished her sandwich, and then said she had some work to do. Less than ten minutes later she was back at my desk carrying a piece of paper. I glanced at the scrawled names, phone numbers, and e-mail addresses.

"Thanks to my superior investigative skills and the power of the Internet, you may now phone or e-mail Caroline's brother and ex-husband," my daughter said. "And before you think of a list of reasons why you shouldn't contact them, let me tell you why you should: You might get some juicy stories for your article or a clue about why Caroline's mother is trying to silence you. At the very least, it will infuriate the Horrible, High-Handed Mrs. Marshall if she hears that the hired help is getting uppity."

I laughed. "I must admit you make it very tempting."

Somewhat to my surprise, the phone number Em provided led me directly to Todd Adams, Caroline's ex-husband. He even answered the phone himself.

Caroline had spoken very little about her ex. I knew they'd married right after college, stayed together less than two years, and he'd been "too materialistic" for Caroline's taste. From what I'd heard, they hadn't had anything to do with each other in years. The man seemed to have been filed away in one of the mental folders of her past life and then forgotten.

I'd been afraid that Adams would refuse to talk to me or say their marriage had been so long ago that he barely remembered it. But instead he said, "Oh, yes, Caroline's brother, Will, told me about you."

"You're still in contact with Caroline's family?" I asked, surprised.

"Will and I were friends in college; that's how I met Caroline. He phoned to tell me she'd died. That was a real shocker. If I hadn't been still working in Costa Rica I would have come to the funeral."

"It was a shock for all of us."

"Have they caught her killer?"

"Not to my knowledge, though the police say they're still working on it."

He was too polite to ask the obvious question: Why exactly are you calling me? I gave him the answer, describing the magazine article I was writing. "I was hoping you might give me your insights about Caroline and your marriage to round out my picture of her."

He snorted: not the response I was hoping for. Then he said, "I've always thought that I barely knew Caroline; I'm not the one to go to for insights about her. We were too young to get married, we realized it was a mistake, and we got divorced. It was an amicable divorce, partly because neither of us was very invested in the marriage and partly because there were no joint assets to fight over. If there had been, I'm sure Caroline would have been more passionate about our parting."

"I'm not sure I understand," I said. "The Caroline I knew was constantly preaching against greed and materialism."

"As was the Caroline I knew, or at least she was by the time we broke up. She discovered frugality when she started working for Eloisa. It was this huge epiphany for her. Caroline became obsessed with the subject. Eloisa was more like a thrifty homemaker who wanted to share her advice, but Caroline saw frugality as a life-changing philosophy, a means of taking control of one's life. She was fanatical about it, like a convert to a new religion. Money—saving money—was all she really cared about."

"She told me once that you and she had different attitudes about spending." She'd said that Todd had a rich kid's view of money. I gathered it was a major source of conflict between them.

He sighed. "That's probably the way she saw it. Things were either black or white with her: I wanted to spend money and she wanted to save it. Except it wasn't that simple. What I wanted was to enjoy life and not think constantly about 'How can I get this cheaper?' I wanted us to be able to go out to a nice restaurant and savor the meal, not fume all evening about the cost and calculate how much money we could have saved by cooking the food ourselves.

"Caroline would come home from the grocery store with all this stale food that she'd bought for pennies because it was past the expiration date. I'd say, 'What's wrong with this cereal? It's tasteless.' She'd say, 'But I got three boxes for a quarter, an incredible bargain.' Then I'd say, 'Who cares? It's disgusting.' And she'd say, 'You're a spoiled, pampered elitist,' and storm out of the room."

"I can see how that would be a problem." I also had no trouble picturing Caroline sanctimoniously lecturing her young husband about why he should cheerfully eat stale cereal.

"She wasn't like that when I first met her," he said, sounding wistful. "She was this shy, uncertain college girl who saw herself as a huge disappointment to her social-climber parents. She used to say, 'They might have liked me if I was an empty-headed sorority girl.' "

I winced, aching for that girl whose parents wouldn't accept her. "It bothered her—what her parents thought of her?"

When he answered his voice had a harder edge. "Their disapproval defined her. They made her feel she wasn't pretty enough, social enough, charming enough. They were terrible parents. Her mother in particular was emotionally abusive. Caroline's father, who died the year after we were married, was cold and dismissive. The only warm parental figure in her life was her grandmother. It was her grandmother's love, I always thought, that saved her from her childhood."

I'd known that Caroline had lived for her summers with her grandmother in the Colorado cabin. "I had the idea that Caroline rejected her parents' values."

"Eventually she did, but not when I first met her. For a long time she believed what her mother said about her: she was a loser. That was why Caroline took up frugality with such a vengeance. It was the antithesis of everything she'd been told growing up, where appearances were all-important and the right possessions proclaimed your worth. And it was a philosophy that valued Caroline's strengths—her resourcefulness, intelligence, and hard work—and said her parents' materialism was an obscene waste of resources. It told her their beliefs—their spending, their social climbing—were warped."

"And how did her parents react to her new views?"

He chuckled. "Not well at all. They thought Caroline was mocking them, spitting in their faces, which, of course, she was. Will tells me that she eventually managed to cut herself off entirely from her parents. When we were married, she wouldn't have had the courage to do that."

I found myself telling Todd about my strange encounter with Mrs. Marshall and her demand that I write nothing more about Caroline.

"I knew she'd never allow Caroline's memoir to be published. I said that to Will when he told me Caroline had been writing a book with you."

"You thought that her mother would have tried to stop the book, even when Caroline was alive?" I asked, incredulous. "How could she possibly do that?"

"I don't know how she'd have managed it. I just know she'd try. What you don't understand is how completely the family's lives used to revolve around maintaining their image—the image her parents wanted to project. They terrorized their children into playing their parts in the perfect-upper-class-family story. The one time Caroline tried to tell a grade-school teacher the truth, her mother locked her in a closet and killed her dog."

For a few seconds I was too shocked to speak. "She killed Caroline's dog? My God. I hope that teacher reported her to Child Protective Services."

"Oh, Mrs. Marshall convinced her that Caroline had an overactive imagination. She made Caroline apologize to the teacher for lying. The dog, in the parents' version, had just accidentally eaten a toxic plant."

"What toxic plant?"

"I believe it was Nandina, a shrub that produces cyanide. Caroline said her mother told her that the dog, who'd never before eaten any plants, suddenly just happened to chew on one that gave him seizures and respiratory failure. Mrs. Marshall, incidentally, had a poison garden in her backyard. She used to joke, 'Just think, I've got the means to poison my enemies just by strolling into my garden.' "

I said good-bye to Todd. Then I wrapped my arms around myself, trying to stop my sudden trembling.

A minute later Em walked into the room. She took one look at me, and asked, "Mom, what's wrong? What happened?"

I shook my head, wanting both to reassure her and to get the unwelcome image of dead pets out of my head. "Nothing happened. I was just hearing about Caroline's very grim childhood from her ex-husband. Her parents should have been reported to CPS."

The ringing of my cell phone cut off Em's questions. Was Todd having second thoughts about what we'd discussed?

But it was another male voice on the line. "Mrs. Prescott, this is Will Marshall, Caroline's brother. Todd just told me about your conversation with him."

Well, that hadn't taken long. Todd must have phoned his former brother-in-law immediately after he hung up. "Yes, we just spoke."

Apparently Will heard the wariness in my voice. "I didn't know about my mother asking you to stop writing about Caroline. The last time she and I spoke she couldn't have cared less what you wrote."

"Well, she cares now. She wants me to sign a contract promising to never write another word—article, book, blog—about Caroline."

He paused. "She didn't give you any explanation for her change in attitude?"

"She said she wanted to be fair to me by paying me the rest of what Caroline owed me, and now that Caroline's house has been sold, she has the funds to do that. Except my final payment, fifteen thousand dollars, was supposed to be for finishing the book. Your mother says she'll pay me for giving her all copies of the manuscript, all my notes and research materials, and signing a contract agreeing to never write anything about Caroline."

"Mother said she wants to be fair to you?" He made a derisive snorting sound. "Fairness to others is not a concept I usually associate with my mother."

Despite myself, I smiled. "I had a similar reaction when she told me. So the question, Mr. Marshall, is what made her change her mind?"

"I have no idea. First I heard about this was from Todd. Only thing Mother mentioned to me was that somebody bought Caroline's house."

"Maybe she just wants to tie up loose ends and settle Caroline's accounts?" I suggested. Perhaps the lawyer she'd consulted had suggested it would be cheaper to just pay me off rather than have to deal with a lawsuit if I decided to sue the estate for breach of contract.

"That's possible, I guess, though frankly it's out of character for Mother to be so generous." He paused. "I'm not sure how to tell you this, Mrs. Prescott, but I called to warn you about Mother. I have no idea why she suddenly doesn't want you to write about Caroline, but whatever the reason, it has nothing to do with fairness."

What was he trying to tell me? Was he saying I shouldn't sign Mrs. Marshall's contract? "I don't understand what you're getting at."

"Sorry. This has kind of thrown me for a loop and I'm not being very articulate. What I'm trying to say is that it would be in your best interests to do what my mother requests—give her all your manuscript and notes, sign the contract, cash her check, and hope to God that you never hear from her again."

"Why do you say that?"

"Because I know her," he said, his voice harsh. "She will stop at nothing—nothing—to get what she wants. At a very early age I realized that life was a whole lot easier if you did what Mother asked. Caroline, unfortunately, was a lot feistier. I used to beg her to just let things go, to pretend, as I did, to be an obedient child. But Caroline wouldn't hear of it; she insisted on fighting back—with some very harsh consequences."

"Like your mother killing her dog?"

"Among other things," he said. "Show the good sense that my sister didn't, Mrs. Prescott, and heed my warning. My mother is a dangerous, unscrupulous woman. You don't want to mess with her."

CHAPTER THIRTY-FIVE

It was Mary Alice's funeral all over again. The service for her twin sister was held in the same funeral home in the same room, with the same serious-looking, balding minister officiating. He even started his sermon with the identical sentiment: "We are here today to celebrate the too-short life of Ellen Buhr."

I scanned the other attendees seated around me. I recognized Mary Alice's two daughters and the young woman with spiky, Goth hair who'd sat next to Ellen at the other service—Ellen's daughter, I presumed. Today a tall, skinny young man, who appeared uncomfortable in his dark suit, and a woman with frizzy, red hair sat next to her. The guy looked so much like Ellen—same color hair, same gray eyes and prominent nose—that he had to be Ellen's son. Ellen's son and daughter-in-law, I remembered, had both lost their jobs and moved back home with her.

Members of the frugal-living class again were well represented. Josie and Ed sat next to Ethan and Margaret and their oldest daughter. Lucy, catching sight of me, smiled and waved, and I waved back.

Seeing Caroline's students seated together like that made me think about all the people who *weren't* here, the class members who couldn't attend this service because, in the scant months since Mary Alice's funeral, they had died: Ophelia, Nathan, Caroline. And now Ellen had joined the list of the deceased. So many people with too-short lives, killed for reasons yet to be determined.

Who would be next? The question pierced through my consciousness, as unwelcome as a lightning strike on a peaceful night.

I tried to refocus on the service, but only stray words, biographical sound bites, seemed to reach me. Ellen had been a real estate agent, mother of two, widowed two years ago after a freak car accident. She liked gardening, reading true-crime books, attending garage sales.

Her daughter, the Goth girl, got up to eulogize her mother. "A little over a month ago my cousin Eleanor told y'all that it sucks to have your mother die. She was right. But my experience is a little different than hers because, you see, this is the second time I lost Mom."

She told us how her father's death two years ago, in a freak traffic accident, had overnight changed their lives. "My mom, who was always bristling with energy and schemes and opinions, trying to control everything and everyone around her, suddenly became this unrecognizable, quiet, muted person. It was as if all the life drained out of her when Dad died. Josh and I felt as if we'd lost two parents the day that truck slammed into Dad's car."

She scanned the room. "Then my family suffered another horrible loss. My mother's twin sister, Aunt Mary Alice, died, and Mom was inconsolable. But a week or two later she decided to renovate her parents' old house and sell it. That was what she used to do: flip houses. But after Dad died, she stopped.

"Working on Grandma's house, the old Mom came back. Suddenly she was once again in her element, doing what she loved. I'd almost forgotten what she'd been like before, she'd become so polite and stoic and boring. Sure, our old Mom had been bossy, demanding, impatient—and, yes, Ethan, I know, she could be a pain in the ass to work for—but she was intensely alive."

In the row ahead of me Lucy giggled. "She said 'pain in the ass,' Daddy." He sent her a stern, shushing look.

"It was great to have that cantankerous, excited, hyper Mom back," Ellen's daughter continued. "I wish she was still with us. Life seems too quiet without her." She paused. "And now my cousin Eleanor wants to say a few words."

Mary Alice's daughter came to the podium. "My mother and Aunt Ellen were twins. They were both what you might call prickly personalities, very big on speaking their minds even if you didn't want to hear it. The house that Susie was telling you about, my grandparents' house, was a big source of friction between the two of them. My mom wanted to keep the house and Aunt Ellen wanted to sell it.

"After Mom died, Aunt Ellen was free to get rid of the house. Because all four of us grandchildren were co-owners of the house, I think that project pulled us together as a family. Aunt Ellen was bossing us all around, giving us little jobs to do. It felt so familiar, as if Mom was still around to nag at us and offer us the great benefit of her life experience: that's what she used to call her unsolicited advice."

This certainly was a family who believed in sharing the warts-and-all pictures of the deceased, I thought. I tried to imagine what my daughters would say about me at my funeral service. Would Katie tell the mourners, "Although Mom tried hard, she was a really lousy cook"? And would Em say, "I loved her, but she tried to talk me out of following my dream to become a private investigator"?

Eleanor cleared her throat and eyed the assembled mourners. "We want to invite all of you to come for refreshments to the house, which our long-suffering carpenter, Ethan Galen, has just finished. Aunt Ellen would have loved it that we're holding an open house in her honor. She'd like it even more if you made an offer to buy the house."

A few people laughed, a bit nervously. That apparently was the end of the service. Ellen's son got up and walked to the doorway, handing out slips of paper that I assumed were directions as people started to leave.

I stood, wondering how many of the forty or so mourners would go to the reception. I myself was thinking about skipping it. I still had to phone Mrs. Marshall this afternoon. Unfortunately, I first had to make up my mind about whether I would do the sensible thing—just take the money—or go for the ill-advised but emotionally satisfying option—inform her I'd write whatever I damn well pleased. The fact that I even considered refusing to sign the contract after her son's frightening warning shocked even me. I was hoping I'd come to my senses before I talked to her. The suddenly healthy balance in my checking account would help assuage my loss of pride.

"Mrs. Prescott?" It was Lucy hurrying over to me. "You are coming to see Daddy's work on the house, aren't you? There's punch and sandwiches and cakes, and I made my zucchini bread just for you." She looked suddenly shy. "I'm really glad you came today."

I couldn't very well turn down an invitation phrased like that. What could it hurt to spend an hour visiting with Lucy and admiring her father's carpentry work? It even gave me a short reprieve from having to phone Caroline's formidable mother.

Fortunately, the site for the reception was not far, which did not mean I got there quickly. By the time I arrived, Lucy was sitting on the porch swing, apparently waiting for me.

"Did you get lost?" she asked, looking concerned.

"Only for a little while," I said. It had always been a joke in my family that if you wanted good directions to anywhere, ask Mom and then do the opposite.

"Mr. O'Neal didn't want to come? Is he your boyfriend? He's very nice."

I took a deep breath. "Mr. O'Neal is out of town today or I'm sure he would have come. Yes, he is very nice, and yes, he's my friend."

"That's not what—"

I took her arm. "Why don't you show me around the house?"

She did. The place was one of the sprawling, brick ranch houses built in the forties and fifties. For an older home, it was in pristine shape and obviously updated.

After giving my condolences to Ellen's son and daughter, I followed Lucy on her tour. She took me to see the new oak kitchen cabinets her dad had installed, the once-screened-in porch he had enclosed to make a charming little sunroom.

I was impressed with the house and even more impressed that Ethan's young daughter was able to point out exactly where Daddy had installed crown molding. "This looks beautiful," I told her. "Your dad does excellent work."

She smiled proudly. "He does." She lowered her voice. "And this was a really tough job."

"You mean the house was in bad shape?"

She shook her head. "No, he's used to old houses. It was Miss Ellen who made it hard. She was always calling to complain about something, trying to get Dad to do everything faster. She was a very difficult client."

I tried not to smile. "I can imagine she would be."

"She was even yelling at him the night you were at our house for dinner. Dad was telling her, 'I won't be pushed around, Ellen.' And she said, 'I'm not fool enough to threaten you, Ethan. Not with your history.' Then she stormed out of the house. Mom was saying she shouldn't be driving and Dad went out to look for her. But he was too late. She'd already crashed her car before he found her."

What "history" of Ethan's was Ellen talking about? It was not something I could very well ask his adoring daughter.

Lucy took my hand and led me into a large walk-in closet in the master bedroom. "I know Miss Ellen had a pretty bad temper, but I thought some of the things that her family said about her at the service were nasty." She shook her head, as if such behavior was incomprehensible to her. "They're really mean to each other. All they do is criticize each other and fight."

What was it that Eleanor had called her mother and aunt in her eulogy—"prickly personalities"? I suspected it was a family trait. Yet Ellen had sobbed with genuine grief at Mary Alice's memorial service. "I think they care for each other, Lucy, but they're not very good at expressing it."

She looked dubious about my conclusion, but too polite to contradict a grown-up. Instead she said, "My dad and mom say that family is the most important thing in life. Even when someone is difficult or sick or did something wrong, we have to support each other." Clearly, in her mind, Ellen, Mary Alice, and their children did not meet these lofty standards.

"You're lucky your family is so good to each other," I said.

The little girl nodded vigorously. "My parents are very good to all our relatives. When I was little my aunt's baby died—the one I told you about who got botulism from eating honey. Her husband, my Uncle John, told Aunt Jane she'd killed their baby by her stupidity and he wanted a divorce."

"That's terrible," I said.

"It was. Aunt Jane came to stay with us, and she cried and cried all day long. I'm not supposed to know this, but my dad went and beat up Uncle John to convince him to do the right thing. Uncle John came to our house, one eye swollen shut and his lip split, and he apologized, telling Aunt Jane he knew it wasn't her fault and would she forgive him."

Nothing like a good beating to help a man appreciate his

wife, I thought. Maybe that was what Ellen was talking about when she said she knew Ethan's history. "What did your Aunt Jane say?"

"She went back to live with him. Uncle John hired a lawyer and said he was going to make sure that the people who really killed his baby were held responsible. He sued the store and the lady who gave Aunt Jane the honey. But he didn't win the cases, and my aunt got very depressed."

Lucy leaned in closer and whispered in my ear, "Then she killed herself."

I put an arm around her. "Oh, honey, that's horrible."

She was trying to surreptitiously swipe at the tears in her eyes as the two of us walked out of the closet.

She jumped when a man in the doorway said, "Lucy, what exactly are you doing in there?"

"I'm—I'm just showing Mrs. Prescott the house, Daddy."

I sent him my most winning smile. "You've done beautiful work, Ethan. Lucy wanted to show me everything."

"Thanks," he said coldly, keeping his eyes on his daughter. "Your mother has been looking for you. She needs your help in the kitchen."

Lucy scurried away without a backward glance. I scowled. Lucy's nice, loyal family seemed to equate childhood with being an indentured servant.

Or maybe I was just overreacting. Ethan looked his former mellow self now. "I'm glad you like my work, Lauren. I hope Lucy wasn't making a pest of herself."

"Not at all. I think she's a great kid." A girl who clearly needed more social contact in her homeschooled, chore-filled life, I thought. Perhaps Em and I could take her out to lunch and maybe go shopping or to a museum. But Ethan had already hurried out the door before I could suggest such an outing.

I returned to the living room. After helping myself to a glass of iced tea and piece of Lucy's zucchini bread, I walked over to Ellen's daughter, who was talking to Josie. "The house looks very nice. You shouldn't have any trouble finding a buyer."

"I hope so. Mom really put a lot of effort into it."

"It's a shame she didn't live to see it finished," Josie said.

Susie turned to her. "You were at the dinner the night Mom died, right?" When Josie nodded, she said, "Did something happen there that upset her—something that would make her drink so much?"

Josie looked at me. "She did seem kind of agitated, now that I think about it. But I'm not really sure why. Can you think of anything that upset her, Lauren?"

"It seemed to bother her that I was writing a magazine article about Caroline Marshall. She went on about what a terrible person Caroline was and if it hadn't been for Caroline, her sister would still be alive."

Susie nodded. "She said that before, even though everybody knows Caroline Marshall didn't kill my aunt. Did you think Mom was drinking a lot, Mrs. Prescott?"

"Yeah, she was beginning to slur her words. Was it unusual for her to drink?"

"No, unfortunately, but because my dad was killed by a drunk driver, she was almost fanatical about not drinking and driving."

"Margaret told me that they offered to let her spend the night or have Ethan drive her home," Josie said. "But Ellen insisted she was fine to drive and didn't have a long way to go."

Susie shook her head. "I wish she'd let him drive her, but Mom always had to do things her way. She'd never admit that she needed help."

Josie patted her hand. "I'm so sorry for your loss, honey."

Susie excused herself. Josie turned to me, shaking her head. "I didn't want to say anything in front of her, but for me the saddest thing is that all the issues Ellen was getting so upset about that night turned out to be insignificant. She was irate that Ethan was taking so long to finish the house—and yet here it is, looking great. She was furious that you were going to publish a flattering article about Caroline that rehashed her sister's murder, and now you're not even writing it."

I stared at her. "Who told you that I wasn't writing the piece about Caroline?"

She looked confused. "I'm not sure. Margaret? Or maybe Ed heard something."

"Well, I haven't decided myself whether or not I'm doing it, so your source is jumping the gun." I didn't know why I felt so angry. Admittedly, I'd always hated gossip, but I was also annoyed with myself. I still hadn't decided what I was going to tell Mrs. Marshall and, unless I wanted her to show up again at my apartment, I had to tell her something. And if I didn't sign her agreement, I needed to finish the damned article. What I had been doing—nothing—was no longer an option.

"I need to get going," I told Josie.

I looked for Lucy to say good-bye, but didn't see her anywhere. I headed out the door, feeling the ever-present Houston humidity enclose me like a sauna.

I felt anxious and, oddly, fearful. There were so many questions I wanted answered—so many murky issues that were unlikely to ever be resolved with the kind of clarity I sought. In the absence of those answers, I had the distinct impression that whatever decision I finally made, it was going to be a bad one.

Chapter Thirty-Six

Caroline's mother had left a curt message on my cell phone: "I need your signed contract today. I'm leaving tomorrow morning after the closing. Call to tell me when you'll drop it off." Not, I noticed, "IF you'll drop it off." This was a woman who was used to having her orders obeyed.

As I drove from Ellen's memorial reception/open house, I listened a second time to the phone message, hearing all the barely-controlled fury in the voice of the woman I'd been warned not to mess with. It was easy to understand why her young son had decided life would be a lot easier if he just did what Mom said. I wondered what price Caroline had paid for her disobedience.

What I needed was to talk to Mrs. Marshall in person. Perhaps if we had a face-to-face discussion we could clear up any misunderstandings and—I hoped—work out some kind of compromise. If she told me, for instance, that she was afraid I intended to write some grisly account of Caroline's murder, I could reassure her that I had no intention of producing such an article. I did not for one moment believe the explanation Mrs. Marshall had given me before—her embarrassment at having her posh friends read her daughter's "advice for blue-collar housewives"—was the real reason she wanted me to quit writing about her daughter.

Perhaps it took Josie telling me that she'd heard I was no longer writing the profile of Caroline to make me recognize how much I wanted to write it. Granted, part of this reaction was my lifelong abhorrence of being told what I could or could not do, but that was only a minor part. Much more important were my realizations that I had some important things to say about Caroline and that the article could be a good, insightful piece.

Caroline Marshall, for all her selfishness and occasional high-handed business tactics, had also had many admirable qualities. She'd been a complex, driven, and highly intelligent woman who'd been brutally murdered before she'd had a chance to bring her dreams to fruition. At the very least, she should have a more nuanced picture of herself and her frugality-as-empowerment philosophy presented to the public. She deserved to be remembered as someone more than the "Dumpster Queen Found Dead in a Dumpster" from the tabloid headlines.

Of course, convincing Mrs. Marshall of this was another matter entirely.

It wasn't too far to Caroline's house and I decided I'd drive there. When I'd sold my own home, the day before the closing I was walking through the place, viewing it one last time and checking to make sure I hadn't left anything behind. While Mrs. Marshall was undoubtedly less nostalgic and better organized than I, there still seemed a chance that I might find her at Caroline's.

Besides, hadn't Caroline herself told her class that a newly vacated house was a good place to find salvageable goods? Who knew: if I didn't find Mrs. Marshall there, maybe I might find something—some once-meaningful belonging or piece of furniture—that I could use in my article.

There was no vehicle parked in front of Caroline's house, only a stack of boxes and a broken, cane-back chair sitting by the curb.

Hoping that, appearances to the contrary, Mrs. Marshall

might nevertheless be inside, I walked up to the door. No one, unfortunately, answered my vigorous knocking. The place looked locked up and uninhabited.

I sighed. Since I had no idea what hotel she was staying in, it seemed as if the only way I was going to be able to contact Caroline's mother was by phone.

On the way back to my car I decided I could spare a few minutes to look through the tossed-out stuff from Caroline's house. At the very least I might get a paragraph for my magazine article: What did the items left on her curb tell us about the woman who believed there were treasures to be found in other people's trash?

Remembering at least a few of Caroline's lessons, I first retrieved some gardening gloves from the trunk for protection from any sharp objects.

The first box I sorted through contained a dented cookie sheet, some chipped ceramic plates and bowls, old sponges, and a pair of canvas gloves that Caroline had undoubtedly used in her work. The second and third box contained gardening paraphernalia, cleaning supplies, and assorted kitchen and bathroom items I had absolutely no interest in.

Perhaps this wasn't such a hot idea after all. I could think of about a dozen better uses of my time—calling Mrs. Marshall and finishing my magazine article topping the list. Then I spotted a big box of books.

Well, at least I could learn what Caroline read in her spare time. How-to books apparently. I picked up cookbooks, a gardening book, crafts book, and guide to money management. There was also a book on Colorado history and one on pioneer women. The only fiction she seemed to like were old mysteries by British authors, Agatha Christie mainly, with a few Dorothy Sayers.

At the bottom of the box were some bigger books. I picked

them up: two high-school yearbooks. I grinned. Now these could be helpful. Picking through this junk hadn't been such a waste of time after all. I might even take some of the other books as well. I'd always meant to read *The Murder of Roger Ackroyd*.

I turned to the index of one of the yearbooks, looking for listings on Caroline. A piece of paper fell out of the book.

A letter! It was a note from her grandmother expressing her concern about what Caroline had written her. I scanned the next paragraphs. Her grandmother said Caroline should move out of her parents' house and move in with her. She would come there to attend Caroline's high-school graduation in a couple weeks. While there she'd "make the necessary arrangements with your deplorable parents and then personally escort you off the premises, honey."

Wow. I wondered if that confrontation had actually happened. Had Caroline moved out after graduation? How had her parents reacted to the accusations?

I paged through the rest of the yearbook, but no other letters seemed to be residing there. The second yearbook didn't contain any, either.

For a few seconds I'd let myself imagine that Caroline had hidden all her private documents—letters, a diary maybe—in these books, tucked away from the prying eyes of her parents. Unfortunately, though, it looked as if Caroline had had other ideas.

Unless . . . I dug out the history of Colorado. Her grandmother's cabin, Caroline's safe haven, was located there. And the book's rather dry topic ensured that not many people were likely to be paging through it.

I flipped through it. An oversized envelope fell out. I opened it and gasped. Could this actually be . . . ? There were two stacks of letters held together by rubber bands. One was to Caroline from her grandmother. The second was letters from

Caroline to her.

Giddily I piled the books and letter back into the box. Maybe if I looked carefully through the other books I might even find some additional information.

I carried the box to my car and deposited it in my trunk. Then I pulled out my cell phone and called my daughter.

Emily, unfortunately, didn't answer, but I left her a message. "Em, I'm at Caroline Marshall's house. You won't *believe* what I found. Call me."

Too late I heard the footsteps behind me. Not that I would have known what to do if I'd turned sooner.

But at least I would have been better prepared for the hand that grabbed my shoulder and the deep voice that said, in a not-very-friendly voice, "Why, Mrs. Prescott, imagine meeting you here."

I stared at him, too shocked to say anything.

He pointed at my phone. "Say good-bye."

I did what he said. "Got to go now, Emma Jean. Love you."

When someone is pointing a gun at your head you comply with his wishes. Quickly, very quickly.

CHAPTER THIRTY-SEVEN

"Ethan?" I stared at the gun. "What—what are you doing?"

"Ridding my family of another obstacle."

Another obstacle? Perhaps it was the moment for a police officer to join the conversation. I still clutched my cell. Could I dial 9-1-1 without Ethan noticing and/or shooting me?

Apparently not. I had only punched in the first number when he wrenched the phone from my hand and threw it into bushes on the side of Caroline's house.

My voice was quivering as I said, "I don't understand. Why am I an obstacle to your family?"

He sent me a look of unvarnished hatred. "You had to keep pumping Lucy for information, didn't you? She's just a naïve little girl. You even got her to like you."

What was he talking about? "I adore Lucy. She's a terrific kid. She became so attached to me just because she's starved for company." Then I remembered the more important part of his accusation. "I have no idea what secrets you're talking about. And I never pumped Lucy for information."

His thin lips curled. "I find that hard to believe. I heard what the two of you were talking about in Ellen's closet."

I mentally ran through that conversation with Lucy. We'd talked about Ethan's work on the house, his friction with Ellen, the way that Ellen's family seemed to be constantly at each other's throats, unlike Lucy's relatives who always put family first. Could Ethan be upset that Lucy had told me he'd beat up

262

his brother-in-law and his sister had committed suicide after the death of her baby? Or was it something that she had confided about Ellen? Maybe Ethan was feeling guilty that he'd known Ellen was too drunk to drive home from his house but had made no effort to stop her. But would any of these admittedly touchy topics have made him angry enough to kill me?

"I don't remember anything particularly notable about my conversation with Lucy," I lied. "I think this all must be a big misunderstanding." I eyed his gun. A potentially lethal misunderstanding—at least for one of us.

He shook his head in disgust. "You had to keep on sticking your nose into other people's business, even though you and your nosy daughter were warned to butt out. I even tried to give you the benefit of the doubt because you've been nice to Lucy. I told myself you were only doing your job, gathering information for your book about Caroline. You had to make a living just like the rest of us."

I nodded my head encouragingly, desperate to encourage this chain of thought. *That's right, I'm just another working stiff doing her job. Don't blame me.*

"But then I solved your problem. I arranged it so you could stop your prying but still get paid." He glared accusingly at me. "There's no reason now for you to write about Caroline. You're getting paid what you're owed and the project's cancelled. But oh, no, you can't do what any sensible person would do. I heard you say this afternoon that you're still writing the article. *You* have to keep digging."

I could feel my mouth drop open. How did he know so much about me? We were the most casual of acquaintances, virtually strangers. "How did you know that Mrs. Marshall offered to pay me to stop writing about Caroline?"

"Because I was the one who put the idea in her head." He motioned for me to move toward the house.

I didn't really want to, but it seemed preferable to being shot. As we walked, I said, "Mrs. Marshall isn't there."

"I know," he said. "But I still have my key from when I did some work here."

Now, I thought, might be a good time to scream or run. Or do anything except go alone into this empty house with a man who wanted to get rid of me.

There was, however, one major problem with my escape plan. Who would hear me scream? I did a quick scan of the street: no one in sight. Caroline's elderly neighbor, I'd heard, had moved in with her daughter's family after Caroline's murder. The house had a "for sale" sign in the yard.

Ethan poked me in the back. "Don't even think about screaming. I won't shoot you if you do what I say."

Did he think I was a complete idiot? Was I supposed to believe that he was taking me into Caroline's house—at gunpoint!—just so we could talk?

I had to stall for time. We were almost at the steps of Caroline's front porch. "Wait a minute. Why would Mrs. Marshall take your advice? Does she even know you?"

He sneered as he pulled a key from his pocket. "I sent a letter—unsigned, of course—warning her that the book you were writing would make her look bad, that you were intending to do a hatchet job on her. Ophelia told my wife once about Caroline's mother's poison garden and her cruelty to Caroline, all while pretending to be a doting mama. I figured a witch like that would be really humiliated if she were exposed in your book as a child abuser. I suggested she could pay you not to write anything about her or her family."

Clearly Mrs. Marshall was not the only person who didn't want me to write about Caroline. Ethan hadn't gone to all that effort just to make sure that I was paid for my work. The crucial question was why did he care what I wrote?

"Listen," I said, "you're wrong about me refusing to take Mrs. Marshall's offer. I need the money and I'm not going to write any more about Caroline. I just phoned Mrs. Marshall to tell her so." *In other words, Ethan, whatever it is you don't want me to* write, *I won't be writing. Problem solved.*

Ethan shook his head. "It's too late." He pushed me onto the porch and started to unlock the door.

I made a quick lunge, pushing him as hard as I could. He staggered for a moment but quickly regained his balance. He caught me on the porch stair, wrapping a muscular arm around me and pulling me back on the porch.

His grip felt tight enough to crack a rib. Glaring down at me, his face was red with fury. "I told you," he said, "that I wouldn't shoot you if you did what I said."

Did that mean he was going to shoot me now? Pain was surging from my ribcage. "But you didn't say you wouldn't kill me."

His grip loosened a tiny bit, enough to feel merely uncomfortable. He half dragged me to the front door, and this time successfully unlocked the front door while keeping me pinned to his side.

"I've never shot anybody," he said, as he opened the door and pushed me inside.

"Is that supposed to make me feel better?" I asked, too incredulous to think about saying the right thing to a prospective killer.

Unbelievably, he laughed. Ethan, the man who never smiled, was suddenly finding his sense of humor. "Actually, it is." He locked the door from the inside, leaving us alone in Caroline's now-empty living room.

"Why?" I wanted to keep him talking, but I also wanted to know.

"I guess it's that I imagine that being shot can be a prolonged and painful way to die. So if I don't have to, I don't want to shoot you."

"You don't have to," I said firmly. "And now that we have that cleared up, let's leave. I can't imagine Mrs. Marshall would appreciate us trespassing."

He laughed again. "I can see why Lucy likes you. You're funny."

Amusing was not what I was going for. "Seriously, I am not going to harm you or anyone in your family. I don't know what you think you heard Lucy tell me. But whatever it is, I will not repeat it to anyone. No one, I promise."

His eyes narrowed and he no longer looked amused. "I wish I could believe that. I don't think you'd intentionally harm my family, but with your unfortunate inquisitiveness, you can't help yourself. You know that old saying 'Curiosity killed the cat'? Well, it's your curiosity and your meddling, Mrs. Prescott, that did you in."

That also was what he'd said in his threatening note to my daughter: Curiosity killed the cat. Too bad we hadn't heeded the warning.

As Ethan moved towards me, I kept wishing I'd paid more attention in that women's self-defense class. I tried to remember some relevant points. When the brittle young instructor had called me a perfect crime victim—middle-aged, out-of-shape, and unaggressive—I'd retorted, "Then I guess I'll have to make a point of avoiding thugs and muggers."

"That's a good start," she'd said. "That's a key concept of a woman's self-defense strategy: Always stay vigilant about your surroundings, keep on the lookout for potentially dangerous situations and people, and then steer clear of them."

Obviously I'd blown Key Concept Number One. My assessment of Ethan as a not-too-bright carpenter and an essentially harmless husband and father had been wrong. Dead wrong.

I scanned the room looking for possible weapons or another exit. The room, unfortunately, was totally empty and Ethan was blocking the nearest exit. The other one—the back door off of the kitchen—was on the opposite side of the house.

"Why are you doing this, Ethan?" I tried once more. "I promise you, I don't know anything—ANYTHING—that would harm you or your family. And I'm not going to write that book about Caroline." It was quite possible I wasn't going to write another word. Ever.

"If you don't know now, you will soon," he said. "You're a born meddler. Just like that Nathan. The two of you are pit bulls—you won't let go."

Nathan? Lucy had said that Nathan had attended the group potluck at their house, the one I hadn't been invited to. He'd asked so many questions about the deaths of Mary Alice, Ophelia, and Caroline that Ellen had dissolved into tears. Nathan had even asked Lucy if her parents grew Barbados nuts in their garden.

Oh, my God!

Ethan must have read my realization on my face. "See," he said pleasantly, "you know more already. Which is why, Mrs. Prescott, I need to get rid of you."

He reached behind him for a backpack I hadn't noticed he was carrying.

"The same way you got rid of Nathan?" I made a quick step backward as he glanced down to unzip the satchel.

He nodded. "And Mary Alice and Ophelia. I feel bad about them. I had nothing against either of them. They just took the poison I intended for Caroline. In the end I decided to kill Caroline by another means."

I tried to slow down my rapid breathing so I could think. "What I don't understand is why you wanted to kill Caroline so badly. What had she ever done to you?"

This time I had no trouble detecting his emotion. His face, pleasant and relaxed a minute earlier, flooded with color, his eyes glinting dangerously. There was something not right about those eyes.

"Caroline killed my niece and my sister, but she said none of it was her fault. The police, the courts, no one, would hold her accountable for what she'd done. The baby's death was a tragic accident, they said. Some people even blamed my sister—said she should have known enough not to feed an infant honey or she shouldn't have taken food that someone else had thrown away. But Caroline told the class that the food they found in the store's dumpster was perfectly safe to eat. Never mind that my niece died from eating it. The way she saw it, she wasn't responsible for anything bad that happened when people followed her advice."

"And after that your sister committed suicide," I half-whispered, remembering the story Lucy had told me.

He nodded. "She killed herself after the courts refused to hear her lawsuit against Caroline. She died thinking it must be her fault, after all, that her baby had died. The last words she said to me were, 'If I hadn't been so stupid and taken that useless class my daughter would still be alive today. I destroyed my family because I wanted to save a few dollars on groceries.' So you can see, Mrs. Prescott, why I didn't have much use for Caroline Marshall."

"And you thought I might write about your family in my book?"

He shrugged. "Caroline's death has already gotten far too much publicity. Your book would have revived public interest in it. And the last thing I want is for Caroline to be portrayed as this noble, martyred teacher who only wanted to help people save money. Caroline deserved to end up in a dumpster, and she shouldn't be remembered at all."

He pulled a foil-wrapped package the size of a sandwich from the backpack. "Look what I brought for you," he said, unwrapping it and showing it to me.

I stared. "Lucy's zucchini bread?"

He nodded. "I know how much you like it."

What was he telling me—that he'd thoughtfully provided me with my last meal? Or was he trying to get rid of me with bread that he'd doctored with something lethal? My mouth went dry as I took another tiny step backwards.

I needed to keep him talking—about something other than the zucchini bread he wanted me to eat. "Why did you poison everyone except Caroline?"

"Originally I'd thought it was fitting that Caroline be killed by food, the same way my niece was, but after two failed attempts to poison her, I decided it didn't make much difference how she died. I just wanted her dead. And having her body found in a dumpster seemed more fitting anyway. I should have thought of it earlier."

"Why Barbados nuts?" I asked as he pulled a small plastic baggie out of his backpack. It seemed to be filled with some kind of ground spice.

"Why not? They're a fast-acting and very toxic poison. I got the idea from Ophelia—not to kill Caroline, of course, but to grow poisonous plants. She and Margaret became friends, and Ophelia couldn't stop talking about Caroline's terrible mother and the poison garden in her backyard. That led me to read about the various types of lethal plants. For a time I even thought about trying to set up Caroline's mother as Caroline's killer, but I decided the logistics were too complicated, with Mrs. Marshall living in another state."

I had a very good idea now of what he was planning for me. Undoubtedly that little baggie I'd thought contained ground spice was actually chopped up Barbados nuts. Maybe he intended to sprinkle them over the zucchini bread.

I backed up another few inches in the direction of the kitchen. If I kept him answering my questions, stalled for more time, maybe Em would listen to my phone message and figure out that something was wrong. Surely she, the would-be private investigator, would then send the police to Caroline's house.

Unless, of course, she didn't listen to my message in time. Em often turned off her phone so her activity of the moment wouldn't be interrupted. If she didn't summon the police for, say, another hour or two, they could well arrive too late.

Ethan shook his head at me, his mouth quirking into a mocking smile. "I can see what you're doing and it won't work. I'm not going to let you get to the kitchen. I told you I don't want to shoot you, but I will if I have to."

He held out his hand, offering me the piece of zucchini bread. "Now be a good girl and come eat the bread I brought here especially for you. Trust me, it's a lot quicker way to die than by a bullet."

Trust him? I'd witnessed Mary Alice writhing and convulsing after eating the dessert laced with Barbados nuts. I doubt very much that she would have said that it was a quick and easy way to die.

But before I could respond, I heard the unmistakable sound of a key turning in a lock. Someone was opening the back door. Oh, my God.

I opened my mouth to yell a warning, but Ethan was next to me in a second, clamping his beefy hand over my mouth as we heard approaching footsteps.

"What the hell do you think you're doing?" an indignant female voice demanded. Mrs. Marshall stood, hands on her hips, glaring at us from the hallway. "You are illegally trespassing on my property."

I tried to signal her with my eyes: Run! Get help! Call 9-1-1!

Unfortunately, she seemed oblivious to my efforts to communicate. Mrs. Marshall, being Mrs. Marshall, ignored me, continuing her shrill tirade. "I should have known that you would betray my trust. You are as stupidly obstinate as Caroline, though at least *she* didn't branch out into criminal activity. What are you and your friend doing here? Looking for some more gossip about my family for your filthy book?"

Didn't the woman notice that my "friend" was holding his hand over my mouth—which, among other things, made my answering her ridiculous accusations impossible?

Apparently not. She dramatically pulled out her cell phone. "I am reporting you right this minute to the police," she announced loudly.

Ethan lunged towards her.

Out of necessity he had to let go of me. I knew an opportunity when I saw it. Ignoring the imminent confrontation in front of me, I turned and sprinted toward the front door.

Behind me Mrs. Marshall let out an ear-piercing scream. I hoped she was as vicious a fighter as I expected her to be. Ethan would not be cowed by threats.

I'd just reached the door when I heard the unmistakable sound of a fist connecting with bone, followed by the thud of a body hitting the floor. The screaming stopped.

Hand shaking, I fumbled to unlock the deadbolt.

"Oh, no, you don't." Strong hands grabbed me from behind.

This time he would kill me.

There was a roaring in my ears. I felt Ethan's hands grasping my waist, pulling me back from the door. In my mind I heard the self-defense teacher screaming at me: *You are a street fighter, Prescott. Kick ass!*

With everything in me I stomped on Ethan's foot. I heard him grunt as I ground my heel into his instep.

He didn't let go but I managed to turn slightly to the side. I drove my elbow into his face, then turned the other way and smashed my other elbow into his head.

With a roar, he let go of me. His face wore a rictus of focused rage. Before I could move, his slap caught me on the side of the head, causing searing pain.

What made me think I could fight him? I'd never fought anyone. I was the smart-mouthed kid who was only good at verbal barbs.

I took in a mouthful of air and yelled. I turned and slammed the bottom of my foot into his knee. *Drive your foot completely through his knee,* the instructor in my head commanded me. *Make sure he can't stand or walk.*

Ethan's face contorted as he fell to the floor. I jumped back to get out of grabbing distance.

"Move!" a voice from behind me ordered.

I glanced over my shoulder. Mrs. Marshall was clutching her jaw with one hand, holding a small aerosol can with the other.

I moved, allowing her to lean in and direct a steady stream of pepper spray into Ethan's eyes.

He roared with pain. His arms were flailing, undoubtedly searching for the gun he'd dropped.

I spotted it on the floor and kicked it far from his reach.

"At least you're good for something, Lauren," Mrs. Marshall shouted. She planted her foot on Ethan's neck. As if she were squashing a bug, she ground her shoe into his neck until he appeared to lose consciousness.

"We've got to get out of here," I told her. Ethan might be temporarily immobilized, but he could recover at any minute. If anything, his injuries would probably make him more brutal.

Mrs. Marshall seemed reluctant to leave. She removed her foot from Ethan's neck and delivered a sharp kick to his head.

I managed—finally—to unlock the front door. "Come on," I told her, "we need to get help." If I didn't get her out of here, she might kill him.

I'd taken only one step onto the front porch when I heard the sirens.

Never in my life had I had been so happy to see a police car. And driving right behind it was my worried-looking daughter.

Chapter Thirty-Eight

It crossed my mind, as I repeatedly answered the same police questions, that while Ethan's entire assault had lasted no more than fifteen or twenty minutes, talking about the assault was taking more than four times as long.

I also had to reassure my anxious daughter that I was fine. "You've got a nasty bruise on the side of your face, Mom," Em said. "Maybe I should take you to the ER to get it looked at."

"Ethan slapped me." Hard. Gingerly I touched the injured area. "No bones seem broken." I'd look like hell for a while, but I'd heal.

Overhearing our conversation, Mrs. Marshall turned from the police officer she'd been talking to. "That bastard probably broke my jaw. But who do the police take to the hospital? The criminal, that's who! Doesn't *that* tell you all you need to know about the priorities of our justice system?"

Frankly I was just as glad that the police had taken him away. Even as Ethan lay on the floor moaning, I'd half-expected him to leap up and murder the one living witness who could testify against him—me. One did not manage to kill four people (maybe five, if he'd been involved in Ellen's fatal car accident), without being determined and resourceful.

"He said he was blinded by your pepper spray," I told her. "And he might have a concussion from that kick to his head."

"So?" Caroline's mother said. "Maybe he should have thought of that before he broke into my house and destroyed my cell phone."

"Not to mention his murdering your daughter," Em added, sotto voce.

Mrs. Marshall's eyes narrowed, looking as if she was trying to decide if she was being insulted. "Of course, that goes without saying," she said stiffly.

The police had stored the slice of zucchini bread and the crushed Barbados nuts in evidence bags to take to the lab for testing. They made detailed notes when I told them what Ethan had confessed to me about the murders of Caroline, Mary Alice, Ophelia, and Nathan.

Mrs. Marshall, unfortunately, had not overheard Nathan's confession. She'd entered the house through the back door, she told the police, and been shocked to see two other people in her house. When she'd announced that she was calling the police, Ethan had grabbed her phone and "viciously assaulted" her. Then he'd gone after me when I tried to leave. In her version of events, Mrs. Marshall then "came to Lauren's rescue," with her pepper spray and neck-stomping.

I managed not to roll my eyes. Probably I should be grateful that she hadn't tried to get me arrested for trespassing.

Ethan himself had refused to tell the police anything other than that he wanted to be taken to a hospital.

An officer had taken him to have his injuries checked out, but, after that, a police woman assured me, he was going to go to jail.

The only thing that worried me was that the police obviously needed a lot more corroborating evidence before they could make a case against him. "I think Ethan was growing the Barbados nuts himself," I said. "He told me he'd researched various kinds of poisonous plants and decided that this one was fast-acting and very toxic. I'm not sure where he was growing them, but his family has a big garden behind their house."

The officer wrote it down, but from her expression I suspected she thought it would be a futile needle-in-a-haystack search.

Finally—after every conceivable question was asked at least three times—the police told us we were free to leave. "But don't go out of town without notifying us."

That caution made Mrs. Marshall immediately launch into a tirade about how she had every intention of leaving tomorrow after the closing for this house. "*I* was not the one who broke the law," she was saying as Em and I headed for our respective vehicles.

I was unlocking my car door when I heard someone calling my name.

"Lauren, wait!" Mrs. Marshall commanded. "I have something to say to you."

I was tempted to pretend I hadn't heard her. I could get into my car and speed away, ignoring the well-dressed woman bellowing at me from the street. While I was certainly grateful that she had interrupted Ethan's attempt to murder me and very happy that she packed pepper spray in her purse, the woman had an unparalleled talent for being irritating.

I took a deep breath and decided I'd better hear what she had to say. If I bolted, she'd just track me down anyway.

She hurried to my car. "About the contract I offered you," she began.

I stared at her. What with Ethan trying to feed me Barbados nuts, I'd totally forgotten about Mrs. Marshall's effort to bribe me into not writing about Caroline.

"I don't know," I began.

"I'm withdrawing my offer," she said at the same time.

"What?"

"I've reconsidered my earlier position. It was only that terrible man's e-mails that made me think you were going to write something scandalous. So you're free to write whatever you want about my daughter." She smiled at me, looking as if she expected to be awarded a medal.

In other words, now that Mrs. Marshall assumed I wasn't going to write about her backyard poison garden and her nonexistent parenting skills—topics Ethan had apparently told her I was eager to pursue—she didn't want to waste any good money paying me off.

"But you will honor Caroline original agreement with me?" I asked, remembering Mrs. Marshall's recent speech about how she only wanted to be fair to me. "She promised to pay me fifteen thousand dollars when I turned in the completed book manuscript—the last installment of our contracted payment."

Mrs. Marshall's eyes narrowed. She waved her hand dismissively. "Well, I don't think that's necessary now, do you? With all the media stories that will be coming out about this poisoning serial killer and his vendetta against Caroline, I'm sure you'll have publishers lining up with lucrative offers. There seems no point for me to offer additional remuneration."

It might be worth fifteen thousand to never have to deal again with this woman. Even her own son had warned me to steer clear of her.

I waved to signal Em that I was leaving and got into my car. My daughter and I had already agreed that we'd meet at our favorite Tex-Mex restaurant. To our way of thinking, we both deserved a big Margarita, and a large order of nachos.

If I was still hungry after that, I might even stop on the way home to pick up a Baby Ruth. It had been that kind of day.

It was not until the next morning that I remembered I still had the box of Caroline's books and letters in my trunk. I hurried to the car, feeling like a kid who suddenly realized she'd forgotten to unwrap a big Christmas present.

I placed the envelope containing all the letters between Caroline and her grandmother on the kitchen table. Then I went through all of Caroline's books to make sure there were no other treasures hidden inside them.

There weren't any more letters, but I found other clues to her past. The nonfiction books were filled with her jottings. She'd underlined sentences and put asterisks next to key points about budgeting, home mortgages, low-cost casserole recipes. She seemed especially fascinated with the lives and day-to-day activities of pioneer women. Years later, when Em and Katie and I had seen Caroline on television, she'd been telling her students to envision themselves as "modern-day pioneers."

Reading the various ideas she wanted to remember, I imagined Caroline piecing together her philosophy. Some of her critics had claimed that she'd started her business merely as a way to make money. They claimed that frugality was merely an expedient choice of topic, owing to her years of working with Nathan's grandmother. When Eloisa died, they said, Caroline had seen a business concept she could steal, and she ran with it.

These books and her margin notes displayed Caroline's genuine passion for her subject. Her ex-husband had told me as much in our phone conversation. Caroline, he said, had been like a "convert, completely obsessed with her new faith." Undoubtedly her strong reaction was also influenced by her disdain for her materialistic parents and her love for her garage-sale–loving grandmother, but it was clear that her interest in frugality-as-empowerment was very real.

Finally though it was time to tear myself from the books and move on to the pièce de résistance: Caroline's letters to and from her beloved grandmother.

I started with the letters written by Caroline. There were thirty of them, starting from the time Caroline was a sophomore in high school and ending right before she graduated. I put them in chronological order and then began to read.

Her letters chronicled the life of a bright, lonely teenaged girl in a just-the-facts manner. Only occasionally could I infer what she must have been feeling, such as when she disclosed that her mother thought her joining the school chess club was "nerdy." Usually she never mentioned her family. The only thing she ever sounded excited about was her summer visit to her grandmother.

Her grandmother's letters to Caroline were more revealing. Besides chatty accounts of what she was doing—the garage sales she'd attended, what she was planting in her garden—she praised her granddaughter's smallest achievements: Caroline's good grade on the advanced algebra test, her moving up to second-chair violin in the school orchestra.

She told Caroline that her mother was wrong about chess club. "She's just jealous because she never could learn how to play chess." She made plans for their annual visit. "The strawberry preserves you and I made last summer sold so well at our church bazaar. This year I think we should take on some new challenges. I promised my friends lots of new items for the next bazaar. How do you feel about learning to make homemade toys? We can try everything from wooden trains to rag dolls. Won't that be fun?"

Caroline, I realized, had apparently learned a lot of the do-it-yourself activities that she later taught in her frugality classes from her grandmother.

It wasn't until Caroline's last letter that she finally laid out her complaints about her parents. They'd "gone ballistic" when she refused to be presented at their county club's debutante ball and announced that she preferred to study business at a state university rather than attend the Ivy League college they'd wanted her to go to. Her mother had screamed at her about what a "huge disappointment" she was, refusing "all the op-

279

portunities we've worked so hard to give you." Her father said she was a "loser."

The letter I'd first read, the one tucked in Caroline's yearbook, had been her grandmother's reply to that: After her high-school graduation in a few weeks, they'd move Caroline out of her "disreputable parents' house" and into her grandmother's home. Grandma would tell Caroline's parents "what's what."

Unfortunately, that was the last letter I had. I only wished I knew what happened after that.

On impulse, I phoned Will, Caroline's brother, and was immensely relieved when he answered.

He told me what I wanted to know. Caroline indeed had moved in with their grandmother immediately after high-school graduation. Grandma had told his parents that if they made any attempt to prevent their daughter from leaving, she would report them to the police for child abuse. His mother and father hadn't been happy about it, but they did nothing to stop the move. Caroline had gone to the state university to study business and marketing.

"She never stepped foot in our parents' house again," Will said. "They saw each other from time to time, though, like at my grandmother's funeral."

"When did your grandmother die?"

"Two years after Caroline moved in with her. But at least by that time Caroline was settled in college and had a life away from my parents. She told me at the funeral that the time she spent with Grandma was the happiest of her life." He paused, then said, "Why do you want to know this?"

"I'm writing a magazine article about Caroline. I just found the letters she and your grandmother wrote to each other. They helped me finally see the way to write my profile."

"I'm glad," he said. "Caroline deserves to have her story told."

"I thought so, too." And, I realized, I was one of the few people who could do her story justice.

I thanked Will for his help and said good-bye. Then I got to work on my article.

I threw away most of what I'd written in my first attempt at the piece. This time I focused on what it was like to be an introverted, bookish girl, too serious and too stubborn for her social-climbing family, having to live with supremely self-absorbed parents whose only interest in her seemed to be whether she looked good in the family photo.

I told about Caroline's vital relationship with her affectionate, penny-pinching grandmother and their precious summers together in the Colorado cabin and about Caroline's first job working for Nathan's grandmother on her newsletter for thrifty homemakers. I tried to show how all these experiences helped Caroline to forge her own life philosophy. She believed that rejecting the rampant consumerism she'd grown up with and embracing a conscious frugality were the only ways for her to gain control of her life. Frugality was synonymous with freedom and empowerment.

Yes, Caroline was ambitious, ruthless in pursuing her goals and sometimes insensitive to the feelings of her employees and students. But she was also a genuine advocate for her beliefs. She was convinced that living frugally would make everyone's lives better.

I concluded the article with a description of her murder. Readers, I hoped, would come away with an appreciation and some sympathy for this complex, driven, and vulnerable woman. I wanted them to remember Caroline Marshall as more than the body found in a dumpster.

★ ★ ★ ★ ★

Katie and Matt were coming for the weekend. I hadn't seen my daughter or son-in-law in almost two months, though we talked on the phone often. Katie reported that now Matt was once again working in Dallas, the two of them had resolved their issues and were happy. I believed her, but I also wanted to see for myself.

They certainly looked happy together. The adoring way Matt watched his wife as she hugged us hello reminded me of the early days of their marriage. And Katie, so despondent only a few months ago, now seemed to radiate contentment.

"I'm so sorry I missed all the excitement," Katie told us. "I feel left out of the family crime solving."

I merely rolled my eyes, but Matt said, "*I'm* glad you weren't here. I don't want you putting your life in danger."

Katie beamed at him.

"The only person who was in danger was Mom," Em said. "I did some investigating, but she was the one who solved the crime—and was almost murdered by the killer."

Reflexively I touched the still-colorful bruise on the side of my face, my memento of Ethan's attack. "I solved the crime, Em, only *after* Ethan grabbed me at Caroline's house. It wasn't exactly a fine example of deductive reasoning. Ethan overheard Lucy tell me about her baby cousin's death from botulism after eating honey from a dumpster and then her aunt's—the baby's mother—suicide. Neither of us knew it, but that was Ethan's motive for murdering Caroline: she'd led the dumpster-diving expedition where his sister got the honey, but Caroline refused to take any responsibility for the baby's death.

"Ethan assumed that once I heard the story, I'd put all the pieces together and turn him in to the police. That's why he followed me when I left the reception, bringing along zucchini bread and chopped Barbados nuts especially for me. But since

Lucy never mentioned Caroline had anything to do with her aunt, I never suspected Ethan—until he assaulted me." Recounting the story, I realized again how lucky I was to be alive to tell it.

"I kind of thought it was a woman who killed Caroline, since her neighbor saw a woman come to her door that afternoon," Em said. "But it turns out that woman—whoever she was—had nothing to do with her death. Ethan admitted that he used his key to Caroline's house to get inside. He sneaked up on her and bashed her over the head, fracturing her skull. Then he shoved her into a body bag, loaded her into his van, and drove to the dumpster where he left her."

Katie shuddered. "When I think how close we came to losing you, Mom . . ."

"Tell me about it," Em said. "I thought I'd throw up when I was driving to Caroline's house behind the police car."

"But you didn't lose me," I said in my firm, changing-the-subject voice. "And it was your quick thinking, Em, that got the police to Caroline's so quickly."

Em looked pleased. "Your calling me Emma Jean on your phone message was a good clue that something was going on."

"This Ethan guy is in jail, right?" Matt asked. "Not out on bond?"

I nodded. "He's in jail and very likely to stay there. I was afraid there wasn't going to be enough corroborating evidence to make a case against him, but, to my complete surprise, he confessed to everything. Apparently, when the police found the Barbados nuts growing in the undergrowth behind his garage, they threatened to bring charges against his wife, Margaret. That's when Ethan decided to confess. He said Margaret was totally unaware of what he'd done, that he'd purposely kept everything secret from her."

"Do you buy that?" Katie asked. "I find it hard to believe

that his wife didn't know anything about four separate murders."

"Five murders," Em said. "He confessed to killing Mary Alice's twin sister, Ellen, too, after that dinner at their house, the one that Mom and Paul went to. He told the police that Ellen got drunk and started threatening him, saying she knew he had some secrets he didn't want exposed. Ethan didn't wait to hear any more. When she drove home that night, he followed her in his truck. Her fatal accident was caused by him pushing her car into a tree."

"I think Margaret probably didn't know any of the specifics," I said. "It would be like Ethan not to tell her—he was very protective of his family. And Margaret appears to be one of those women who sees only what she wants to see. In any case, I'm glad Lucy and her siblings will have one parent who's able to look after them."

I had yet to talk to Lucy, uncertain of what to say to her. Did she know that her father had tried to poison me with her homemade zucchini bread—sprinkled, of course, with poisonous nuts? I certainly hoped she was unaware that it was only after her dad overheard what Lucy told me about the deaths of her aunt and baby cousin that he decided to get rid of me. Would Lucy always think of me as the person who sent Daddy to prison? Or would she want a friend during the tough times that were sure to follow?

I decided I'd wait a few weeks to call her. She might very well tell me she never wanted to lay eyes on me again, but I still needed to let her know that I cared about her.

"Mom," Katie said in a voice that indicated it was not the first time she'd said it. "I was saying that those roses are gorgeous." She nodded at a vase containing a lovely arrangement of pale peach and white flowers.

I smiled. "Yes, they're beautiful, aren't they? Paul sent them."

"It's too bad he can't be with us today," she said. "I'd like to see him."

I recalled her first meeting with Paul, when she seemed to develop an instant antipathy toward him because he was so unlike her father. But the more time that Paul spent with Katie and Em, the more both of my girls grew to like him. And now the two of them sounded like very unsubtle matchmakers.

"Paul's in Seattle this week, moving in to his new place," I said, well aware that she already knew this.

"I bet you really miss him," Katie said.

In fact, I really did, but her comments were starting to irritate me. Didn't she realize that it was mothers who were allowed to nag their children, not vice versa?

"I do miss him, but he's coming to visit next weekend."

Now Em had to leap into the Canonizing Paul Conversation. "That's great. I've missed him, too. He's a really nice guy. Did you know, Katie, that he sent me flowers, too?" She nodded at an arrangement of carnations on a side table.

"Why'd he send *you* flowers?" Matt asked.

Em grinned. "Because he wanted to thank me for making Mom go to that women's self-defense workshop. He said she'd never have gone if I hadn't pushed her into it, and without the class, she wouldn't have been able to kick Ethan's butt."

"I didn't attack him," I said. "I was defending myself. Though Paul's right about my owing my very limited self-defense moves to Em."

"I think we should all drink to that," Em said.

Matt nodded. "We've got a lot to celebrate."

Emily stood up to take beverage orders. She made a guess at what everyone would pick. "Beer, Matt? White Zinfandel for Mom and Katie?"

"I think I'll just have a glass of water," Katie said.

"Why?" her sister asked. Katie almost never turned down an

offer of her favorite wine. "We're celebrating."

I stared at my elder daughter, my eyes wide. Then I glanced at Matt. Both of them were beaming. "Are you . . . ?"

"Yes!" Katie shouted happily. "In eight months you're going to become a grandmother."

I could feel tears welling in my eyes. I leaped up to give her a hug. "Now *that's* something to celebrate."

CHAPTER THIRTY-NINE

"You're becoming famous," Paul told me with a big smile.

I rolled my eyes. "Yeah, right." Nevertheless, I was proud of my just-published magazine profile of Caroline. I was pleased with the article and delighted it had made the cover of the magazine. I didn't kid myself that it was my stellar writing that had made it the featured story; my unwitting role in discovering Caroline's murderer—and the killer of four other innocent people—undoubtedly had a lot more to do with the article's prominent position.

I took another sip of coffee. It was so comfortable to have Paul sitting across from me at my kitchen table—wonderful, I had to admit, to have him in the same city as me. Unfortunately, it was only a weekend visit. He'd be flying back to Seattle Sunday night.

"Did I tell you that Caroline's mother phoned to yell at me about the article?" I said. "She told me that everyone who knew her said she'd been a very supportive mother to her 'difficult daughter.' "

"What did you say to that?"

"I said I was only quoting Caroline's letters to her grandmother, and, apparently, Caroline hadn't viewed her mother as being so supportive. I wanted to add that caring mothers didn't usually poison their children's dogs, but I decided against it."

"And how did Mrs. Marshall respond to your explanation?"

I grinned. "She hung up on me, before I even had a chance

to tell her I'd just been offered a contract to write a book about Caroline."

"A very lucrative contract," Paul added. He chuckled. "Which was just what Mrs. Marshall predicted would happen when she was weaseling out of paying the money Caroline promised you for the completed manuscript."

"At least this way Mrs. Marshall won't have any idea what I do or don't write about her daughter until she reads the published book." In truth I was both very nervous and extremely excited at the prospect of writing that book. Taking Mrs. Marshall out of the equation was a definite relief.

"And Caroline's brother and her ex-husband also phoned me about the article," I said. "Fortunately, they both loved it. Her brother said he thought I'd really captured what Caroline was like. He said he and his family spread her ashes right behind their grandmother's Colorado cabin when they went there this summer." I blinked away some sudden tears. "Will said that up there he felt that his sister was finally at peace."

Paul reached over and squeezed my hand. He really was the most tender and empathetic man.

As if sensing what I was thinking, he said, "You know, Lauren, you could write your book in Seattle just as easily as in Houston. The temperature's a good twenty-five degrees cooler, and it would give you a chance to see how you like living in the Pacific Northwest. It's not as if you have to be here, now that Em's happy and back in school in Austin."

"And Katie's happy in Dallas, now that her morning sickness has stopped," I added.

He sent me a look that showed everything he was feeling—his nervousness, his hopefulness, his yearning. "I would really love to share my life with you," he said, "no matter where we live, no matter how much commuting is involved."

His beautiful, expressive eyes suddenly twinkled. "And I

promise to always keep a supply of Baby Ruths on hand."

I leaned forward and cupped his face in my hands. "Now how could I possibly pass up a tempting offer like that?" I said right before I kissed him.

ABOUT THE AUTHOR

Karen Hanson Stuyck is the author of six previous mystery novels. Her novel *Fit to Die* first introduced reluctant amateur sleuth Lauren Prescott and her two daughters. Her other mystery novels include *Do You Remember Me Now?*, *A Novel Way to Die*, *Cry for Help*, *Held Accountable*, and *Lethal Lessons*. She has worked as a newspaper reporter, an editor, and a public-relations writer for hospitals and a mental health institution. Her short stories have been published in *Redbook*, *Cosmopolitan*, *Woman's World*, and other magazines. She lives with her husband in Houston.